The Cursed Canoe

FRANKIE BOW

The Cursed Canoe

Published by Hawaiian Heritage Press

Edited by Maria de Pillis-Shintaku
Hardcover ISBN: 978-1-943476-14-5
Paperback ISBN: 978-1-943476-15-2

Library of Congress Control Number 2016933621

DEDICATION

To my favorite canoe paddler, with love.

ACKNOWLEDGMENTS

I could not have written this without the tireless support of my family. Thank you.

CHAPTER ONE

Emma Nakamura's crew was out near the breakwall, but even at that distance I could tell her canoe was moving fast. She'd promised us she'd finish paddling practice in time for sunset happy hour (half price drinks and free pupus) at the Pair-O-Dice Bar and Grill. But the sun had already sunk out of sight, and Emma's canoe continued to zip back and forth with no sign of slowing down.

It wouldn't be any use complaining to Patrick Flanagan, who was standing next to me on the black sand beach. Pat is indifferent to food and looks it.

"Emma's pushing them hard," I said.

"Probably trying to get in as many sprints as she can before it gets dark. Was that your stomach growling?"

"Ooh, Pat, I hope Emma doesn't end up giving someone a heart attack or anything."

"Careful what you wish for. You might get it."

"Okay, I guess I'm not actually wishing for anyone to have a heart attack. That wouldn't be nice."

"Lightning strike?" Pat suggested.

"Maybe a little one."

I imagined Zeus astride the dormant volcano that dominated the island (Mount Olympus being impractically far away), aiming a thunderbolt directly at seat five of Emma's canoe. Just enough voltage to knock Kathy Banks out of commission for a while.

It's not like me to wish someone ill. I try to get along with everyone, not always an easy task for a new department chair. But seeing the good in the officious and incurious Kathy Banks, my liaison in Mahina State's Student Retention Office, is beyond my ability. I squinted at the distant outline of the canoe.

"Why does Emma tolerate her?"

"Kathy's a strong paddler. That's why Emma keeps her on. You know, Emma doesn't like Kathy any more than you do, but she doesn't really have a good reason to kick her off the crew."

"Flirting with Yoshi doesn't count as a reason?"

"You know Emma will ignore that kind of stuff if it has anything to do with one of her big canoe races," Pat said. "Besides, I don't think Kathy's flirting is completely a one-way street."

"That's probably true. Emma told me her spineless husband, those were her words, doesn't initiate it, but he doesn't exactly try to—oh hi Yoshi, I didn't see you standing there!"

"Did they come in yet?" Yoshi shaded his eyes and peered out at the dark ocean. I wondered why he didn't simply turn the bill of his baseball cap around to face the front.

"It's getting a little dark to see them now," I said. "But Emma's canoe is out there."

"The sun sets so fast here. I'm still not used to that. It's so different from upstate New York. I feel like we're the only ones on the beach."

"We're not," I said.

A man leaned on the wall of the halau, the open-sided shed housing the crew's canoes and equipment. He was texting or playing a game on a handheld device, slouched against the halau's weathered siding as if he were doing a fashion shoot. His leather pants were so snug it looked like the lower half of his body had been dipped in black latex.

Pat followed my line of sight.

"Enjoying the view?"

"He's more your type than mine. Besides, I'm not looking."

"Careful, Molly. I think Gorgeous George there is with one of the ladies in Emma's crew. Does Donnie know about your roving eye?"

I tried to formulate a devastating comeback, but couldn't think of anything wittier than, "Shut up, Pat."

"I'm starving," Yoshi said. "I paddled for almost an hour today."

"I guess I could eat something," Pat agreed. "You

think we should head over to the Pair-O-Dice and get a table? Emma can meet us there whenever she's done torturing her crew."

I was about to chime in with my support for Pat's idea when a distant voice yelled,

"Call 911!"

Pat was already on his phone to the emergency dispatcher before I could locate my own phone in my purse. I wondered whether I should look into getting one of those bags that lights up when you open it, like a refrigerator.

"Yes, I'm sure we need an ambulance," Pat enunciated into his phone. "No, I can't tell you the exact nature of the emergency. Someone shouted, 'Call 911', so—Medical. Yes. I'm sure. Look, the boat's not on fire, and I'm pretty sure they didn't get attacked by pirates. Yes. No, I'm not trying to be…Okay, thank you."

Still on the phone, Pat touched my arm to get my attention and pointed at Emma's canoe. As it crept closer to shore, we saw what the problem was. Only three women were paddling. Behind the boat, three more shapes trailed in the black water. Two were swimming, holding up a limp figure between them. Yoshi, now waist-deep in the surf, gripped the side of the canoe and pushed it hard to point it up toward the shore. Emma and the two remaining paddlers hopped out of the canoe and pushed it until it rested on the sand. An ambulance pulled up, and two men in white hurried down to the water's edge.

Even with her blonde hair stringy and wet, I

recognized her immediately. The men in white bundled Kathy Banks into the back of the ambulance and pulled away slowly. Yoshi stood and watched until the ambulance was out of sight.

CHAPTER TWO

The women in Emma's crew hosed the boat down and hauled it into the halau. The paddlers worked quietly and dispersed quickly, leaving the four of us—Pat, Emma, Yoshi, and me—on the dark beach.

You might imagine a Hawaiian sunset as a florid blaze over the water, edged with pinks and golds, but here you would be wrong. Those sunsets happen on the west side of the island, the dry sunny side that draws all the tourists. Here on the rainy windward side, the sky darkens, and the palm trees become black silhouettes, and it's nighttime. If you really want to see something, stand on the beach at dawn. When the rising sun lights the ocean, then creeps up the forested slopes rising up from the shore, and finally illuminates the snowy peak of the volcano…well, I've heard it's spectacular. I don't usually get up that early myself.

"One minute everything's fine," Emma fumed, "an' next minute she falls into the water in front of me. No warning at all."

I seemed to be the only one who was feeling the cold. Emma was fairly incandescent with rage. She seemed to think Kathy Banks had keeled over on purpose, specifically to ruin paddling practice.

"Was she breathing when they took her out of the water?" Pat asked.

"How should I know?" Emma crossed her sturdy arms. "Sherry and Pam were the ones who pulled her up. That was all we could do. None of us had a phone out there. Man, I knew something like this was gonna happen."

"Cause of the diet?" Yoshi asked.

"You put your crew on a diet?" I was glad I had resisted Emma's attempts to persuade me to join her crew. The thought of daily workouts was bad enough, but a diet on top of everything else sounded downright totalitarian.

"No, I did not put anyone on a diet. I mean, I might have told 'em that we could all stand to lose a little weight."

A chill breeze sliced through my loose knit angora sweater. I hugged myself and rubbed my upper arms.

"Can't you eat whatever you want?" I said. "With all the exercise you guys do?"

"You don't want extra weight in the boat," Emma said. "You gotta be light so your boat rides higher in the water. That way there's less drag, and you go faster. But look, I did not encourage this. In fact, I told them, you can't train on five hundred calories a day."

"Five hundred calories a day! Plus hours of paddling? You guys are like galley slaves. How does anyone think this is fun?"

"Molly, when you start paddling with us? Once you're out on the water? You'll understand."

"No," I said. "That is not going to happen."

You can't equivocate with Emma. You show any hint of indecisiveness, and she'll steamroll right over you.

"I mean, when the Labor Day Race is over," she said. "Right now I'm dealing with seven crew members and only six spots in the boat. Everyone wants to race, so it can get a little ugly."

"Can?" Pat said. "Looks like it already has."

"We call it paddletics," Yoshi said. "When paddlers get too competitive within their crew and turn on each other."

Yoshi has mellowed a lot since he first moved here with Emma as a freshly minted MBA. At first, he didn't like living in Mahina. He claimed there were no decent jobs to be had, and would say things like, "I can't live in a place where no one can tell I'm wearing a two-thousand-dollar suit."

Tired of his grumping around the house, Emma got him into canoe paddling, which he embraced with the zeal of a convert. Most of his time is now spent paddling and hanging out at the beach. Today he wore board shorts, a souvenir t-shirt from the previous year's Labor Day canoe race, and a cap with the logo of a local paddling shop.

One thing that hasn't changed about Yoshi is his need to be the Expert. His favorite pastime is explaining things to people.

"Paddletics!" Pat exclaimed before Yoshi could expound further. "Molly, isn't that one of those words you hate? What do the Word Police have to say?"

Pat knows I hate sloppy neologisms: Homophobe. Anything-gate. The worst of the bunch is the suffix –holic, which got snapped off the end of 'alcoholic' and now is attached to any word you can think of to indicate addiction or even mere affinity. Normally I enjoy arguing etymology with Pat, but right now, I wasn't in the mood.

"I've heard worse. Paddletics could mean affairs of the paddle, in the same way that politics means affairs of the city."

A fire truck pulled up, lights flashing. Pat shook his head and went over to talk to the driver.

"Okay, Molly. We're gonna head home. I hafta change. Sorry about making you miss the Pair-O-Dice."

"It's okay, Emma. I wasn't even thinking about happy hour. You should get going. You must be freezing." Emma's wet rash guard and board shorts clung to her sturdy frame. I shivered in sympathy.

"Nah, not really. It's not that cold. Oh, I dunno if I can have lunch tomorrow. I gotta follow up with Kathy. I'm gonna visit her tomorrow at the hospital if she's still there."

Emma and Yoshi started back to the parking lot. I called after them,

"Give me a call tomorrow. I'll go with you to visit Kathy."

Emma paused and turned back.

"Seriously?"

"Yes. Of course, I know her too. I mean, I work with her."

"Sure. Okay." Emma sounded unconvinced.

An hour ago the ocean sparkled cobalt blue. Now whitecaps foamed on the black water, illuminated by a cloudy sliver of moon. I was lightheaded with hunger, and I doubted I would ever feel warm again. Pat came back as the fire truck pulled away.

"What's going on?" I asked.

Pat shook his head.

"Who knows? I told them the ambulance came and went already. They tried to argue with me."

"Maybe you shouldn't have been so sassy on the phone."

"I told them to go take it up with their dispatcher. Molly. Molly!" Pat gripped my shoulder. "Are you okay?"

"I'm fine. No, I'm not. I will be, though."

My two-tone turquoise Thunderbird looked unfamiliar, black and white under the sodium light. Pat gently removed my keys from my hand, opened the car door, and deposited me on the driver's side. I pulled the heavy door shut, cranked the window open, rested my hands on the wheel, and started doing the breathing exercises from the video that came with my yoga ball. I didn't want to be sick all over my new-old-stock upholstery. Pat braced his hands on the door and bent down to eye level.

"I told you, you have to see someone about this."

"This breathing is supposed to fill me with peace and calm," I said.

"It doesn't seem to be working."

I leaned forward and rested on the hard steering wheel, focusing on the sensation of the cool Bakelite pressing on my forehead.

"No. It's not working."

"Do you want me to drive you home? You can probably leave your car here overnight. Who would be stupid enough to steal a 1959 Thunderbird?"

"I'll be okay." I hoped I really would be. "It's a little unnerving, the way Kathy collapsed at the exact moment we were talking about her."

I expected Pat to say something to reassure me. Emma's crew simply got overzealous with their diet, he could have said; Kathy probably overexerted herself.

Instead, he squinted out at the black water.

"Something about this doesn't feel right to me. I don't think this is going to turn out well for Kathy."

He pulled his attention back to me. "I hope I'm wrong. Molly, you go home and get a good night's sleep."

"Pat, why did you say that? Why do you think this isn't going to turn out well for Kathy? What doesn't feel right?"

I wondered whether years of reporting on murder

and mayhem had made Pat paranoid. He used to be a reporter for the *County Courier*, before the layoffs. Now he teaches freshman composition part-time at our university and runs his own news blog, *Island Confidential.*

"Go see a doctor about this." Pat wasn't going to answer any of my questions. "Before you keel over. I'm serious."

CHAPTER THREE

The temperamental climate control in my office was working this morning. My wall thermometer showed seventy-nine degrees Fahrenheit. Warmer than I'd like, but significantly cooler than outside. I brewed a strong cup of coffee, tried to get comfortable on my yoga ball chair, and prepared to tackle my to-do list.

You might think my recent promotion to interim department chair would be some kind of ego-inflating power trip. Allow me to disabuse you of that notion right now. In addition to teaching my classes and trying to keep my research going, this is how I spend my days:

First and foremost, I attempt to comply with the often conflicting, and always paperwork-intensive, diktats from our university's Student Retention Office. I also run department meetings, schedule classes, counsel students, and listen to complaints.

Oh, the complaining: Students complain about professors, professors complain about administration, the Student Retention Office complains about my faculty members failing to complete their reports on time, and so on. All I can do is listen and try to appear sympathetic.

Here's what I can't do: I can't force faculty members to fill out their weekly Teaching Philosophy Statements and Customer Interaction Reports for the Student Retention Office. I can't make money appear in the department budget, no matter how badly someone might need office furniture or whiteboard markers or copier paper. And I can't tell people how to teach their classes.

I have to explain this to our two most senior professors, Hanson Harrison and Larry Schneider, whenever they come storming into my office to gripe about our colleague, Roger Cowper. "Dr. Rodge," as he tells his students to call him, doesn't give midterms or final exams, assigns no homework, and gives A's to everyone who signs up for his Human Potential class. I can't force Rodge to "maintain academic standards worthy of our university" (Hanson's words) or "teach a real college class and knock off that feel-good bullshit" (Hanson's contemporary, Dr. Larry Schneider). As long as Rodge shows up when he's supposed to and stays out of trouble with the students, there's not much else I can do. Especially not when the Student Retention Office keeps nominating him for the campus-wide teaching award every year.

The top message in my email inbox was an announcement for what was politely termed a "destination conference." The call for papers invited "original contributions on topics related to any of these topics or others" and proceeded to list just about every discipline in existence as well as a few that the organizers had apparently invented. I could certainly use another presentation on my vita when I went up for tenure, but I wasn't desperate enough to sign up for a phony conference sponsored by the nonexistent "Las Vegas University." I deleted the message and the one after it, a reminder to attend Tuesday's emergency faculty senate meeting.

The next message was from the Student Retention Office.

ANNOUNCEMENT.

This was uncharacteristically cryptic. Normally the SRO's email headers are more descriptive: *Meet Our New Student Parking Advocates! Learning Styles Workbooks Now Available Online! Fifty Shades of Play: Show Your Students Some Love This Valentine's Day with These Engaging Classroom Role Play Exercises!*

A tentative knock on my door interrupted my reading. The SRO's announcement, along with the hundreds of other unread messages in my inbox, would have to wait until after lunch.

Lunch! One more thing on my to-do list. I had told Emma I would go with her to see Kathy Banks. I hoped the visit wouldn't take too long. With any luck, Kathy would be resting quietly, and we wouldn't even be allowed in to see her in person. I could drop off a card and slip away. Kathy would probably want something with glittery flowers or a kitten in a basket.

I opened the door to a line of students stretching down the hallway, all waiting for me to sign off on their late adds to one of the courses in the management department. Maybe their financial aid didn't arrive in time, or they wanted to switch to an easier professor or a more convenient time slot. My heart broke a little for them. We were already in the second week of the semester. I had seen the numbers from past semesters. I knew that students who joined a class after the first week had practically no chance of passing. But our administration had made it clear: maximizing enrollment (and tuition dollars) was Job One. My standing orders were to let everyone in.

Despite their eagerness to accommodate late registrants, the administration wasn't able to waive the late registration restriction (something to do with our IT department), so I, as department chair, had to process each course-add request manually. I was starting to understand why Dan Watanabe, my predecessor, had always gone around looking like he'd been trampled by elephants.

I finally had a chance to call Emma at around one in the afternoon. She answered after half a ring.

"Molly! How come you didn't answer? I musta called you about a hundred times."

"I was doing registration overrides all morning, so I had my ringer off. Are we still going up to see

Kathy at lunch? Or did you already go?"

"Don't you read your email?"

I jiggled the mouse to wake up my computer, but the screen stayed black.

"Not recently. What's going on?"

"You didn't get the email from the Student Retention Office?"

"I get about a hundred emails a day from the Student Retention Office," I said.

"Yeah, I know. I didn't get it until after I already left for the hospital. Wasted trip."

"You went without me? What do you mean wasted trip? Is Kathy better already?"

"I'll read it to you. Announcement: We are saddened to announce the loss of one of our 'Ohana. Associate Student Success Advocate Kathy Banks passed away over the weekend. We will miss her."

I stared at the computer screen as it blinked awake.

"Emma," I stammered, "I'm so sorry."

"Eh, no need apologize to me. Wanna go get lunch now?"

"Better not," I said. "I've got students coming by nonstop. In fact, I see one waiting for me now. Maritime Club tonight, though?"

"Yeah, Maritime Club sounds good. Mind if I invite someone from the crew?"

"Fine with me." I waved the next student into my office.

"Don't be late," Emma said as I hung up.

CHAPTER FOUR

St. Damien's Catholic Church is an incongruous pink confection, conspicuous on a narrow street of rusty-roofed plantation shacks and jungle-infested vacant lots. It's not exactly on the way to the Maritime Club, but I made the twenty-minute detour. I wanted to stop in before I met Pat and Emma for dinner.

The church's wide double doors were open, and the interior was quiet and dim. I slid into a pew in the back and allowed my vision to adjust to the candlelight. The only other person in the sanctuary sat in the front. The round head looked familiar. I stood and approached him.

"Iker?" I whispered.

"Molly." Iker stood up and clasped my hands, his plump fingers squeezing mine with enthusiasm. Iker is probably around my age, but with his shiny side-parted helmet of brown hair and his plump, pink face, he seems both old and baby-like: ageless. I wondered whether he was uncomfortable in his red sweater vest and long-sleeved madras shirt. St. Damien's isn't air conditioned, and the air was sticky and warm.

"I have not seen you in Mass," Iker said.

"I know," I said. "I've been sleeping in. I need to be better about my attendance. What are you doing here?"

"At the start of the school year, we are distracted by so many things. It is good to rest and worship and remember. These things are not for the Sabbath only, yes? Molly, you are troubled. Please sit with me."

Iker Legazpi is one of my favorite colleagues, despite his sunny attitude. He must get the same underachievers, plagiarists, and grade-grubbers in his accounting classes as the rest of us have, but he never complains. He gives every student his full attention and the benefit of the doubt.

"Did you go to the Student Retention Office meeting this morning?" I asked. "I couldn't make it. I was doing late registrations."

"Yes," Iker said. "It was a long meeting of many hours."

"Anything interesting?"

"Oh, Molly, these meetings, they are as dull as a dishwasher. Many people stood and left."

"But you stayed until the end?"

"I did not wish to be impolite," he said.

Iker is a saint. Not a real one, of course. You have

to be dead for that. But close enough.

"So Iker," I said, "You're right. I do have something on my mind. Could I ask you about it? I'd love to get your perspective."

Iker studied my face. "Perhaps this is a matter for Confession?"

"No. I mean, this is a hypothetical situation."

Was that a lie? I just told Iker a self-serving lie. Great. Now I really was going to have to go to Confession. Not all lies are bad, of course. Some are deployed to spare feelings and soften hard truths: I'm so sorry you have to leave; that was such an interesting story; there's no such thing as a stupid question.

"Molly, if you do no wrong, you need not to be afraid."

"How do you know I did something wrong?"

"It is only a proverb. I mean to say that you should not be worried over something that is hypothetical only. Perhaps you can explain me the situation."

I inhaled deeply.

"Okay. What if, and I'm sure you've never experienced this, but bear with me. Imagine there was someone you really didn't like."

"What a terrible thing!"

"Well, wait. What I just told you wasn't supposed to be the terrible part. So it occurs to you that the world might be a better place without her. Them. Without them, I mean."

"Oh, Molly." Iker clasped his plump hands

together in dismay.

"It gets worse. Suppose in this hypothetical example, the person actually goes and, um, passes away."

Iker's silence made me uncomfortable, so I continued to talk.

"In this fictional case," I asked, "am I, I mean, is hypothetical person A responsible for hypothetical person B's, uh, demise? At all?"

Iker's sigh was compassionate, rather than impatient. "Molly, you know First John 3:15, yes?"

"Um, sure, it's, uh…" No. I wasn't going to sit here in church and lie to Iker's face.

"I don't quite recall the exact verse," I said.

"It is simply this. Everyone who hates a brother or sister is a murderer."

"What? Seriously?"

"Yes. The main character of your story, Person A as you say, is already guilty of murder. This is even before someone dies."

"Does it really say that?"

Well of course it did. Iker wouldn't make it up. This conversation wasn't going at all the way I had hoped it would.

"And Matthew 5:22," Iker continued. "It is also like that. One who is angry at his brother, it is the same as a murder."

Iker must have been raised Catholic, as I was. So where on earth had he learned all these Bible verses?

"I'm so sorry I bothered you with this, Iker." That was no lie.

"I believe you know the answer to your question," Iker said. "You already knew it before you asked me."

I shook my head, hopeless.

"But what if it's too late to fix it?"

"No. It is not too late, Molly. It is never so late that one must abandon what is right."

I walked out alone to my car. I should have invited Iker to join us at the Maritime Club, but I couldn't bring myself to do it. Pat and Emma both like Iker, so they wouldn't have minded. I was the problem. Although I knew Iker had only meant to be helpful, my conversation with him had felt like a reproach. I couldn't face sharing a meal with someone who thought I was a murderer.

CHAPTER FIVE

By the time I arrived at the Maritime Club, Pat had already secured a table out on the lanai, with a full view of the ocean. Emma, who had made a point of warning me not to be late, wasn't there yet.

"Did you make an appointment to see someone about your nerves?" Pat asked. "Like you promised?"

"I'll get around to it." I shielded my eyes from the sparkling ocean, too distressed to enjoy the view. "Did you say my nerves? Like I need to loosen my corsets and lie down on my fainting couch?"

"That's a fab jacket, Molly. Is that what you wore to work today?"

"Yeah, what's wrong with it?"

My vintage wardrobe isn't particularly comfortable in the tropical humidity, and my dry-cleaning bills are horrific, but there's really no modern substitute for a 1940s Lilli Ann suit jacket in carnelian red with black piping.

"Nothing's wrong with it," he said. "It's fab. Molly, I can tell you're stressing out. Try to calm down. Breathe. Do you want something to drink?"

"I'll wait till Emma gets here. And you don't have to tell me to breathe. I do know how to do that."

"Okay." Pat watched me carefully.

"Don't look at me in that tone of voice."

I took a slow, deep breath (which I was going to do anyway).

"It's not your fault, Molly. What happened to Kathy."

"Who said it was my fault? You? Do you think it's my fault too?"

Pat placed his elbows on the table and leaned toward me. "Molly. I just said it isn't your fault. Remember what I said—"

"I do remember. You said you didn't think it was going to turn out well for Kathy. How did you know?"

"I didn't. But I've covered enough murder cases. Sorry to be so blunt about it, but something about this stinks."

"So you think there's a story here for *Island Confidential*? Are you going to investigate?"

"Yeah. I am."

I sighed. "I still feel a little bit responsible. I mean, I was having not-very-kind thoughts about her."

"That's fine, Molly. Go ahead and wallow in your Catholic guilt if that's what you want to do. But whoever did this is still out there. How do we know this'll stop at Kathy?"

Pat half-rose from his chair and I turned to see Emma bustling in through the back gate, her husband Yoshi close behind her. Following Yoshi I saw a pale, skinny woman with an outsized nimbus of curly black hair, walking with the blond muscleman I'd seen at the beach. These two leaned close together, hands in each other's back pockets. The woman looked vaguely familiar.

Pat leaned over to me and muttered, "There he is, Molly. Feast your eyes."

"Pat, stop it."

"Oh, pardon me. I guess your eyes aren't in the mood for junk food today."

The man was wearing a metallic silver leather blazer with cutoff sleeves, matching low-rise leather trousers, and no shirt. He sported a clump of leather bracelets and steel chains at each wrist. A studded dog collar circled his throat.

"At least he's wearing a collar," Pat said. "He's technically complying with the club's dress code."

As they got closer, I noticed the artificial, sculpted look of the man's face. His perfectly tousled beach boy hair had about an eighth of an inch of mousy roots.

I nudged Pat. "Bet you a hundred dollars he's from California," I said.

Pat and I got up to help scoot two of the plastic outdoor tables together.

"Oh hey, Doctor B," said the big-haired woman, extending a slim, chiseled arm. Her East Coast rasp was like chain link fence scraping concrete. As I accepted her handshake she said, "I'm Sherry. I'm in your business planning class."

"Right," I said. "Of course."

"I'm on Emma's crew," she added. She introduced her companion as Glenn, two n's. Up close, his face looked weathered. I guessed he'd spent a lot of time in the sun.

"I was so sorry to hear about Kathy," I said, as we all got ourselves seated. Across the table, I heard Yoshi say, "You went up there to see Kathy? Emma, why didn't you tell me?" I looked up to see Emma aiming a look at Yoshi that should have frozen him solid on the spot.

"She's about to take our order," Emma snapped. "You better choose."

I turned my attention to the waitress. She smiled at me.

"Hey, you two are sisters, right? Are you twins?"

I realized she was talking about Sherry and me.

Sherry broke out in a gravelly laugh. "Yeah, you're my evil twin. Right, Doctor B?"

"Sure," I agreed. Why not? Sherry had clearly partied hard in her youth, but she still looked good. I'm vain enough not to mind being told that I look like an attractive person.

"I'm ready to order," I smiled back at the waitress. "I don't need to hear the specials. I'd like the prime rib, end cut if you have it. And a baked potato with sour cream and butter. Real butter, please, not margarine."

"Whoa, Dr. B," Sherry exclaimed. "That's kinda rich, huh?"

Yes, well, I thought, this is why I'm the fat sister.

"I'll work it off later," I said.

"Really?" Emma interjected rudely.

Yoshi ordered filet mignon, and Emma chose seafood pasta. Glenn and Pat both opted for the vegetarian curry. Sherry requested a green salad, no dressing.

"Girl, you still on that crazy diet?" Emma shook her head at Sherry.

"Yes, ma'am. I want to be sure I get to race on Labor Day."

The table fell awkwardly quiet. Kathy's demise had brought the number of Emma's crew from seven down to six, the exact number of seats in the canoe. The odds of Sherry getting a spot had just jumped up to one hundred percent.

"I don't want to weigh down the boat," Sherry added quickly, patting her bare hipbone. She wore snug low-rise jeans and a shrunken t-shirt that showed off her belly button jewel. For long-lost sisters, Sherry and I sure didn't inherit the same style sense.

Yoshi glanced warily at Emma. "Do they know what happened? With Kathy? I can't believe it. So unexpected."

"They didn't give us the gory details, Yoshi."

"I wonder if there's anyone who misses her."

I had meant to be kind, but my words came out sounding mean.

"What I meant was," I added quickly, "I wonder if she has any family or longtime friends or anything. It's sad to think you can go, and no one would miss you."

Another uncomfortable silence. No one at the table claimed to be sad about Kathy Banks. Yoshi opened his mouth as if to speak, but Emma shot him a death glare and he clammed up.

"Kathy seemed like a very forceful person," Pat said. "Always convinced that she was right." He glanced at me. "I think she got people's backs up."

"She could be a little rough around the edges," Sherry placed her hand on Glenn's evenly tanned bicep. "I wonder if she attracted some bad energy. Glenn's crystallologist told him if someone sends you too much negative energy, you could get hurt. Maybe even die."

"Oh yeah," he agreed. "That's totally true. Most people don't realize how powerful the chi is. Negative energy is literally deadly."

"I owe you a hundred dollars," Pat murmured.

"How does that work? Has negative energy ever actually killed someone?" I could hear the contempt in Emma's voice, although I don't think Glenn caught it.

"Totally! There's this thing called Voodoo death? Where if you hate someone enough, and totally want them dead? They die. It's proven. The only problem is, it comes back and hurts you too. It's totally toxic. Hating someone is like drinking poison and expecting the other person to die."

"Voodoo death," Emma repeated, with a caustic edge to her voice. Emma, who is an accomplished biologist, has no patience whatsoever with anything she deems pseudoscience (a category that in her mind includes not only crystallology but also sociology, psychology, economics, and management).

"Yeah, Voodoo Death," Glenn repeated. "It's seriously real. You can look it up."

CHAPTER SIX

The library's interior featured a terrazzo floor and faux-walnut and chrome tables that had been around so long, they had gone out of fashion and come back in. My plan was to read up on "Voodoo Death" without logging into our library database and leaving an electronic trail. I hadn't mentioned any of this to Emma or Pat. Instead, I had made the case that spending Saturday morning in an air-conditioned library would be a great opportunity for all three of us to catch up on grading, class prep, and writing. Someone said being a writer is like having homework every night for the rest of your life. That's also a pretty good description of what it's like to be a college professor.

I recognized the young man who hurried up to greet us as one of my former students.

"E komo mai, Professor Barda." He smiled. "Welcome to our information literacy resource center."

"Oh, hi…" I glanced down at his ID card, "Micah. It's nice to see you again. I thought you graduated?"

"Did. Job market on the island kinda junk, but."

"No kidding," Pat said.

"But they was hiring here," Micah said. "I was lucky to get one job. Anyways, may I help you to find anything in particular today?"

"We reserved study room C," I said. "We might need someone to unlock it for us."

"I can do that," he announced happily. "Follow me."

"So what is your job here, Micah?" I asked as he led us toward the back of the library, the hard floor ringing with our footsteps. "What do you do?"

"Knowledge Curator. Means I could help you look stuff up. I know you don't need any help, but, Professor. Choke guys, I mean a lot of us working here." He gestured around the library, and sure enough, it was teeming with young people shelving books, straightening chairs, and wiping down desks. Micah led us to a door, unlocked it, let us into the windowless, beige-walled study room and left us to it. As soon as Micah had left, I went out to the stacks and retrieved several dusty volumes of bound journals.

The three of us worked quietly for a few minutes. Emma tapped away on her laptop while Pat graded papers.

Emma looked up. "What are you doing, Molly?"

I was perusing a journal whose focus was mental health, religion, and culture. "Looking up some information for my class. On belief systems around the world."

Many of which, I did not add, believed in something called "Voodoo death." People who had broken taboos, or who believed they had been cursed or put under a spell, often seemed to give up and die.

"The mechanisms for this phenomenon," the article stated dryly, "which we term psychogenic death, remain controversial."

The authors were maddeningly vague about whether psychogenic death could be inflicted on an unaware victim such as Kathy Banks. At least I assumed she was unaware. Kathy had never struck me as someone who was particularly sensitive to other peoples' feelings.

"Speaking of Kathy Banks. I never told you guys the latest about that student in Larry Schneider's class."

"Were we speaking of Kathy Banks?" Emma glared at me. "I thought I was trying to get some work done."

"Oh, Phone Boy?" Pat leaned back in his chair and crossed his arms. "Did you ever figure out whether the letter he left in your guys' mailboxes was supposed to be a death threat or a suicide note?"

"No. Either way, though, not good. So I filled out the paperwork to have him removed from Larry's class. Instead of signing off on it, Kathy Banks called me into her office. Want to guess what happened?"

"She congratulated you for preventing a classroom massacre," Pat said, "and told you that the student would be referred to psychiatric services immediately."

"Ha! No. She lectured me about how I had failed our university's mission to serve every student. She accused me of imposing my value system on him."

"Are you sure you want to talk about this?" Pat asked.

"Obviously, she does." Emma doesn't like interruptions, and I could tell I'd made her a little grumpy.

"Our safety, our students' safety, meant nothing to her. It was all about, I don't even know. Implementing the Student Retention Office's feel-good initiative du jour. checking off the right box on some grant renewal form."

"Maybe you need to check your privilege," Pat said. "Maybe she was right. You and Larry assumed his note was threatening, but it sounds like you might be imposing your cultural—"

"How about you give your White Savior complex a rest, Pat. He's the orthopedist's kid."

Pat raised his hands in surrender and went back to his grading.

"Well, Kathy's dead now," Emma said. "So you can be happy."

"I'm not happy she's dead." I stood and stacked the volumes on the table. "I don't think I can use these."

“Just leave them on the table,” Emma said. “They’ll reshelve it.”

“That’s okay.” I hoisted up the entire stack of books and did a sort of controlled stagger toward the door. “I’ve been sitting too long. I’ll put them back where I found them. It’ll be like I was never even here.”

"Want to take a break and get some coffee?" Emma asked.

"Thanks, Emma, but I just remembered I have some errands to run. I'll see you guys Sunday at the Pair-O-Dice."

I didn’t feel like spending any more time with Emma or Pat. I wanted to talk to Donnie.

CHAPTER SEVEN

Water drops quivered on the hood of my 1959 Thunderbird as I drove out of the Wiki-Wash. The two-tone turquoise and white paint job gleamed in the afternoon sun. This was one of those times I was glad I'd had my car shipped over to Hawaii.

The times when I'm less glad usually involve my mechanic, Earl Miyashiro of Miyashiro Motors. Earl keeps telling me I should give up on my temperamental Squarebird and buy something more reliable. Maybe my car does handle like a leaky boat with a broken rudder, and a two-year-old Toyota wouldn't rack up repair bills that rivaled my student loan payments. But there's no car built today that can make my heart sing, and I don't care what kind of funny looks Earl gives me when I say things like that. I would go to someone less judgmental and literal-minded, but Earl is the only auto mechanic on the island who will go near my car.

My sparkling T-bird and I headed over to Donnie's Drive-Inn for a late takeout lunch. Merrie Musubis, the Drive-Inn's biggest competitor, has better-tasting food, no question. But Donnie's Drive-Inn has Donnie Gonsalves.

Donnie spotted me at the takeout window and came over just as the server was handing me a big Styrofoam bowl brimming with my Sumo Saimin.

"No knee da kava?" The young woman asked me.

As I was trying to parse her question, Donnie intervened.

"Did you need a cover for your bowl, Molly?" he translated.

"Oh. No. No, thank you. I was going to eat here."

Donnie called back into the kitchen that he was taking five minutes, and led me to a clean picnic table. Cleanliness is the one outstanding feature of Donnie's Drive-Inn. The seating is all outdoors, and the food is nothing special, but every surface is spotless. The floor, the tables, the restrooms, the service windows. Immaculate.

"Molly, this is a nice surprise." Donnie slid onto the bench opposite me. Even toward the end of the lunchtime rush, he looked cool and unruffled. His black hair, graying slightly at the top and sides, was trimmed short and perfectly in place. His red Donnie's Drive-Inn polo shirt looked freshly pressed, a sharp crease down each sleeve. He had the top two buttons of his placket undone, as he always did. Never one, never three. I used to wonder why even his casual shirts always looked like someone had ironed them until I found out he sends his clothes out to be professionally laundered. Someone actually does iron them. I suppose that makes sense for someone like Donnie. He has a lot more money than free time.

"I heard the news about Kathy Banks," he said. "I'm sorry."

Of course, he had already heard the news about Kathy Banks. The coconut wireless is faster than any newfangled fiber-optic network. Heaven help anyone who needs to keep a secret in this town.

I set my Sumo Saimin bowl between us to share. I'd been planning to gobble up the whole thing myself, but I didn't want Donnie to sit there and watch me plow through a giant bowl of noodles, fish cake, and fried Spam. Besides, he hadn't let me pay for it, so not sharing would have seemed selfish.

"Was she the one from the office that's always giving you trouble? Her name sounds familiar."

"No one's giving me trouble, Donnie. I mean, I might have had some minor disagreements with the Student Retention Office. But I didn't hate her or anything. You're right, it was sudden. It's kind of hard to believe."

I sighed and gazed into the golden depths of the Sumo Saimin Bowl. "In an instant, everything's changed. She's actually gone."

"That's always hard," he said, "when someone passes on, and you weren't on good terms. There's no way to make your peace."

"I *was* on good terms with her!" I insisted. "At

least I wasn't *not* on good terms with her."

Donnie smiled knowingly and turned his attention to lunch. He slid a pair of wooden chopsticks out of their paper packaging, snapped them apart, and rubbed them together to smooth the splinters.

"Is your school going to close for a half day or anything?" he asked.

"Oh, no. What happened to poor Kathy Banks isn't going to slow down the machine at all. You'd think at least the Student Retention Office might take some time off to mourn her or something, but no. The Student Retention Office never sleeps. In fact, you know what? I just found out they're inflicting a fresh atrocity on our university even as we speak."

He smiled, dug his chopsticks into the bowl and pulled out a knot of noodles. "Is this what you were telling me about using professors' online ratings for hiring and firing?"

"No, that's already a done deal," I said. "And we have the ratings thing under control anyway."

"Do they know you guys write your own reviews?"

"I'll tell anyone who will listen, but the SRO people just keep saying, Crowdsourcing! Crowdsourcing! As if it's a magic spell. It seems like you don't have to be very smart to get a job in the Student Retention Office. Anyway, the latest thing is that they're lobbying to rid of our general history requirement. Because, you know, history is hard and boring and Today's Millennial Digital Native doesn't want to waste time studying all of those old dead people. The faculty are going to get together and try to fight it, but you know, by the time administration asks us for our opinion, the decision's already been made."

"So your students don't like having to take history?"

Donnie plunged his chopsticks into the bowl. Watching the bands of his sleeves strain over his well-developed biceps made me lose my train of thought for a moment. Donnie doesn't have time to go to the gym, but he doesn't have to. He spends his day hauling around stainless-steel cooking equipment and pallets of frozen food in a crowded, steamy kitchen. I could never do his job. I wouldn't even know where to begin. After so many decades of schooling, I thought, I have remarkably few practical skills. Come the apocalypse, I'll either have to get myself into a supervisory position, or end up as a protein source.

"Of course they don't like having to take history," I said. "They don't like having to take anything. I can think of a few who probably wish we'd mail them their degrees and cut out all of that tedious learning stuff in between."

"You don't have any students who are that bad, do you?"

I'd had at least one who was that bad, and worse. Donnie's beloved son Davison, as it happens.

"Oh, no, of course not," I said quickly. "I'm exaggerating to make a point. I have wonderful students. You know that."

Davison had taken, and barely passed, my IBM class (that's Intro to Business Management). Gonsalves *fils* was an unrepentant cheater and a lying suckup, among other things. I had been greatly relieved when Donnie moved him to a fancy private college on the mainland.

The way Donnie spoils his son is probably the only thing that causes real tension between us. Whenever the subject comes up, though, all Donnie has to say to win the argument is, "Wouldn't your parents do this for you?" And he's right; they would try to shield me from the consequences of my own actions if they could. The difference is they would have the decency to make me feel guilty about it for the rest of my life.

In any event, I've come to realize honesty is not the best policy when it comes to the topic of young Davison Gonsalves. It's easier to let Donnie believe that I adore his demon spawn every bit as much as he does.

"Aren't the students your customers?" Donnie asked. "Why not just give your customers what they want? If my customers want their Sumo Saimin bowl without kamaboko, they can have it." He gestured with his chopsticks at a D-shaped piece of fish cake, white edged with hot pink. "That's kamaboko, by the way."

I already knew what kamaboko was.

"It's fish cake," he explained.

"The students are not our customers, Donnie.

And a college education is not a bowl of noodle soup."

CHAPTER EIGHT

"You don't think the student is your customer?" Donnie asked, as if such a thought had never occurred to him.

I indicated a delivery truck in the parking lot.

"No more than Palila Ranch thinks their cattle are their customers."

"Interesting way to look at it," he said. "So who is?"

"You are."

"I mean who's your customer."

"You. Employers. You're the one who's going to hire them. You want us to send you a pack of illiterate dunderheads?"

Donnie laughed. "I can find all the...what did you call them? Illiterate dunderheads I need on my own, thanks. Molly, this history thing sounds like it's above your pay grade. You said they've already made up their minds, right? You shouldn't stress out about it."

Donnie had started working right out of high school and had built Donnie's Drive-Inn without the benefit of any formal higher education. Things like general education requirements don't mean much to him. Even the relentless dastardliness of the Student Retention Office seems to strike him as amusing. He doesn't see the cracks spreading in the very foundation of civilization, the way I do.

"I watched our university lose a multimillion-dollar donation," I said.

Now I had his attention.

"You know Skip Kojima?" I asked.

"Kojima Surfwear? Yeah. Met him a few times. He's a good guy."

"One of our students told him he was such an inspiration to her that she wanted to start her own clothing line. Called Tokyo Rose."

Donnie raised his eyebrows.

"And not to be hip and edgy so she could sell it in some store on Melrose or anything like that," I added.

"Some store where?"

"In Hollywood," I said. "Not really the point. The point is, she actually thought it was a good name for a brand because it sounded pretty. She said this to a man whose father fought in the four hundred forty-second."

"Not good," Donnie agreed.

"You know what else she said? She said she thought Japanese tourists would like it."

"Maybe your history requirement isn't working too well to begin with."

"Touché," I sighed. "Actually, the student I'm talking about was a history major. Not only that, I found out there already is a Tokyo Rose label. So if she had simply taken a few minutes to do a quick search beforehand—sorry. I didn't mean to dominate the conversation with shop talk. You know, the history department should've seen this coming. The Student Retention Office told them to cut down their writing requirements and they refused. They should've played ball like—anyway. I'm really done now. What's new with you?"

"I've been collecting recipes, believe it or not."

"To sell at the Drive-Inn?" I asked. "Like a souvenir cookbook?" I wondered who would buy such a thing. Donnie's Drive-Inn is great for a quick bowl of Sumo Saimin or a plateful of candy-sweet teriyaki beef slices, but what would be the point of reproducing the Drive-Inn's dishes at home? All of the blandness and none of the convenience?

"I hadn't thought of doing a whole cookbook," he said. "I'm just pulling together some easy recipes for Davison. I think he's living off instant noodles and beer right now."

"It sounds like he's really putting down roots on the mainland," I said optimistically. "That's great, you helping him to become more self-sufficient. And hey, there's nothing wrong with noodles, right?"

I scooped some out of the soup and wound them around my chopsticks.

"Davison's in a great program," Donnie mused, "but sometimes I wish he were back here taking classes with you."

The slippery noodles almost squirted out of my mouth. "What?" I sputtered. "Why?"

"I think you're a good maternal influence on him," Donnie grinned. "He behaves himself when you're around."

I nodded and tried not to choke. I like Donnie a lot. But I'm not ready to take on the role of mom. And stepmother to Davison Gonsalves is the last job I'd ever want to sign up for, right behind prying out my own kidneys with a plastic spoon.

"He's not actually thinking of coming back, is he?" I asked. "And walking away from that great scholarship?"

"No, just dad's wishful thinking," Donnie said. "I'm glad you have his academic interests at heart. It's good he has someone like you on his side."

"Don't mention it. By the way, Donnie, can I ask your opinion about something?"

"Sure."

"Do you think it's possible to make something happen just because you're hoping for it to happen? You know, with the power of your mind, or emotions, or whatever?"

"Are you thinking Kathy Banks passed away because you wished it? Why are you looking at me like that? Isn't that what you were leading up to?"

"I was. You're very perceptive. Because here's the thing. I was down there at the bay when it happened."

"I didn't know that," Donnie said.

"I was standing there with Pat and Yoshi, you know Emma's husband, and of course you know Pat."

One look at Donnie's face told me I should have edited Pat out of the story. Pat and I had already been close friends when I met Donnie, so Donnie tolerates him, but that's as good as it's ever going to get.

"Anyway," I continued quickly, "I knew Kathy was out there paddling, so we were talking about how Emma was working her crew really hard, and we hoped no one would drop dead from the strain. You know, idle musing."

He nodded. "And then?"

"Well, that's when it happened. One minute everything was fine, and suddenly we heard all this shouting, and it turned out Kathy had fallen into the water and I guess you heard the rest."

"So you're asking me, are you responsible? Because you were thinking about something bad happening to her, right before it actually happened?"

"Right. I guess I am asking that. So what do you think?"

"Molly, sometimes things just happen. You know that."

"Yeah. Now we're talking about it I realize how silly it sounds. Hey, are you going to eat this piece of Spam?"

"All yours. Enjoy. I have to get back. Are you still

coming for lunch Tuesday? I got some real buffalo mozzarella for Caprese." He stood up and took the Styrofoam bowl to throw away.

"I'm looking forward to it."

I meant it. Donnie's home cooking is extraordinary; it's nothing like what you get at Donnie's Drive-Inn.

My sense of having received absolution on the Kathy Banks question faded as I drove away. I remembered a bit of bad luck had befallen one of Donnie's competitors not long ago. It had made things awkward all around. Donnie doesn't like to talk about it. But I realized his take on my situation might not have been completely objective.

CHAPTER NINE

Pat's banged-up 1979 Honda Prelude was parked on the curb outside the dilapidated wooden storefront of the Pair-O-Dice Bar and Grill. The car used to be bronze, but the sun had bleached the horizontal surfaces to chalky white. Pat hadn't bothered to remove the stickers applied by a previous owner: "FBI-From Big Island" on the driver's side door; "Hawaiian Force" on the taillight; and a cursive "In Loving Memory of Aunty Rose Kahananui" across the tinted back window.

The hood of Pat's car was barely warm, meaning Pat had probably been sitting inside the Pair-O-Dice for a while. I didn't think I was that late. Maybe a half hour, tops. I hoped Emma was already there. Pat gets grumpy when he has to wait by himself.

I stepped from the bright sidewalk into the dim interior of the Pair-O-Dice and waited for my eyes to adjust. It felt a little cooler inside, thanks to a lone wobbling fan beating the humid air. I saw Pat seated at a wooden table in the corner with a half-finished basket of plastic-cheese nachos in front of him. He was perusing a copy of the *County Courier* and drinking a cup of what I guessed was the Pair-O-Dice's dismal bar coffee. I went up to the bar, ordered a scotch and soda and fries, and joined Pat.

The bartender would have no trouble finding me when my order was ready. Pat and I were the only customers.

"You know," I said as I sat down, "at some point you're going to cross paths with someone who actually knew Aunty Rose Kahananui. What are you going to say to them?"

Pat barely glanced up from the newspaper, shrugged, and returned to his reading.

"Checking out your competition?"

"Uh huh."

I looked around the desolate bar.

"How on earth does this place stay in business?" I tested the wobbly table.

"I dunno," he said. "If they're a front for a gambling operation, you'd think they'd pick a less obvious name than the Pair-O-Dice."

"So how is your Kathy Banks story coming?"

Pat set down the newspaper and turned his attention to me.

"I'll tell you how it's going, Molly. Kathy Banks is a non-person. That 911 call I made? Recorded as a false alarm. No record of the ambulance, even though you and I both saw the paramedics put

Kathy into it and drive away. The police don't have anything on her at all because no one reported a missing person or a murder."

"The hospital must have something," I said. "There's only one emergency room—"

"And patient records are private," Pat interrupted. "They claim they can't tell me anything, not even whether Kathy was admitted."

"Well, that sounds frustrating."

"And another thing. Kathy Banks is a perfect name to have if you don't want people finding you online. Do you know how many people out there are named Kathy Banks?"

"You think it's a fake name?" I asked. "Maybe she had to change her identity for some reason?"

"She seem like a Mafia wife to you?"

"No, you're right," I said. "She lacked the gentle refinement. Pat, maybe the reason you're not finding anything is there's nothing to find. Kathy Banks was an average person with a common name, and she died of natural causes."

"So where's her family?" Pat demanded. "Her friends?"

"Maybe she alienated them all. Hey, I did see your story about our going up in the rankings, though. Great news for us, huh? It almost seems too good to be true."

"I know," he said. "Our graduates' employment rates and salaries are up? I almost can't believe it. Alumni donations are up too."

"I wonder who these graduates are who are doing

so well in this economy. I mean, of course I'm happy to hear about it, but I sure haven't met any of them myself. Remember Micah, my student? Got his degree and the only job he can find is working in the library?"

"Yeah, and no one will put me in touch with any of these supposed high paid alumni," Pat said. "I saw the numbers, but it doesn't add up with what I've seen. I'm still digging. Hey, did you see Bob Wilson's letter to the editor?"

"Oh, Bob from the history department?" I said. "No, but I can imagine. In *Island Confidential* or the *County Courier*?"

"He sent it to both—"

The bartender, who looked too young to be serving alcohol, brought my drink and fries. When he had gone back behind the bar, I took a sip and started to sputter and cough. Pat reached across the table and pounded my back with his giant hand. That never helps, by the way.

"Molly, what's wrong? Are you okay?" His concerned expression gave way to laughter. "That bad?"

I grabbed a napkin from the dispenser and patted my mouth. "I don't know what this is. It isn't what I ordered." I took my drink and marched back up to the bar.

I returned to the table with my fresh drink.

"So what was the problem?" Pat asked.

"He made my scotch and soda with actual soda."

"So? Why didn't you drink it?"

"Because first of all, ew, and second, soda in this country is all made with high fructose corn syrup now. That stuff is murder on your liver."

"So what did you get?"

"Bourbon straight. I didn't want him to get confused again. Anyway, Bob Wilson's letter to the editor?"

"Oh yeah. You heard about the group of for-profit colleges that's getting sued?"

"Oh. I might've heard about it. Something about how they did their recruiting?"

"Among other things. The recruiters were paid based on how many students they could sign up. Then after they had 'em on the hook, they'd get 'em to take out loans with a group of financial institutions that they had some kind of relationship with. The students didn't understand what they'd signed, and after they flunked out, they didn't realize they were obliged to pay back the loans."

"How awful." I felt a pang of sympathy. How many times had I checked I have read and agree to the terms of the agreement, without actually having read, much less agreed? I could've signed away my house for all I knew. "So what did Bob have to say?"

Pat picked up the *County Courier* and read:

"Are we any better? Our departments are funded based on how many students we can attract, retain, and graduate."

"Well, he's not wrong about that."

Pat lowered the paper. "It gets better." He picked up the *County Courier* and continued reading. "The university can't attract enough qualified students to meet our headcount goals, so we lower our standards. We spin students' lack of preparedness into a virtue by invoking Access, and we reframe failure to learn as Diverse Ways of Knowing. And all the while, we're raking in their financial aid dollars."

"Whoa. What possessed Bob to put all this in writing?"

"Bob's in the history department," Pat said. "He probably feels like he has nothing to lose. Oh, here's Emma. And she brought company."

CHAPTER TEN

Two female silhouettes, one slender, the other more substantial, stood in the narrow doorway, backlit by sunshine. Sherry (the thin one) headed to the back of the Pair-O-Dice, to the ladies' room, I supposed. Emma came over to our table, sat down, and started helping herself to my fries.

"Hey!" I protested. "Are those on your diet?"

"Mmmph." She swallowed a mouthful. "You know I don't believe in diets. Yuck. These aren't very good. They're leathery." She grabbed another handful.

"How's your crew adjusting to the news about Kathy?" I asked.

"I think it's finally sinking in," Emma said. "Going out on the water today without Kathy, it kind of made it real for us. I don't think Sherry's taking it too well."

"I'm kind of sad about it too," I said.

“You didn’t even like her,” Pat said.

“Even so. It’s a stark reminder of your own mortality, isn’t it? I was expecting Kathy to stay a couple of days in the hospital with a bad cold or something. I thought everything was going to go back to normal.”

“Everything kind of is back to normal.” Emma brandished a French fry emphatically. “That’s what makes it so tragic. She sank like a pebble in the water. A few ripples, and then silence.”

Having made this pronouncement, Emma turned her attention back to wiping out the local french fry population.

“It was sad to hear the news,” I said, “but at the same time, I feel bad because I don't feel worse about Kathy. I mean, I didn't feel that bad when I read the news, but not feeling bad made me feel guilty so now I feel awful."

"Make sure you write that down," Pat said, "in case there's a memorial service and they call on you to say a few words."

"I’m not surprised you don’t feel bad about Kathy being gone, Molly. I remember you got a stomachache every time you had a meeting with her."

“If I were you, I’d probably be glad she’s gone too,” Pat added.

"I’m *not* glad she’s gone. I mean I’d be glad if she was gone because she found another job or something. I’m not glad she, you know. I didn’t hate her. We had structural conflict. My job is quality control, and her job was maximizing throughput. Of course we were going to see things differently. Nothing against her as a person."

"I had something against her as a person," Emma said. "I think she was seriously trying to move in on Yoshi. You know, she told him she was a natural blonde."

Pat quietly checked out of the conversation and focused his attention on the *County Courier.*

"That doesn't necessarily mean she's coming on to him," I said.

"She offered to prove it to him."

"Ah. So Emma, are you guys going to be okay for the Labor Day race?"

"We're hanging in there. Everyone showed up to practice today."

I refrained from mentioning how neatly Kathy's demise had solved Emma's seven crew members, six seats problem.

Pat glanced up from his newspaper. "Well," he said, "I guess Kathy just solved your six seats, seven crew members problem."

"Thanks, Pat," she said. "Real helpful of you to point that out since I don't know how to subtract single digit numbers. You know what, though. I'm worried about Sherry, now. She's still smoking. And she's diabetic. I hate to say it, but I hope she's not next."

"Then you'll only have five crew members," Pat said.

"If that happens, we'll have to shanghai Molly

into paddling with us."

Sherry came over and sat down, interrupting our conversation before Emma could explore this appalling idea any further.

"How was paddling practice?" I asked.

Emma and Sherry were both wearing their sleek yellow paddling jerseys. Emma's arms were sturdy and brown, and Sherry's were slender and pale, but both had the muscularity that was the reward of hundreds of hours of exercise. I felt self-conscious and flabby in my sleeveless top.

"Oh, hey Dr. B." Sherry offered a fist bump, which I fumbled. "It was sunny when we started out, didn't stay that way, we got rained on, but it's all good. You huli, you get wet anyway."

"We were just talking about Kathy," Pat said.

Sherry nodded. "Yeah."

"You were pretty good friends?" he asked.

"I still can't believe it."

"What was Kathy's story?" Pat prodded. "What was she doing before she moved here to Mahina?"

"She lived on the mainland before," Sherry said. "She was glad she moved. She liked it here."

"She did?" I could hear the surprise in my own voice. My only interactions with Kathy had involved her being dissatisfied with something I had (or hadn't) done. I had never thought of Kathy Banks as a person who could feel emotions like joy and delight.

"Yeah," Sherry said. "She used to say how nice it was to get a fresh start at a new job. And she loved paddling."

"Did she have anyone back home?" Pat persisted. "Any family? Anyone special?"

The dark quiet of the Pair-O-Dice was abruptly pierced by a tinny version of an Eighties power ballad. Sherry fumbled in her purse and pulled out her phone.

"Glenn." She stepped outside to take his call.

Pat turned his hands up despairingly.

"Kathy really didn't talk about her past," Emma said. "What Sherry just told you? That's about as much as I ever heard. Hey Molly, what's the deal?"

"What do you mean?"

Pat laughed. "When Sherry's phone rang you jumped so high, I thought we'd have to peel you off the ceiling."

"I did not."

"Molly, he's right," Emma said. "You've had a lot of stress lately being department chair and everything. And for some reason, you seem to be taking this thing with Kathy kinda hard."

I smelled Sherry's cigarette smoke drifting in through the open door. I hate breathing cigarette smoke, but I didn't want to make a big deal about it, so I put a paper napkin over my face.

"I'm not the real department chair," I said through the napkin. "I'm only the interim department chair. I don't have tenure, remember?"

"Right," Pat said. "Same responsibilities, with no authority."

"Pretty much." I reached for the basket of fries

and found it empty. Emma had left only the translucent red-and-white-checkered paper and a few crumbs of salt.

"I'm going to get another order of fries." I stood up and took the empty plastic basket. "Mine are all gone and for some mysterious reason, I'm still hungry. Anyone want anything?"

"No thanks," Pat said.

"I'm full," Emma added.

"Molly, you gonna see a doctor about your stress?" Pat asked. I shrugged dismissively and walked up to the bar. I had made an appointment for Monday morning, but I didn't think it was any of their business.

CHAPTER ELEVEN

Being the first person in the waiting room was like being the first customer at a salad bar. The molded beige fiberglass seats sparkled, and the magazines were fanned out in perfect formation. I liked to savor those initial few moments of cleanliness before other people came crowding in to ruin everything with their germs. I started to pick up a magazine but reconsidered when I thought of the hordes of sick people who had handled them. I wondered whether the magazines got disinfected somehow and decided they probably did not.

At two minutes after the hour, a young woman entered the room and went behind the reception desk. She wore a black appliqué skirt with yellow and magenta flowers, a plain gray t-shirt, and no makeup. Her wiry black hair was pulled back in a bun. She busied herself at the computer terminal, and I checked the news on my phone as I waited for her to pull up my record.

"Hello, Professor." She grinned at me, flashing gold dental work.

"Oh, hi Hermina!" I tried to sound nonchalant, as if encountering a former student as I was waiting for my appointment with a mental health professional were no big deal. "I didn't know you were working at the clinic. Didn't you graduate?"

"Yeah, last spring. I went home, but there wasn't no good jobs there. I came back and worked at the library for a while, but that didn't work out. So here I am."

I wanted to ask her about the library job, but I didn't know whether her separation had been voluntary, and I didn't want to risk embarrassing her. My recent visit to our library had made me curious. How was our cash-strapped university able to hire dozens of library helpers?

"Well, it's nice to have you back in town."

Of course I'm happy whenever one of our graduates finds gainful employment. Unfortunately, I knew Hermina still had friends on campus. I wondered how long it would take before the entire student body knew I was seeing a shrink. I knew there was no shame in it, of course, but I was well aware that not everyone is similarly enlightened.

"It'll be just a minute, Professor," Hermina said. "Make yourself comfortable. Someone will call you."

Nothing about this situation was comfortable, but the way she said it made it sound like I would be there awhile. At least I could get some work done while I was waiting. The Student Retention Office had recently upgraded their website to make it mobile-friendly. I navigated to the For Faculty page. It was the last tab, of course, after For Students, For Parents, For Community, For Media, and For Accreditors. The Student Retention Office always put faculty last. Every chance they got. To them we were a necessary evil, to be endured until the Ed-Tech Singularity or The Great Disruption or whatever they were hoping would finally make us obsolete.

I pulled up the Weekly Departmental Report form.

1. For each class in the department, list

a) The instructor of record,

b) The current enrollment expressed as a whole integer, and

c) The number of student absences during the week, expressed as a whole integer.

I don't think anyone in our department actually takes attendance. Rodge Cowper, whose classroom usually looks half full at best, always reports 100% attendance. Larry Schneider rages that babysitting isn't in our job description. Hanson Harrison proclaims that he's opposed to checking attendance because his students are adults (I don't think anyone in Hanson's social circle has ever had to punch a timecard). I don't mind taking attendance, as it helps me to memorize students' names, but even I have given up. Our classes have become increasingly crowded as our university admits more students to increase tuition revenue (without hiring additional faculty), so we're now at the point where reading through the roster of names takes up half the class period.

2. For each class in the department, list the course learning outcomes for the week, describe how each learning outcome ties into the Strategic Plan of the University, and indicate each student's achievements along these learning outcomes.

No one ever fills this one in. One of our accounting professors once calculated that with our current course load, this task alone would take more than forty hours per week. No matter. I knew if I turned in incomplete paperwork again, Kathy Banks would—oh, right. Not Kathy Banks. One of the nine who had presumably sprung up in her place, then. I began to feel an unpleasant throbbing behind my right eye.

You may copy and paste the current class roster from the enrollment management system. Irregardless of whether letter or numerical grades were assigned, please provide a qualitative description of each student's efforts and how the faculty member honored the student's unique learning style.

Irregardless? I placed my hands over my eyes and took a deep breath.

"Amelia?"

I looked around the empty waiting room. Was I

hearing voices now? Who was Amelia?

"Amelia?"

A young woman in pink scrubs stood in the entryway to the inner offices, looking right at me. We were the only two people in the waiting room.

"Amelia Barda?" she said.

I put away my phone and stood up.

"Amalia," I corrected her. "I go by Molly. Not Amelia."

"What a pretty name," she soothed, using her now-put- the-knife-down-like-a-good-girl voice.

She led me down a hallway into a small room that looked more like a corporate cubicle than a doctor's office. A pale, desiccated man sat behind a hulking desk, twirling back and forth in his swivel chair. He braced his bony hands on the lip of the fake mahogany desktop and swiveled from one side to the other. Back, and forth. Back, and forth. It was making me dizzy. I sat in one of the two matching beige fabric chairs and read the nameplate on his desk. Dr. Gregory Spiner. That was unfortunate. I was going to think of him as Dr. Spinner from now on, whether I wanted to or not.

Dr. Spinner peered at the computer terminal on his desk, then at me.

"Amelia Barda? What brings you in today?"

He looked sickly, his fair eyebrows invisible on his fragile skin.

"My name is Amalia," I said. "Not Amelia."

He started to type. The only objects on Dr. Spinner's desk were the computer terminal and an oversized candy jar. In my rush to arrive early, I hadn't stopped to eat breakfast. The candy jar lurked in my peripheral vision, tempting me, but I didn't want to stare at it. I didn't want him to start asking questions about sugar addiction.

"A good friend of mine thought I seemed kind of stressed out," I said. "It was his idea for me to come here. I've never been in before, so I'm not sure how this works. Do you ask me questions, or do I just start talking, or what?"

Doctor Spinner stopped typing and looked at me.

"Let's start with a question, Amelia. What's troubling you right now?"

I thought of my conversation with Iker Legazpi.

Everyone who hates a brother or sister is a murderer.

"That I may have committed murder?"

He resumed typing.

"No. Please stop typing! That's not what I meant. I was joking."

He paused and looked up at me.

"Um, I didn't mean it was a joke-joke, I mean obviously it's not funny. I would never joke about murder. I mean, not to you. Are you going to have to write one of those warning letters now? Here, let me start over."

CHAPTER TWELVE

"A coworker recently passed away. Some kind of boating accident, I guess. I'm not exactly sure how it happened. I was there, on the beach, though. And I…"

Dr. Spinner watched me for a moment and started typing again. I shifted my position in an attempt to see his screen in the reflection of the glass cabinet doors behind him. No luck.

"Okay. Here's the thing. Maybe if I'd known she was going to pass away I would've been nicer to her when she was alive. I missed an opportunity and now I won't have another chance."

Doctor Spinner kept typing.

"She works, worked, I mean, for the Student Retention Office," I said. "They have this enormous grant, and their whole job is to keep students from dropping out and to raise our graduation rate. Which is an admirable goal. No one could argue with that.

Except we're not allowed to use the grant money to do the things that might actually work. Make the dorms habitable, hire more professors so students can get the classes they need, or even just give out more scholarships so students can afford to stay in school. Everything we do has to be 'new' and 'disruptive' so the Student Retention Office forces one weird fad after another on us. Then when that doesn't work, because of course it doesn't, they lean on us to pass everyone anyway, and they drown us in paperwork to make it look like they're doing something. In fact, I was just trying to fill out one of my weekly reports while I was waiting."

Doctor Spinner stopped typing and looked at me.

"You know, Amelia, women like yourself sometimes get caught in the role of people-pleasers. Have you thought about saying no?"

"Say no to the SRO? The history department tried that. Why don't we ask the history department how that's working out for them? Better hurry, though, because pretty soon we're not going to have a history department."

Doctor Spinner typed for what seemed like an unnecessarily long time.

"You said you wish you had been kinder to your colleague when she was alive," he said, finally.

"I guess so."

"And yet I still sense some anger, Amelia."

"It's Amalia, not Amelia. Or Molly. Everyone calls me Molly. It was frustrating to deal with Kathy Banks. It was like trying to reason with a robot sometimes. As if she'd been pre-programmed with these few catch phrases. Honor each student's way of knowing. Be a Guide on the Side, not the Sage on the Stage. Provide peak customer satisfaction. I could never talk to her like a human being."

"But she was a human being."

"I guess. You know, there was one conversation we had. We were going back and forth over some marginal student she wanted to place into our management program. I told her, this kid has no chance of succeeding in this program and we both know it. If we admitted him, we'd simply be shaking him down for his financial aid money. We'd be no better than those schools that advertise on daytime television. Of all things, that seemed to upset her. I don't know why it touched a nerve, but it did."

I waited for Doctor Spinner to weigh in on this, but he sat with his fingers poised over his keyboard.

"Well, of course she insisted I was wrong, Mahina State's mission was access and so on. What was strange, though, is I saw tears in her eyes. I couldn't believe it. I pretended to change my mind and agree with her in the end, because I felt bad about hurting her feelings."

He pushed against the desk and launched himself around, holding his hands in the air as if he were riding a roller coaster. As he completed the full 360-degree turn, he grabbed the edge of his desk to decelerate.

"Sometimes you have to trust people, Amelia. What did you learn from this experience?"

He readied his fingers to start typing again.

"I don't know. The poor kid stuck around long enough to burn most of his financial aid and dropped out. So I was right, and Kathy was wrong. Maybe the lesson is people should listen to my good advice."

Dr. Spinner stopped typing and watched me. Wrong answer. I tried again.

"Don't let myself be manipulated by tears?"

Doctor Spinner launched himself and his chair into another full turn. On the way back around he plunged his hand into the candy jar, pulled out a fistful of cellophane-wrapped goodies, and set them down in front of me. I reached for one of the wrapped candies and started to open it.

"Now hold your horses there, Amelia. Let's discuss this first."

"Discuss? Why?" I picked one of the candies up and examined it. It was an oval shape, and blue. Blueberry? Vanilla?

"Take one when you feel anxious," he said, "or twenty minutes before you think you might encounter a stressful situation. It can take our pharmacy a few days to get your prescription in, so these samples are for you to take with you today."

"Oh. A prescription." I set the pill back down, hoping my disappointment wasn't too obvious. "What is this a prescription for, exactly?"

"Anxiety. You will be pleased with this, I guarantee."

"Anxiety? Huh. Fair enough. Are there any side

effects, interactions, anything I should know about?"

"Oh no. Nothing at all."

"Nothing? Are you sure? That's unusual. Well, I guess I can check the package insert. Just to be on the safe side."

He giggled as if I had made a clever joke. "Package insert. How quaint. I'm certain you know how to use the internet, Amelia."

He pushed off the edge of his desk and whirled around once more, and slid a printed piece of paper across the desk toward me.

I gathered up the wrapped drug samples and the discharge slip. I considered shaking his hand, but he was busy spinning himself around. I left his office and found my way back to the reception area.

"Hey, Professor!"

The cheery voice was coming from behind the pharmacy window.

"Oh, hi, uh…Peter. It's been a while. Biz com, right?"

I was proud I'd remembered his name. He was one of hundreds of students I'd had over the past few years. He seemed to take it for granted.

"Professor, I graduated and then did my Pharm. D. on the mainland and now I'm back! Cool, huh?"

"Yes, that's wonderful. How do you like working here?"

"I love it. I'm like the hub of the communication network, like we talked about in class. Pretty good I remembered that, yeah?"

"Impressive."

"You know what I mean, though? I get to talk to everyone. Like Professor Watanabe, the department chair?"

"He's our interim dean now," I said.

"Cool. Tell him congratulations! I see him here once in a while. We special-order him those cases of antacid tablets. He likes the sugar-free ones, cause he takes so many of them, if he had the regular ones, his teeth would all be rotten by now."

"And I saw Hermina on the way in."

He grinned.

"Yeah, we have a little alumni network going on here. It's awesome. Hey, did you hear about us going up in the rankings?"

"Yes. I was happy to see our graduates doing so well."

"Yeah, me too. Anyway, I got your order from Dr. Spinner here in the computer. It'll take a couple days to get it in."

"You call him Dr. Spinner?"

"Sorry," he laughed, "Did I say that? I meant Dr. Spiner. Anyway, it'll be ready in a couple days. We'll call you. It's worth the wait, though. You'll love it."

"Really? I'll *love* it?"

"Oh yeah. Even people who are super uptight, no offense Professor, it calms 'em right down."

"Thanks, Peter. Good to know."

I walked back out to my car, tucked the pills into the side pocket of my purse, and forgot about them.

CHAPTER THIRTEEN

The appointment at Behavioral Health had taken a little longer than I'd expected. I walked into the classroom right on time, which was almost as bad as being late. The whiteboard was covered with leftover notes from Rodge Cowper's Human Potential class.

Think outside the box!! was scrawled across the top of the board. Underneath was the famous drawing of nine dots run through by four connected straight lines. The rest of the board was filled with pairs of first names and positive adjectives in various handwriting styles. *Heather: Helpful. Rick: Righteous. Nancy: Nice.*

I wiped Rodge's insights from the board as my students entered and got seated in their discussion groups. When I'd finally erased everything, I turned around to face the class.

"Today we're going to brainstorm brand-new ideas for your start-up businesses. No restaurants, no sports bars. Okay? And no grumbling. Listen. You've all done the break-even, so I'm not telling you anything you don't already know. None of those businesses made it. The problem with food and beverage type businesses is they have high fixed costs, many competitors and substitutes, and a fickle market. We can't all be the next Donnie Gonsalves. You have to pivot. When your first idea doesn't work, think of a better one."

I wrote on the board:

Technology.

Culture.

Sustainability.

"These are your prompts. I'll come around and talk to you individually. Go."

Sherry's throaty rasp rose above the background murmur of discussions getting started around the room. "Sweetheart," she was admonishing one of her tablemates, "you can talk about aloha all you want but when you actually look into it? Most of the time it's a big pile of—"

I rushed over to Sherry's table in time to prevent her from finishing her thought.

"Let's try to keep it clean," I said.

I try to instill professionalism in my students, and that includes using appropriate language. This dictum usually needs some reinforcement throughout the semester.

"Sorry, Dr. B. We were trying to do the culture prompt. I don't know how we ended up talking about my control freak ex-husband."

"Well, the culture prompt doesn't seem like it's working for your group. Why don't we try another direction? How about technology? Do you remember the story I posted about those entrepreneurs in Berlin? The ones doing custom clothing fittings online?"

The group exchanged glances.

"I just sent out the link," I prompted gently. "The customers posed with a CD-ROM disk, and from that, the entrepreneurs could calculate the customers' body measurements?"

Their uncomprehending stares made me wonder whether any of them had read my post. I tried again.

"Forget about clothing. Here's something that's been on people's minds. Privacy. Right?"

Everyone nodded, which could have meant anything from "I've been keeping up with the relevant news on privacy issues" to "I am nodding my head."

"The internet has changed our ability to be anonymous. And some people have more anonymity than others. If your parents had the foresight to name you something like Kathy Ba—like Bill Smith, you're in good shape. A search would turn up so many hits, you could never be sure you found the right person."

"Yeah, my name's pretty unique," Sherry said. "DiNapoli. Sherrine DiNapoli."

"Oh. Sherrine is a very pretty name. Anyway—"

"DiNapoli's Italian," she interrupted cheerfully. "Like you, right? Barda?"

"Barda is actually an Albanian name."

"Ohhh." Sherry nodded knowingly. "Like Mother Teresa."

I was impressed Sherry knew this. People generally assume I'm Italian because of my last name, or Irish because of my first. The first time I met Pat's mother, she had perked up when I introduced myself as Molly and asked me what my last name was and where my people were from.

"My people?" I'd asked, naively. "Albania, I guess, originally."

"Oh, no one knows what that is, dear." Mrs. Flanagan immediately changed the subject to where we were going to have lunch. I had apparently made a good impression on her despite my obvious character flaw, not being Irish. Pat was kind enough to inform me that according to his mother, I was "really quite pretty, if you like that kind of thing."

"My Ma has a picture of Mother Teresa up in the living room," Sherry said, "next to the Pope. Mother Teresa must've been a big deal at your house, Dr. B."

I glanced around the table to see if anyone else wanted to participate in the conversation. Sherry's group members seemed content to watch.

"We did admire Mother Teresa's work with the poor," I said.

My parents knew who Mother Teresa was. She was a big deal at our church, no question. In private, though, my mother the obstetrician and my father the science teacher agreed Blessed Teresa of Calcutta could have done a lot more good by handing out free birth control. That's the kind of Catholics we are. Practical.

"Has any one of you ever searched for someone online?" I asked.

"It was easy to Google you, Professor Barda," said one ponytailed young man, who I remembered was on exchange from Washington State. "I searched for the professors before I transferred over here. I read all the online reviews."

"And you still signed up for my class? That was brave of you."

"The thing about you being half human made me curious," he said. "You seem pretty normal to me, though."

"Yes, well. I make an effort to blend in."

As the students packed up to leave, I erased the board, making sure to wipe away any stray mark. I wondered whether I was the only one who cared about maintaining a clean learning environment. Rodge apparently didn't think it was important to erase the board after class. Maybe I didn't need to be so conscientious about it either. One of these days, I mused daringly, maybe after I get tenure, I might leave my notes up on the board and let Rodge erase them.

CHAPTER FOURTEEN

Over afternoon coffee, I vented to Pat and Emma about Rodge Cowper's unsatisfactory whiteboard hygiene. Emma occupied my visitor chair. Pat was perched on the edge of my desk, his long legs almost reaching the wall of my tiny office. I used to have two chairs but the plastic one had cracked and finally split in two. I, of course, was enthroned on my fifteen-dollar yoga ball from Galimba's Bargain Boyz.

The dim fluorescent lighting made Pat and Emma look bilious. To save money on the electric bill, our administration had ordered half the light tubes removed from most of the buildings on campus. The effect is like one of those video games where you have to go into an abandoned warehouse and kill zombies.

"Everyone knows Rodge does that," Emma said. "You're lucky it was just the whiteboard this time.

Sometimes he writes off the edge onto the wall."

"You'd almost think Rodge is someone who doesn't recognize boundaries," Pat added.

"How come you're worried about it now?" Emma asked. "Rodge has been writing all over the walls forever."

"Yeah, don't bite my head off for saying this, but you've been kind of irritable."

I sighed. "You're right. I haven't been sleeping well. I've been--I know this sounds ridiculous, but do you remember what Sherry's boyfriend said? About death from bad vibes or whatever? I looked it up. There actually is something called psychogenic death. Also known as Voodoo death."

"You don't believe that." Emma set down her coffee mug. "Where did you read this, anyway?"

"Old anthropology journal."

"You know anthropology's not an actual science, right?"

"Not even going to dignify that, Emma. The thing is, I feel responsible for what happened to Kathy Banks."

"Molly, that's idiotic." Emma glanced at the wall separating my office from Rodge Cowper's and lowered her voice. "You never killed Kathy Banks. Even if your stupid Voodoo death thing was true, which it's not, there's a lot of people who hated her worse than you did, so if you want to take the blame, you're gonna hafta to get in line."

"So maybe I just laid on the last straw. With my bad juju or whatever, I don't know. Ow!"

I clapped my hand over my aching right eye.

"What you're describing isn't anything magical, Molly," Pat said. "Peoples' own minds exact the punishment they think they deserve. It's the same thing as when you get those eyeball headaches whenever you're feeling guilty about something. By the way, what happened when you saw the…" Pat lowered his voice. "with your appointment?"

"Oh, the psychiatrist?" I said.

"You went to a psychiatrist?" Emma asked. "Good for you, Molly."

"I thought you said psychiatry was all tommyrot and balderdash, Emma."

"Nah. You're thinking of psychology," Emma said. "Psychiatrists are real doctors. They can get you the good drugs."

"Well, I did keep my appointment. I'm not sure it did much good. There are people out there in the world who are genuinely sick, and here I wasted the doctor's time, not to mention mine, just because I've been kind of stressed out."

Emma raised her eyebrows. "Kind of stressed out?"

"You can actually see hairline cracks forming at your temples," Pat added.

"Oh, and, by the way, the receptionist was one of my former students. As was the pharmacist. So that was fun."

"Well, what happened?" Pat seemed to have a proprietary interest in my experience with mental health services.

"I don't know. Some glassy-eyed guy with a scraggly ponytail twirled around in his chair a couple of times like the Mad Hatter, stuffed a bunch of pills into my hand and pushed me out the door."

"Didn't he even give you any follow-up instructions or anything?" Pat asked.

"No. Oh, wait, he handed me this printed form with my discharge papers. It had some kind of boilerplate with a lot of stuff about 'eat right, avoid alcohol and caffeine, get regular exercise,' all that kind of quackery."

"Molly, come with me to the gym later. I'm doing one last upper body workout before the race. You can keep me company, and you might get inspired to do a few deadlifts or something. Pat, you wanna come too?"

"Much as I'd love to, I have a lead on this alumni thing. I'm going to have a chance to meet some of our high-earning graduates."

"So Molly, you're coming then."

"I don't know," I said. "I still have all this paperwork I have to do for the Student Retention Office—"

"Put it off. I'll come by your house and get you after dinner."

"The gym?" I protested. "But I…"

"I'll be there at seven. Try not to eat too much for dinner."

"Wait a minute. Pat, did you say high-earning graduates? Where are our graduates working that they're making all this money?"

Pat laughed.

"Good catch, Molly. Would you believe the library?"

CHAPTER FIFTEEN

The student gym is open 24 hours a day. Like the Student Retention Office complex, the student gym is gleaming and well-appointed. In fact, the SRO helped to fund its construction. Students and their guests can use it for free. After faculty and staff raised a stink, it was decided we would be allowed to use the facility too. During certain hours. For a fee.

It was already after nine at night when we arrived. We walked in past the juice bar, paid our admission to the sullen student worker, and entered a warehouse-sized room ringing with metallic clanging and crowd noise. Despite the crush of sweaty bodies, the state-of-the-art climate control was keeping the air fresh and chilled. The SRO funding had also provided recessed halogen lighting and polished hardwood floors.

"It'd be nice if we could get some of this lighting in my lab," Emma said. "Or at least put back the lights they took away."

"They can't use the SRO grant for general maintenance," I said. "Believe me, I've asked about it."

When the facilities crew came through my office to remove two of my four fluorescent light tubes, they accidentally broke the plastic diffuser cover. They apologized good-naturedly and explained that replacing it wasn't in the budget. Pat thinks the bare fluorescent tubing has a stylish industrial look. Emma says the exposed fixture makes my office look like a Kuewa meth garage. I don't want to pay for a replacement light cover, so I'm siding with Pat.

Emma pointed out a couple of her students from her introductory biology class. They were shirtless, sweaty, grunting and utterly focused on working the leg press machines.

"At least I know they're capable of expending effort on something," Emma said. "Even if it's not biology class."

"Great example of contextual motivation," I observed.

"Hey, look," Emma nudged me. "There's Glenn."

"Who's Glenn? Oh. Sherry's boyfriend Glenn."

He was enmeshed in an elaborate contraption that would have filled a small room. If I didn't know he was in that machine voluntarily, I would have guessed he was being subjected to some kind of high-tech torture. He spotted us and smiled, and extricated himself from the machine as Emma and I approached. He was wearing a black fishnet tank top, shiny black leggings, red and black wrestling shoes, and fingerless red weightlifting gloves. A lacquered yin/yang symbol hung from a black leather choker. In the warm lighting of the workout room, his orangey tan made him look like a human Creamsicle.

"Hey, Glenn," Emma bustled over to his machine as I struggled to keep up with her. Emma's short legs moved quickly, covering a surprising amount of ground. "Where's Sherry?"

"She's out back, having a smoke—Oh." He grinned, realizing he had just ratted out Sherry to her paddling coach. His teeth were so white, they were almost blue. "She totally wants to quit. She's trying, I swear."

"It's okay," Emma assured him. "I know all about it. She says it helps to keep her weight under control. It's killing her endurance, though."

I noticed that the black netting of Glenn's shirt had caught on his nipple ring. I winced and folded my arms tightly.

"I'm trying to help her cut down." Glenn shook his highlighted hair out of his face, misting all three of us with his sweat. I noticed he'd had his hair redone, luminous gold and caramel streaking from his no-longer-grey roots to his perfectly tousled tips. I wondered what color my hair would be if I stopped getting it dyed. I hadn't seen my natural color in over a decade.

"But you can't make Sherry do anything she doesn't want to," Glenn was saying. "I gotta tell you, she's really looking forward to the race. I mean, she was sad about what happened to that lady on your team, her friend, what was her name? Karen?"

"Kathy," Emma corrected him.

"Oh yeah, Kathy. Anyway, Sherry's super excited now she knows she'll have a seat in the boat for sure."

"Sherry and Kathy were good friends?" I asked, and immediately wished I hadn't. Now Glenn was going to tell Sherry, my student, that I was asking nosy questions about her. Or worse, that I suspected she had a role in Kathy's death. Which, I suddenly realized, was not such a far-fetched idea.

Kathy and Sherry had been the two slowest paddlers on the crew, and Emma was only going to pick one of them to paddle in the Labor Day race. Kathy had been the one thing standing between Sherry and a spot in the team canoe.

Fortunately, Glenn didn't seem to find anything strange about my question.

"Oh, yeah!" he said. "I mean, the whole crew was pretty close. You know, Sherry's kinda competitive, but yeah, they were pretty tight. They were all doing that weird diet together."

I glanced at myself in the wall mirror. "So how does that diet work again?" I asked.

"It's kinda hardcore," he said. "Only five hundred calories a day."

"Oh, right," I said. "Never mind."

"And Sherry has to inject herself with this stuff at the same time every day. It's called human, uh…"

"Human chorionic gonadotropin," Emma said.

"Uh, yeah, thanks, Emma. Yeah. It's hard for Sherry, cause her diabetes? She's gotta take insulin, and it's got these little bitty needles, exactly like the, uh…"

He gestured, searching for the words.

"Human chorionic gonadotropin," Emma repeated. "You can just call it HCG."

"Cool, thanks, Emma. Yeah, the HCG. Those little needles look exactly the same, so Sherry has to be super careful not to get them mixed up. She told me it would be bad if she took two doses of insulin by mistake."

Glenn shook his layered hair again. This time, I stepped back to avoid the sweat spray.

"That diet sounds complicated," I said.

"Seriously," he agreed. "But she's totally into it. I told her I think she's already skinny enough, but she wants you guys to do good at the Labor Day race and she says she doesn't want to slow the team down. Sherry's totally, I don't know what the word is, but when she wants something, she gets it." Glenn flashed a flawless blue-white smile. "I kinda dig that about her."

CHAPTER SIXTEEN

I had a late lunch date with Donnie. He works through the lunch rush at the Drive-Inn, so he doesn't take his lunch break until around two. The timing meant I was going to miss an important meeting. At one-thirty, my faculty colleagues were convening to forge a sternly worded resolution concerning the Student Retention Office's "streamlining" of our curriculum (that is, removing the history requirement).

The real reason for my absence wasn't simply a schedule conflict. It was pure, self-serving cowardice. Attending the meeting would be tantamount to opposing the Student Retention Office publicly. I would have to be out of my mind to do such a thing, especially before I had tenure. It was better for me to be off-campus entirely while the meeting was going on.

The aroma of garlicky puttanesca sauce tickled my

nose as I approached the front door. Donnie makes his puttanesca with plenty of green and Kalamata olives, goes light on the capers, and serves a generous helping over perfectly al dente linguine. I reached for the doorbell but paused when I heard my stomach growling. I hadn't eaten since breakfast, and I was starving. Once the visceral clamor had subsided, I rang the bell.

Donnie greeted me with a kiss on the cheek.

"I have to show you something." He took me by the hand and started to lead me down the hallway. Where the bedrooms were, or so I remembered from the one time he'd given me a full tour of his house. Donnie's master bedroom, I recalled, was as elegant as the rest of his place. A low-slung platform squatted on the luminous, perfectly inlaid maple floor. Three framed lithographs by a local artist depicted the Hawaiian creation story in sepia ink on cream paper.

Was he actually planning on our rumpling those raw silk sheets while puttanesca sauce bubbled away on the stovetop? This was so oddly out of character for him that I wasn't sure how to react. Should I feel flattered? Annoyed? Concerned?

We paused at a closed door, and he released my hand. As it turned out, I wasn't going to see the master bedroom today.

"Do you remember Davison's room?" he asked.

"Not really."

"This used to be a little boy's room. Now Davison's a grown man, the bunk bed and posters, all those little-boy things, those aren't quite appropriate anymore. I thought I should buy him some grown up furniture."

"To mark his being an independent adult," I said.

"Exactly. I have a furniture wholesaler in L.A. I like. I sent Davison a catalog and let him pick out the bedroom set he wanted. And he did, all by himself."

"You must be very proud of him."

"You'll appreciate this, Molly. He chose something from the 'Italian Classic Bedroom' collection. It's called Barocco."

Had I ever mentioned to Donnie that I'm not actually Italian? I couldn't remember. It would seem petty to bring it up now.

"Davison told me he liked this bedroom set because it reminded him of his truck."

"His truck? How does a bedroom set remind someone of a truck?"

"It's black with a lot of silver trim. It took a while to get everything shipped in and set up, but it's finally done."

Donnie swung the door open with a flourish.

I gasped.

The hulking bed had a headboard and footboard of rococo silver leaf, set off with tufted black leather insets. Like Davison's truck, it was massive and black and gaudy. At least I didn't see a "Power Stroke Turbo" badge anywhere. The matching dresser was black lacquer, festooned with some kind of curly silver trim and topped with a smoked, silver-veined mirror. A gold-framed print of Botticelli's Birth of Venus hung over the headboard.

"Oh my goodness," I stammered, grasping for something nice to say. "Is that a, uh, heart shape in the trim on the headboard?" The headboard design only vaguely resembled a heart. What it really looked like was an angry little fat face, with two hostile button eyes.

"I didn't see that before. It's sweet that you noticed, Molly." How could Donnie look at this and sound so happy?

"Didn't this room used to have a hardwood floor? Like the rest of the house?" I asked, poking a tentative toe at the plush carpet. "The red color is definitely striking. Have you read The Masque of the Red Death by any chance?"

"No, doesn't sound familiar. The hardwood's still under there."

"And look at that chandelier! Are those candles made out of black leather? Isn't that a fire hazard?"

"They're not real candles. They just look like it."

Donnie reached into the room and flipped a switch. The "flames" on the "candles" flickered mechanically.

Donnie must have a real blind spot when it comes to Davison, I thought. An actual, literal blind spot. It was the only explanation. The rest of Donnie's house looked like it sprang into three dimensions from the slick pages of an architecture magazine or a high-end furniture catalog.

I think I keep my house clean and well organized.

Pat and Emma would even say I take my penchant for tidiness a little too far. But then I go and spend time in Donnie's perfect house, and I come away feeling like one of the Collyer brothers.

"Gosh, Donnie, it's a very different aesthetic from your…" I flopped my hands helplessly as I searched for a synonym for "good taste."

I finally came up with,

"…your more understated décor."

"It's only missing one thing now," Donnie said.

The severed horse's head?

"Davison." Donnie put his arm around my shoulders and gave me an affectionate squeeze. "Now his room is the way he likes it, I think he'll be spending more time here. He can come back and stay whenever he has a break from school. Summer vacation, spring break, whenever."

"Oh," I faltered. "That's, um, great."

"In fact, I'm trying to bring him back for a short visit before his school term starts. And Molly, I know you're already teaching, but I think it would be nice if you two could spend some time together and get to know each other better."

"Oh, I think I know Davison pretty well. Remember, he was my student. I mean, of course I'd be delighted."

At least the part about Davison being my student was true.

"You know he's calling himself 'Dave' now. It sounds more Californian, I suppose."

Donnie gave me another quick squeeze and

released me.

"Let's go eat."

Even Donnie's delicious pasta couldn't soften the shock of seeing Davison's bedroom. The new decor was hideous, of course, but I could live with that. I mean, I could always close the door. The problem was what Donnie had said about making sure Davison spent as much time here as possible, with me acting as some kind of mother figure. I allowed Donnie to refill my wine glass. Was this my second glass? My third? In my distraught state, I had lost track. And I still had to drive back up to campus after this. So much for my Mother-Figure of the Year award.

I couldn't think of anything positive to say about Davison's new room, so I steered clear of the topic. Instead, I chatted about Emma's upcoming canoe race. I mentioned I'd be going to the leeward side of the island with Emma to keep her company and enjoy the long Labor Day weekend.

"I might have business over there," Donnie said. "Where are you staying?"

I told him.

"Isn't that a coincidence." He grinned. "I might be over there too. Should we plan to meet for dinner?"

"What a wonderful idea." I smiled back. At least there wouldn't be anything over on the other side of the island to remind him of how much he missed his awful son.

CHAPTER SEVENTEEN

I returned to campus with a few minutes to spare before the start of the all-campus Student Retention Office faculty development session. I wasn't thrilled about the prospect of sitting through yet another SRO retreat, but I didn't want to stay in my office either. Rodge Cowper, whose office adjoins mine, was playing his confidence-building recordings again. Pachelbel's Canon, rendered on what sounded like a twenty-dollar toy keyboard, wheedled through the thin wall separating us.

"My intelligence, creativity, and potential is perfect and infinite," announced the disembodied voice from Rodge's office.

Your subject-verb agreement is another story, I reflected.

I dispensed a cup of coffee from my espresso machine and tried to ignore Rodge's monotone affirmations. The first few times, I had considered asking Rodge to turn it down, but I couldn't think of a way to do it that wouldn't be horribly embarrassing for both of us. So I did nothing, and now I was stuck. I couldn't say anything now. Not after weeks of hearing Rodge assuring himself that he is a sexual, self-confident and dominant male.

Emma pushed into my office, followed by Pat.

"Ready?" Emma asked.

"Almost. We still have a few minutes."

"So what is this one about again?" Pat asked.

"What do you think it's about?" Emma snapped. "Retention, retention, retention. It's the Student Retention Office. They're gonna tell us how we hafta keep our seats filled with warm bodies."

"I think we're reconsidering the 'warm' requirement," Pat said. "Too stringent."

"I walk with confidence," the affirming voice intoned from next door. "Women are drawn to me." I wondered whether Pachelbel's Canon could go on forever on an infinite loop.

"Isn't that right, Molly?" Emma was saying.

"Sorry?"

"Retention is all about selection," Emma said. "Get smart, wealthy students. They're up to the academic demands, and they can spend time studying cause they don't have to work. That's how you get a high graduation rate."

"I reject those claims," Pat said. "I refuse to agree with a system that reproduces privilege so blatantly."

"Sorry, Pat. You don't get to pretend that something isn't true just cause you don't like it."

"We have to go to this thing anyway," I said.

"Let's keep an open mind. Maybe this time they'll actually teach us something useful."

"Yeah, maybe they'll teach us how to be in touch with reality," Emma said. "Even those of us who teach in the English department."

"Or maybe they'll teach us how not to scare students away," Pat replied pointedly. Emma's introductory biology class has one of the highest drop rates in the university. It's not her fault. The Student Retention Office had convinced Emma's department chair to remove the course prerequisites in order to maximize enrollment. Hordes of hopeful and utterly unprepared students sign up every semester for Emma's class. Her first midterm invariably plays out like the invasion of Normandy, only more bloody. About half the class drops right afterward, but by then it's too late for them to get their tuition refunded.

"I exude confidence, sex, power, and self-esteem," announced Rodge's affirmation through the wall.

Emma snorted. "I can't believe the sorry crew I have this semester. I *wish* I could scare them away. I'm never going to get them to drop because they 'need' my class. They all think they're going to medical school. Do you know what happened to me today? I just gave them a little quiz, with a simple question about the nucleotide bases of DNA. So the quizzes come back, and I'm getting every letter of the alphabet!"

She looked from Pat to me and back again.

"You two have no idea what I'm talking about, do you? Never mind. The point is I'm worried I'm gonna have to dumb down my class even more than I already have, otherwise I won't get tenure."

"Oh, don't worry about tenure," I said. "They're using our online evaluations for tenure decisions now, remember?"

"That's right," Pat said. "Crowdsourcing."

"Oh yeah? I'll be okay then."

Emma, Pat and I had originally used the anonymous professor rating site as a source of entertainment. When our administration started to use it to evaluate faculty performance, we stepped up to power-user status, flooding the site with positive evaluations for ourselves and for one another. Thanks to this strategy, Pat, Emma, and I were the three highest-ranked faculty members at Mahina State University.

"That reminds me," I said. "My stock wasn't very high at the Student Retention Office when Kathy Banks passed away, and I hate to think about what kind of notes she must have left for her replacement. Maybe you guys should send me a little ratings love, to give me some headroom."

"Right now?" Pat asked.

"Not this minute. I think it's time for us to head up there. Pat, are you coming?"

"You don't have to go, Pat," Emma said. "Part-timers don't have to do the professional development stuff."

"Nah, I'll go. There's free food, and I don't have

anything better to do."

"Good. It'll be less boring that way."

I pushed myself up off my yoga ball and retrieved my laptop bag from my lower left desk drawer.

"What did I tell you about the lower left drawer?" Pat said.

"The lower left drawer is the first place purse thieves look. Look, this office is not exactly a tempting target. I think I'm okay."

"Yeah, look around, Pat," Emma said.

With its stained, corroded ceiling tiles, bare fluorescent tubes, and rusty file cabinets, my office has little to covet. And any burglar who did manage to venture behind my desk would probably trip over my yoga ball on the way out.

Rodge's eight-bit version of Pachelbel's Canon swelled. *Deedle deedle deeeeee, deedle deedle deeeee…*

A wave of nausea engulfed me as I reached for my purse. We were only going up to the Student Retention Office. I'd been there a million times. What was wrong with me?

Emma was next to me, holding my wrist. "Molly, what is it? You just went white, and your skin feels clammy."

"She's actually kind of greenish," Pat observed helpfully.

"Women are drawn to me," Rodge's affirmation added. "I am a self-assured, confident, sexual and dominant male."

I could feel rebel forces gathering in my stomach. This wasn't going to turn out well. Emma glanced down at her wristwatch. "Molly, your pulse! Nineteen beats in ten seconds."

"What does that mean? Why are you taking my pulse with the metric system?" I felt myself sway. Emma grabbed my shoulders to stabilize me.

"Molly, where's your prescription?" Pat sounded a little panicky. Pat never sounds panicky.

"No prescription. Please. I don't want to swallow anything. Especially not some pill from Doctor Glassy-Eyes."

I reached for the handle of my laptop bag. For some reason, I couldn't grab it. My hands refused to obey me. Then the room started to lurch. Out of the corner of my eye, I could catch it shifting.

"You know what, Pat? I changed my mind. Can you hand me my bag? Quick."

My office had started to spin, and it was picking up momentum. I was about to be sick. Anything was worth a try. I fumbled in my purse, hands shaking, and found the wrapped samples in the zipped side pocket.

"Here, Molly." Pat gently removed the pills from my grasp. "Let me do that. How many are you supposed to take?"

"I don't know. I don't remember! Two? I think?"

Pat unwrapped the pills and handed them to me. I gulped them down with warm coffee.

"You haven't had any alcohol today, right?" Emma asked.

"I had wine at lunch."

"How much?" Pat demanded.

"I don't know. Donnie and I shared a bottle. So I guess a half-bottle?"

Pat and Emma exchanged a glance.

"You'll be fine," Emma assured me. "If anyone's liver can handle it, yours can."

"What's that supposed to—"

"You okay now, Molly?" Pat took my elbow and hoisted me to my feet with one hand. "Come on, ladies. Let's not be late."

"I hope these pills don't make me sleepy. I still have two more meetings after this SRO thing."

"I read and meditate every day," said the voice from Rodge's office. "I possess all the knowledge in the universe."

"What are we waiting for?" I said. "Let's get out of here."

"I am well groomed," added Rodge's affirmation. "And my hair is attractively styled."

CHAPTER EIGHTEEN

Emma, Pat and I made our way up to where the new Student Retention Office complex loomed over our decrepit campus like some warlord's compound. It seemed bigger than the last time I was there. This probably wasn't an illusion. They're constantly adding on new wings and remodeling the old ones. The chilled air hit us as soon as we walked through the sliding glass doors, and I felt better immediately.

"You okay now?" Pat asked. "Your color's back."

"Yes," I said. "I guess it was just a passing thing." I inhaled deeply, smelling drywall and new carpeting.

SRO Conference Room Five had several hundred seats and a fancy audio system that was overkill for the few dozen faculty members in attendance. These meetings were supposed to be mandatory, but there was no way to enforce that. Yet.

We stopped at a side table and loaded up little plates with brownies and melon slices. I waved to

Iker Legazpi, who was sitting in the front row. He beamed at me and waved back. Pat, Emma, and I took our seats near the back and I started to relax.

Conference Room Five had recently been remodeled in the new school colors (as decided by student vote): red, green and gold. Dozens of last year's chairs were going to go into surplus. When Central Supply's next auction rolled around, I would line up with dozens of other faculty members, hoping to get a good deal on the Student Retention Office's throwaways. The mauve color wasn't my favorite, but the chairs were top of the line, and nearly new. There's no way I could afford to buy one otherwise.

"How long until this thing starts?" Pat took out his phone and started typing. "We have a couple minutes, right? How's this: Dr. Barda's coffee mug is carved from the thigh bone of the first student who ever plagiarized an essay in her Business Communication class."

"Is that for the professor rating site?" I asked. "It's perfect. Can you tell on your phone if I'm back up to a smiley face?"

"Why are you asking me? Don't you check it yourself?"

"I try not to look unless I have to."

"Yes, you're back up to a smiley face," Pat said. "And of course you have a chili pepper, because you're hot."

"Gross," Emma said. "That chili pepper thing creeps me out."

"Me too. I'd prefer my students to think of me as a disembodied brain."

"Sorry to nitpick," Emma said, "but Pat, your coffee cup thing is impossible. Even if you didn't need a handle, how could you carve a coffee cup out of a femur? It would be way too narrow, and the bone is too porous—"

Pat was unfazed by Emma's criticism.

"I'm writing for a scientifically illiterate audience. Now here's one for you, Emma."

He cleared his throat.

"Professor Emma Nakamura changed my life. I was gonna drop out of school but now I'm gonna be a famos scientist, spelled f-a-m-o-s."

"Not even funny," she sighed.

"The SRO will love that one," I said. "Oh, and speaking of."

A woman with cascading copper-colored hair and watery blue eyes stepped to the podium in the front of the room and picked up the microphone. The room resonated with screeching feedback. She covered the mike with the end of her sari to quiet the noise and started over.

"How come they get a lecture setup?" Emma muttered. "They're always telling us to step away from the podium and be the Guide on the Side and not the Sage on the Stage, blah blah blah, but look, that's exactly what they do. Bet you a hundred dollars no one's gonna honor *our* Unique Ways of Knowing."

The brownies were delicious, I mused as I took a

bite. I wondered how the baker had achieved the crisp, glossy layer on top. I settled in and listened to the Student Retention Officer greet the room full of college professors as if we were all four years old. Her singsong cadence soothed away the last of my anxiety.

These were the best brownies I'd ever tasted. I wished I had taken a stack of them. Why hadn't I ever noticed the high quality of the refreshments at these SRO sessions? It was the fresh-baked cookies, the chewy brownies, and the rich Kona coffee that made these events bearable. I regretted the restraint I had exercised during my first pass at the refreshment table. Unfortunately, I couldn't go up there again without drawing attention to myself. I was sitting in the middle of a row, and the session was well underway.

The Student Retention Officer had started her slide show, which I think was supposed to illustrate how to engage students and parents during a campus interview. There was the familiar "think outside the box" illustration with the nine dots and four connected lines. After think-outside-the-box came the graph purporting to show that people remember ten percent of what they read, twenty percent of what they see, and so on, all the way up to recalling eighty percent of what they do. Betty Jackson from the psychology department once told me this popular claim isn't based on any research or evidence, but it sounds right, so people keep repeating it.

Compared to my office, Student Retention Office Conference Room Five was dazzling. High-end recessed lights studded the vast ceiling. The cushioning of my green chair sproinged agreeably when I bounced against it. I felt strangely buoyant. Everything in this room sang of newness and promise and an unlimited budget.

Maybe these Student Retention Office sessions weren't so bad. I must have been feeling the sugar buzz from the excellent brownies, I decided. I felt both relaxed and alert. No, better than alert. Aware.

My thoughts percolated brightly on opposite sides of my brain. From my right and left hemispheres, the strands of my consciousness flowed together like two streams, joining in a bright white river of enlightenment rushing over my hippocampus like a glittering waterfall.

A river! We're all one, I realized. Pat and Emma, seated on either side of me, smirking and sulking, respectively. The copper-haired Student Retention Officer with her hypnotically-swaying bronze earrings and sparkling sari. Even the hulking campus security officer who's always posted by the door now, ever since that one incident. Each of us a tiny human tributary trickling into the mighty—

"Molly, you're so creative, let's have you come up first."

Pat nudged me gently. "Molly. They're calling you up for the role play."

CHAPTER NINETEEN

"Now we need someone to play the Prospective Student," the Student Retention Officer announced.

Pat's hand shot up.

Pat, the Student Retention Officer and I sat in a semicircle in front of the room.

The Student Retention Officer, playing the Parent of the Prospective Student, went first.

"Good afternoon, Professor Barda. Thank you for meeting with us. My son…"

She turned to Pat to give him the opportunity to introduce himself.

"My name is Carlo Ponzi," said Pat. "Nice to meet you."

"My son Carlo is interested in the School of Business," the Student Retention Officer explained to me. "What can you tell us about it?"

I could have told her our college is called the College of Commerce, not the School of Business, but I realized it didn't matter. Usually it annoyed me when someone from the Student Retention Office got our name wrong, but not today. She meant well, after all. I realized I was feeling charitable toward the Student Retention Office.

It was a strange sensation.

I recited the College of Commerce's standard spiel to Pat: "We offer an innovative curriculum," I said, making sure to speak loudly enough to reach the distant back row. "Students benefit from practical real-world experience, with opportunities such as the Mercedes Yamashiro Sustainability Fellowship and the James Hisashi Tanaka Scholarship for students planning to go into the hospitality business—"

"I want to learn how to package up subprime mortgages and sell them as triple-A-rated bonds," Pat declared, getting into the spirit of the role play.

The Student Retention Officer added, "We've loved visiting your island, but it's very different from our home. I know moving will be an adjustment for my son Carlo."

She beamed at her "son" slouched in the chair with his arms crossed, his gangly legs and filthy black work boots sticking out in front of him. The long, unpaved driveway that leads to Pat's remote, mountainside house is mud most of the time. Normally Pat's mucky shoes annoy me. Why can't he just rinse them off with a hose or something, I wonder? But today I realized Pat's neglected shoes were a marker of his evolved consciousness, his focus on the things in life that genuinely matter. I was so lucky Pat was my friend!

"Before we make our decision," said the Student Retention Officer, "can you help us to understand, Professor Barda, what we can expect? Maybe you can tell us, what do you enjoy about living here?"

I thought about my time in graduate school, before I moved out to Hawaii. Freeway shootings, summer fires raging across the dry desert, the entertainment industry so pervasive you could walk into any coffee shop and ask a random person, "How is your screenplay going?" And they'd answer, "Almost finished."

Life in Mahina was blissfully uneventful by comparison. No one had any grandiose ambitions, and everyone knew all your business. People put up with you anyway because, hey, it's an island and we're going to have to run into each other again, so we might as well all get along.

I had come to accept that fact of life, although I have to admit the complete loss of privacy had taken some getting used to. People seemed to know what was going on in my life almost before I did. For example, the first time I broke up with Stephen Park—

"Molly? I mean, Professor Barda?"

"Oh! What I like about living here." The picture clicked into focus. I knew exactly what I should say. I took a deep breath and beamed at the audience.

"There are so many things to love about living here: No gangs. No freeway shootings. No freeway, in fact."

The Student Retention Officer nodded encouragingly.

I looked directly into her eyes. So blue! Flecks of cobalt-blue mascara were sprinkled across the top of her cheeks.

"No freeway," I repeated. "No snakes. No clowns."

It was true. I've never seen any of those things here. Freeways, gangs, snakes, clowns. I saw a transient flicker of confusion on the face of the Student Retention Officer. I took that as a signal I needed to elaborate further.

"Well, there's that one little blind snake," I admitted, "But it doesn't count. It's more of a worm, really." I waved my hand dismissively. Out in the audience, Emma clapped her hand over her face. She gets all picky and literal about things like how worms and snakes aren't the same thing, supposedly. She didn't have the advantage of my more holistic perspective. Science can only take you so far.

"But clowns!" I exclaimed. "Absolutely not. We don't allow them here."

"She's right." Pat nodded gravely. "You have to be careful. You let clowns in, and it changes the whole ecosystem. The next thing you know your island is getting overrun by bears on tiny bicycles."

I thought it was callous of Pat to pile on like that. It struck me that perhaps we were being unfair to clowns. Hating clowns is so common it's a cliché, exactly like hating that band, I forgot their name, but you probably know them as the band everyone hates, and maybe the members of the band don't care, but I'll bet the clowns do. How many are there, I wondered? Enough to populate a small country, probably. A nation of rainbow-wigged, bulb-nosed despair. Tears stung my eyes.

"I don't want to talk about clowns anymore," I stammered, my voice cracking. "I've made my decision."

I extended my hand to Pat, preparing to welcome him to the James Hisashi Tanaka College of Commerce. I smiled and nodded magnanimously to the Student Retention Officer. And I opened my mouth to speak.

"I am well groomed," I announced. "And my hair is attractively styled."

CHAPTER TWENTY

Emma, Pat and I sat quietly around one of the Maritime Club's plastic outdoor tables. I was so obviously miserable even Pat was reluctant to rib me. Emma sipped her beer thoughtfully. Pat nursed a cup of coffee. I had a cup of coffee too, but I wasn't drinking it. Instead, I cupped my hands around it to feel the warmth. I was starting to feel the throbbing behind one eye that prefigures one of those screaming headaches where I feel like my eyeballs are going to pop out of my skull and shoot across the room.

Pat finally spoke. "I don't think it was a mistake, Molly." He sounded a little defensive. "I think it's good you went in to see someone about your anxiety. You can't keep having these panic attacks and not do anything about it."

"We're not blaming you, Pat," Emma assured him. "It's just that Molly should have tried the medication over the weekend or something, so she'd know how she reacted to it."

"I shouldn't have taken it after the wine," I said.

"The wine probably didn't help," Emma agreed.

"When we were about to walk up to the Student Retention Office, though, I thought my heart was going to explode. I had to do something. And you know, the medication did feel like it was working. I don't know how it looked from the outside, but from my perspective? It was magical."

I let my head slump down onto my folded arms.

"Now I'm never going to get tenure," I mumbled into the tabletop.

"Oh, I don't know," Pat tried to reassure me. "That's the nicest you've ever been to Linda. She might put in a good word for you."

"Linda?" I picked my head up. "I thought Linda was the blonde one with the long-sleeved muumuus."

"Different Linda," Emma said. "This Linda is the one who was leading the discussion today. The one you were doing the role play with. You actually were smiling at her. The whole time."

"Instead of cursing her in Sicilian and spitting on the ground," Pat added.

"So, what, then? Are you saying I should stay medicated at all times? Because it gives me a completely different personality? One that's clearly superior to my actual personality?"

Pat and Emma were quiet for a few moments. Finally Pat said,

"I think it's wearing off."

"Did you ever read the package insert?" Emma asked.

"No. The doctor told me to look it up online. I can do it now."

I pulled out my phone and found the drug information with a simple search. I expanded the tiny font so that only a few words showed on the screen at a time.

"Unusual risk-taking behavior," I read. "Decreased inhibitions. No fear of danger."

I glanced at Pat. He nodded approvingly and, I thought, a little smugly.

"Sounds like exactly what the doctor ordered."

"Actually, Pat, you're supposed to call the doctor if those things happen to you. Oh, and look at these."

I scrolled down and read through the list of possible side effects.

I handed Pat my phone.

"What's this?"

"The side effects. Read it. You know what? I don't think I should take these anymore. Maybe I can just rely on my supportive friends to help me deal with the stress in my life. Right?"

"Well, you're not going to get all of these at once." Pat slid my phone back over to me.

By this time, my head was throbbing in earnest. I reached into my water glass, pulled out a handful of ice cubes, wrapped them in a napkin and pressed the whole thing against my forehead. It helped a little.

"How did your other meetings go?" Pat asked.

Emma shook her head. "I can't believe you went to more meetings after that. I'm so glad I'm not a department chair."

"I think they went okay I had to talk Hanson Harrison down. One of his students from last semester is filing a lawsuit against him for giving him a C-minus. Then after Hanson, I had a meeting with that other poor kid. The one I had to remove from Larry's class."

"Phone Boy," Pat said.

"Yes. Him. So you know how the Student Retention Office has been pressuring me to give him priority seating in class. I told them no, the class is already full."

"Why was this kid getting special treatment?" Emma asked.

"My guess is he's from out of state, so he pays the higher tuition."

"Right," Pat said. "We never want to lose a customer."

"Especially not when Daddy's a rich doctor," Emma said.

"So he wanted to get readmitted?" Pat asked.

"No. Not exactly. He didn't say anything about the class, in fact. He gave me a long speech about how our government has been complicit in terrorist attacks, how the moon landing was faked and there are all of these videos online that prove it, and he was going to email me the links because I absolutely had to know about this. But of course he had to be careful what he put in his email because there were certain people, the bad lizard people, who have infiltrated the ranks of our administration."

"Sounds plausible to me," Pat said. "At least the last part about the administration being staffed by lizard people."

"Were you still high on your meds when you talked to him?" Emma asked.

"No, thanks for asking. I'm telling you exactly what happened. And there's more. Somehow, he segued into how social networking was funded by the CIA and the military and there are already facial recognition systems set up in public places, and we're all probably being watched right now."

"Not on our campus," Emma scoffed. "Facial recognition systems? They can't even keep our overhead projectors working."

"I wonder how much of the kid's paranoid rant is true," Pat mused. "Maybe he's onto something, and the knowledge drove him mad."

"And then he told me my necklace was super cool and he couldn't stop looking at it. Should I be worried?"

Pat shrugged "He's probably planning to kill you, steal your necklace, and go strangle Larry with it. Was there anything else about the facial recognition? That sounds kind of interesting."

"I think I'm going to talk to the SRO about him again," I said. "Maybe the lizard people thing will be enough to get him referred to counseling. Anyway, yeah, the perfect end to a perfect workday. Top that."

"I got nothing," said Emma. "The SRO meeting was pretty much the highlight of my year."

"Oh, I almost forgot," Pat said. "I found out more about those high paying library jobs. Namely, how high-paying they actually are."

Pat told us a number, and Emma and I gasped as if we had each been punched in the stomach.

"So why did I bother to get a Ph.D.?" Emma said.

"Seriously," I agreed. "I wonder if any of them want to trade with me."

"I'd put in my application tomorrow," Pat said, "If those jobs weren't reserved for our graduates. Someone obviously set this up to make our graduates' employment numbers look good."

"I guess I'm okay with the idea of subsidized employment, in principle," I said. "We're taking care of our own."

"I'd sure like to get paid that much for shelving books," Emma said.

"Yeah, me too. Anyway, this was fun, but I think I'm ready to wrap it up. I need to rest up for class tomorrow."

My head was pounding. More than anything else, I wanted to be home, lying down in the dark with a real ice bag on my head.

CHAPTER TWENTY-ONE

Even after coming home from the Maritime Club, heading straight to bed, and sleeping for twelve hours, I was feeling the aftereffects of Doctor Spinner's anxiety pills. They were not pleasant. My only desire for the moment was to sit, calm and undisturbed, in my dim little office with the blinds drawn, with a few moments to myself before class.

A jaunty knock shattered the quiet. It felt like the sound waves were making my brain bob up and down in my cerebral fluid like a cork. Was that physically possible? I'd have to ask Emma.

I trudged over to my door and opened it.

"Oh. Hi, Sherry." I tried to muster an enthusiastic tone. "Come in."

I held the door open and stepped aside.

"Hey, Dr. B! It's super dark in your office. Ya want me to turn the light on?"

"No! Uh, no thank you."

Sherry seated herself in the visitor chair. I stepped carefully around my desk and lowered myself slowly onto my yoga ball.

"I don't care for the artificial light," I said. "I prefer the natural daylight." I gestured at the tiny slivers of sunlight filtering through my tightly closed blinds.

"So Dr. B, we love the idea of doing something technical for our business plan. I've been working on something I think is gonna be pretty great. I just had some questions about the assignment."

Sherry's bright enthusiasm made me feel like someone was shining a klieg light in my face. I longed to be back in my bed with a blanket pulled over my head. As fleeing my office was not a realistic option, I rested my head in my hands in a pose that I hoped looked thoughtful, rather than hung-over.

"Terrific," I whispered. "I'm glad your group is getting started on this."

"I don't want to say too much yet, but I think you're gonna like it. Glenn's been helping. That's cool, right? I was gonna ask you about it, actually. Glenn's not doing the work for me or anything. He's helping me out with some of the details. Giving me advice and stuff."

"You may interview experts for your business plan, as long as you're doing your own work. It's in the assignment guidelines. Did you say Glenn is helping you?"

"Yeah. He's a doll."

"So what is his area of expertise?"

"He's real good with electronics," she said.

"Glenn? Your Glenn?"

"Oh, yeah. He's awesome at that stuff. You should see how he set up our TV. He got two different game consoles and the cable box hooked up, and he got it all working on one remote."

"Impressive," I said.

"It works perfect. I mean, as long as you don't need to change the volume."

"Well, that's better than I could do," I conceded.

"He's good at computers, too."

"That's wonderful. He sounds like a real Renaissance man." I pressed my hands to the sides of my head to still the throbbing. Why did Sherry have to be so chatty this morning?

"Yeah! He knows all about sharing and privacy settings, like how you can put up a post but make sure only your friends can see it? Oh, that reminds me. I just sent you a friend request. Anyway, Glenn left town for some work thing, and he might be gone for a while, so I dunno what I'm gonna do."

"About your business plan?" I asked.

"Oh yeah, that too," she laughed.

"How can I help?"

"I got some ideas, but I feel like I need to learn more. I was hoping you had some recommended reading for me."

"You'll want to get a general idea of what products are already out there, and where the unmet needs are." I recommended a couple of established technology blogs and a computer security podcast I listen to when I'm having trouble sleeping. I didn't tell Sherry the part about sleeping, of course.

"Oh. And Sherry. I just remembered. Here's something else you may want to look up. Facial recognition software? Have a look at the technology. It might inspire some ideas."

She reached into her purse for a pen and I glimpsed an open pack of cigarettes. "Facial recognition. Lemme write it down. Sounds cool. Oh, you think you could wear sunglasses to confuse the facial recognition software? Like the ones you're wearing? Hey, how come you're wearing sunglasses? Oh, don't tell me. Hangover, right? Listen, I'm not judging, I've been there."

"Factors that confuse the facial recognition software. Good. Your group can investigate that too." I nodded cautiously, lest I set my brain banging around inside my skull again.

"Oh yeah, I gotta bunch of ideas. I don't know which one is gonna work out. Dr. B, I gotta tell you, I'm loving this class. It's like, opening a whole new world for me. I never thought of myself as a businesswoman, but now I feel like yeah, I could be one."

"Of course you can." I managed a weak smile. Sherry's remark was a spark of hope in an otherwise miserable morning. This is what makes it all worthwhile, I reflected. The students who are here to learn, not to appease their parents or wait out a bad job market. Give me one or two of these a semester, and I can deal with the rest.

"My biggest problem right now is putting in the time for class, though," Sherry said. "You know, paddling practice has been pretty intense lately. Emma's been working us hard."

"Are you ready for the big race? I know it's going to be a little sad not having Kathy there."

"I'm so excited! I can't believe it's this weekend already."

"Make sure to take good care of yourself" I wondered whether I looked as hypocritical as I felt.

I caught sight of a broad-shouldered figure standing in the doorway, and for a second, I thought it was Donnie. My heart raced a little, and then… cue the needle-scratch.

It wasn't Donnie Gonsalves at all. It was his son, Davison.

Just when I thought my headache couldn't get any worse.

CHAPTER TWENTY-TWO

The first thing you notice about Davison Gonsalves—aside from the fact that he looks like a baseball-capped, acne-sprinkled knockoff of his father—is his tattoos. Apparently the "tribal" designs and kanji characters so popular with his peers were not obnoxious enough for him. Giant brown centipedes writhed repulsively on his arms as he reached up to grasp the lintel of my office door.

"Eh, Aunty Molly!" Davison gripped my door frame, showing off his muscles and blocking my exit. "Check it out. I'm back in town."

"Look at that!" I chirped. "You sure are." I suppressed the impulse to clutch my head as pain stabbed through my right eye.

"Don't get your hopes up, though." His grin showed off his expensively-straightened teeth. "I'm not staying long. I had to pick up some transcripts and stuff and Dad said I should come by and say hi.

Eh, how you like my new bedroom? Sweet, ah?"

I couldn't begin to think of an appropriate response, and Davison didn't wait for one. Sherry had turned around in her chair and was eying him with interest. His deep-cut tank top was designed to show off as much ink and muscle as possible while still technically serving as a "shirt."

Davison released his grip on my door frame and sauntered into my dim office, overpowering the tiny space with a noxious plume of cologne.

"Hey." He dropped his voice about an octave. "I'm Dave."

Sherry took his hand and held it in both of hers. I could have leaned over and waved my arm between their two faces and neither of them would have blinked.

"I'm Sherry," she rasped coquettishly. "Like the drink."

Somehow, she managed to signal to Davison (sorry, I mean *Dave*) that she was dying for a smoke, and he indicated he could oblige her. She had apparently forgotten about the pack of cigarettes in her purse. I reminded them smoking was not permitted in the building, which was fine with them. They left my office together, giggling and leaning in close to each other as if it were freezing and they had to conserve their body heat. My wall thermometer showed eighty-one degrees Fahrenheit.

When they had gone, I logged onto my computer and accepted Sherry's friend request. Pat refuses to "friend" students, but I don't see the harm. It's a nice, low-commitment way to stay in touch. For me, the asynchronous, take-it-or-leave-it interaction of social media is an agreeable substitute for face-to-face conversation, which I find exhausting.

I'm even online friends with Kathy Banks. Or *was* friends, I should say. I checked my contact list and felt a chill when I saw her account was still active. Well, of course it was. Who was going to deactivate it? I was tempted to click through to her wall to see whether anyone had written on it but decided it would be too depressing. Instead, I spent about thirty seconds perusing my contacts' baby pictures, food photos, and pithy quotes. Then I packed up to go to class.

My sunglasses steamed up as soon as I stepped out of my building. Between my misted-over vision and my pounding headache, I nearly walked right past my classroom door. I groped my way inside and switched off the overhead lights. Hazy daylight filtered through the blinds. The classroom was warm and humid, the feeble air conditioning no match for the wall-to-wall bodies.

"Good morning," I murmured as I fumbled with my sunglasses. I winced as they clattered onto the floor. I retrieved them and stuffed them into my bag.

"We're going to try something different today. We'll keep the lighting dim. Just as they did in the Hawthorne Studies."

A young blonde woman raised her hand.

"Excuse me Doctor Barda, but didn't the Hawthorne Studies—"

"Yes. I know. You're absolutely right. We're going to keep the lights down anyway." I turned to the whiteboard, only to find it covered with Rodge Cowper's class notes. The students arranged themselves into their discussion groups. I spent the first few minutes of class erasing Rodge Cowper's notes from the whiteboard with one hand while shielding my eyes with the other.

A leader knows the way, goes the way, and shows the way.

Become a leader by following best practices.

In it to win it!

The last phrase stayed on the whiteboard, no matter how much I scrubbed with the eraser. Rodge, or someone, must have written "in it to win it!" with a permanent marker. I hoped I would make it through the class period without my skull exploding like a shrapnel grenade.

Sherry slipped in half an hour late and silently joined her group. A few minutes later, they called me over. Sherry had her laptop open.

"You were right, Dr. B," she said. "That face recognition software is out there. We might wanna do something with it. But we're having trouble coming up with a business idea. It's true sunglasses can fool the software, but any sunglasses work, so you don't need special ones."

Standing next to Sherry, I was hit by the stench of cigarette smoke, mingled with Davison's powerful cologne. My stomach, already feeling delicate, rebelled at the sensory assault. I slowly inched away from Sherry to stand at the opposite side of her group's table.

A young woman in her group piped up, "We had the idea that you could put cameras in nightclubs and have something online like, right now there's sixty percent girls and forty percent guys, and people would go to wherever the percentages are the best for them. But we found some bar in Chicago already doing that."

Someone else suggested, "What about a service that finds your high school classmates using yearbook photos? For class reunions?"

Then Sherry said, "Nah. I don't like it. The creepiest kid in your high school would use it to stalk everyone else."

"That might already be happening," I said. I wondered about my own online presence, and whether my photo on our college's website could lead to anything embarrassing.

Sherry laughed, "Guess you can't keep a secret these days. We all better behave ourselves."

"That's great advice, Sherry." I pressed the heels of my hands to my eyes to still my throbbing headache.

CHAPTER TWENTY-THREE

Emma was in high spirits, anticipating tomorrow's canoe race. I was looking forward to meeting Donnie for a pleasant dinner on the sunny side of the island while Davison was back home on the windward side with Sherry. No, wait, Sherry would be paddling tomorrow with Emma. Davison was probably already on his way back to the mainland.

I was driving Emma's little hybrid. Emma sat beside me in the passenger seat, and her husband Yoshi rode in the back. I missed the majestic heave and sway of my Thunderbird, but with a two-hour drive across the island in each direction, there was no way to justify taking a car that gets eleven miles to the gallon. The dense jungle crowded the narrow road from both sides, and droplets of mist speckled the windshield. I could feel my ears pop although the road didn't seem steep. We were gradually ascending, approaching the center of the island.

Yoshi was regaling us with the history of the Labor Day race. I already know all about the Labor Day Race, and I knew Emma did as well, as she was the one who had told me all about it. Neither of us reminded Yoshi of this, however. Yoshi enjoys explaining things to people, and I suppose we didn't want to spoil his fun.

"It's the world's biggest long-distance outrigger canoe race," he explained. "Paddlers come here from all over the world to compete." He went on to recite dates, locations, and key personnel associated with the history of the Labor Day race as we made our way up the gentle incline of the cross-island road. Yoshi kept talking until eventually he ran out of gas and fell asleep.

We emerged from the cloud cover into a bright blue afternoon. The lush greenery had thinned out, yielding to scrubby cloud forest. Up here it was cool, dry, and windy. We still had about thirty minutes to go until we reached the halfway point. Emma would take over driving, and we would start to descend to the chunky black lava fields and misty vog of the west side.

One reason I didn't mind taking my turn at the wheel is the driver gets to choose the music. Emma knows my musical tastes—I wrote my dissertation on punk rock, after all—but she still likes to act like each new song that comes up on my playlist is an unpleasant surprise.

"So what happened to Pat?" Emma asked. "Why didn't he –"

She paused in mid-sentence and wrinkled her nose.

"Is this supposed to be singing?"

"What were you saying about Pat?"

"Why didn't he come with us?" Emma leaned forward and turned down the volume. "I thought he'd want to write something about the race. Lots of local color with the motorcycle clubs and everything."

"He said he had a bunch of papers to grade."

I glanced at the back seat, where Yoshi was dozing through the rough-edged vocal stylings of a band that had broken up sometime before vinyl had been displaced by CDs. "I don't think Pat could afford a room at the hotel," I said. "Now I'm department chair, I know what the lecturer salary schedule is. I have a pretty good idea what Pat makes." I told her the figure.

"What?" Emma shrieked. "That's less than you'd make working at the place in the mall that sells corn dogs!"

"And they get those snappy uniforms too. Yeah, I know."

"Poor Pat," Emma said.

"No wonder he hates capitalism," I agreed.

Emma picked up my phone (which doubled as my music repository) and examined my playlists.

"What's this?" she asked. "Shostakovich. Khachaturian. Saint something. This looks like classical music. Let's listen to classical music, ah Molly? It's gotta be better than this!"

"Oh, no. Those are my mad, bombastic waltzes. They're not exactly appropriate for a nice drive across the island. They're more for when you're riding out to get revenge on someone."

Emma laughed. "Only you would have a soundtrack for going out to get revenge on someone."

"Seriously. Listen to Khachaturian's *Masquerade Waltz* and tell me I'm wrong."

"So if Pat couldn't afford a room, why didn't you offer to share yours? It's not like anything would happen."

"Well, because Donnie's going to meet me over there."

"Oh, Donnie's going to stay with you?"

"No. I'm meeting him over there. If he can get away from work, which I hope he can."

"I don't understand. If Donnie's not staying with you, and Pat's not staying with you, who is staying with you?"

"No one. I just got a room for myself." I said.

"I still don't understand why Pat couldn't stay in your room."

"I don't want Pat staying with me if I'm going to meet Donnie. Donnie's kind of old fashioned."

"But doesn't Donnie know Pat's—"

"Of course he does."

"So what's his problem with Pat then?"

Emma had a point. Donnie would never admit it, but it was pretty clear he did have a problem with Pat.

"He's never said anything about it," I said, "but I think it's because Pat and I have so much in common. We like the same music, we have a lot of inside jokes, we can complain about work, you know what I mean. Donnie and I never really laugh together, and he's not all that into current events either. Unless it's something to do directly with running the restaurant, you know, Chamber of Commerce stuff."

"The music thing is a mystery," Emma said. "I'm amazed I know one person who likes this kind of music, let alone two."

"I have to make sure Donnie doesn't feel excluded."

"So don't exclude him," Emma said. "Invite him to stay in your room. Come on. You two have been together for a while. He can't be that old-fashioned."

"Oh yes, he can. And I'm a good Catholic girl, don't forget."

I glanced at the back seat and was relieved to see Yoshi still fast asleep. "Wow, Yoshi can sleep through anything, can't he?"

Emma made a disparaging guttural sound. "Just crinkle a bag of chips next to his ear if you want him to wake up."

"I don't want to rush into anything with Donnie," I said. "It would be so easy to mess things up with him. You know how he is. Everything about him is perfect and has to be a certain way, you know what I mean? His house, his car, his perfectly pressed shirts—"

"He is pretty OCD," Emma agreed. "I guess that's something you two have in common."

"Emma, OCD is a noun, not an adjective. It stands for Obsessive-Compulsive Disorder. You can say someone *has* OCD, but you can't say someone *is* OCD. If you want to do an armchair diagnosis you can say the person is obsessive-compulsive."

"Thanks for illustrating my point. Anyway, Molly, you have to get to know him sometime. What if you do end up getting married and it turns out he's into something you didn't know about? Like he shows up on your wedding night wearing nothing but a hot dog bun?"

"I don't see us getting married," I said.

"How come? Cause of the kid?"

"Exactly. Davison. The poison pill in this merger deal."

"Isn't he on the mainland?" Emma asked.

"I almost forgot to tell you. Donnie's already brought him back for a visit. And Donnie just finished redecorating Davison's room for him. I guess he thought Davison was getting too old for Winnie the Pooh bed sheets or whatever."

"The new room must look nice," Emma said. "Donnie has good taste."

"Nice? No, it does not look nice. Davison picked out the furniture himself, apparently from the Rococo Monstrosity Catalog."

"So Donnie's idiot son is part of the deal. But look Molly, no one's perfect. At least Donnie has a job."

Emma glared at Yoshi, who was snoring in the back seat.

CHAPTER TWENTY-FOUR

"Is this the song about the sentient amoeba? Do we have to listen to this?"

Emma's criticism of my musical taste was starting to annoy me. I nudged the volume up.

"Anyway," she continued, raising her voice to compete with the increased noise level, "what's your plan for meeting Donnie?"

"We didn't set a specific time. I guess we're going to play it by ear."

"He's coming all the way across the island just to see you and you didn't bother to make any plans? Molly, you gotta call him right now and figure out when you're gonna get together. You don't want this whole weekend to go to waste. Pull over, I'll drive."

"Are you sure? It's not your turn yet."

"Your lifelong happiness is at stake here," Emma said. "It's worth it to me."

"Wow, okay. Thanks!"

We pulled over. On either side of the narrow strip of road, green-tinged scrub stretched to the horizon, punctuated here and there by skinny, dark green ohia trees. Emma and I climbed out and switched places while Yoshi continued to snore in the back seat. Emma settled into the driver's seat and plugged her phone into the sound system. Gentle slack key guitar strumming filled the car.

"That was sneaky, Emma."

"Sorry, I couldn't take any more of your music, no offense. Every song on your playlist is so angry! It was starting to stress me out."

She waited until the road was clear and pulled back out.

"It's not angry-angry," I said. "It's satirical, self-deprecating angry. It's—"

My phone hummed. Donnie was calling.

"See?" Emma said. "Good thing you're not driving."

Donnie hadn't left Mahina yet. He sounded like he wasn't in a very good mood.

"Are you going to be able to come out?" I asked him.

"Sure. I'll be there. I just have to take care of some things first."

I thought of something that might lift his spirits.

"Oh, Donnie, I forgot to tell you. When I saw Davison the other day at my office? He mentioned the new bedroom furniture you got him. He seemed to like it very much. So, success, right?"

I thought that would cheer him up, but it seemed

to make his mood even worse.

"Davison only has a short time in Mahina. I thought I'd get a chance to spend some time with him, but I've hardly seen him at all."

"Oh. He's still in town? Hasn't he gone back to the mainland yet? Well, maybe he wanted to reconnect with his old friends or something?"

"No, I think Davison's met a girl. At least, that's what I gathered from the few words we exchanged the one time he stopped by the house."

"He's only been home once?"

"After I picked him up at the airport, he went to campus to get some paperwork. Then he came by to get his overnight bag. That's the last time I saw him. It wasn't easy to find a flight for him this time of year, with school starting. Fares are really high. And my customers are spending less per order and less overall than they were last year."

"Oh." I had no idea what else to say. *Your kid's kind of a jerk, Donnie. Everyone seems to see it except you.*

"The competition isn't sitting still, either, Molly. Merrie Musubis just added a new Mexican food line."

"I don't think that'll last. Once the novelty wears off, I'm sure your customers will be back."

I didn't tell him I'd actually tried Merrie Musubis' new Carlos Spamtana Burrito. It was awful. Whoever came up with the recipe was apparently unfamiliar with the idea of spices. You can't throw together pasty unseasoned refried beans and Spam chunks and call it a day.

"Davison doesn't care how hard it was to get him a ticket, how long it's been since I've seen him," Donnie went on. "He gets distracted by a shiny object, and off he goes."

"Mm," I nodded.

"He's as bad as Sherry," Donnie said.

"Oh, tell me about it. Wait, what?"

"He hasn't even had a chance to spend the night in his new room."

"Did you say he's as bad as Sherry?" I asked.

Emma shot me a quizzical look.

"Yes, I did," he said. "Sherry."

The long silence made me wonder if the call had been dropped. Finally, Donnie said,

"She left on Davison's eighth birthday."

"Oh."

"Did I tell you about this already?"

"No."

All I knew was that Donnie was a divorced single father. He had never told me anything about his ex. I'd been dying to find out more, but I was never able to figure out a tactful way to ask.

"What happened?" I prodded.

Donnie went quiet again, and for a moment I feared I had pushed too hard. But then he said,

"I never saw it coming, Molly. The day started out perfectly normal. We'd had a disagreement about Davison's birthday cake. I thought at the time she was overreacting. Now I realize she was looking for an excuse."

Maybe it was easier for him to open up on the

telephone, rather than face to face. Awkward as it was, I could understand it.

"She walked out at eleven-oh-two," he said. "Just walked out and closed the door."

"So what did you do?"

Donnie exhaled.

"I let Davison open his birthday presents, and we waited for her to come back. She didn't. I left Davison with a neighbor and drove around town trying to find her."

"Her name was Sherry?" I asked, stupidly.

"Yes. It was short for Sherrine. Unusual name."

"Sherrine?"

I realized I was starting to sound like some not-very-intelligent artificial intelligence program. Maybe it would be better if I stopped talking.

"I always suspected she had a—had someone else. I was working long hours at the restaurant and we didn't get to spend much time with one another. But suspecting is one thing. I never thought she was going to act on it. I was wrong. And I…she wouldn't change her mind."

I tried to picture a desperate Donnie pursuing Sherry all over town and begging her to come back. It didn't square at all with the Donnie I knew. I couldn't imagine Donnie being that infatuated with me. Our relationship, I realized, felt a little like Donnie was sizing me up as a potential business partner. Not falling for me. More like assessing me. On the bright side, so far I seemed to be meeting the benchmarks.

"I stopped by the ice cream shop on the way back home," he said. "I bought Davison the biggest cake they had. It had little orange basketballs on it, made out of frosting. Davison and I ate ice cream cake and watched Davison's favorite cartoons over and over."

"Donnie, I'm so sorry. How did you explain all this to Davison?"

"I told him, Mama had to go away."

I wondered whether I should say something to Donnie about Davison's new paramour. But what would I tell him? It would all be speculation anyway. No, the best course of action was to keep my mouth shut. It was probably an unfortunate coincidence about the name.

"Do you think Davison still remembers any of it?" I asked. How much had Sherry changed over the years, I wondered? Davison had obviously been drawn to her.

"I don't know. He never talks about it. Sorry, Molly. I don't know how we got onto this. Hey. Are you reading anything good?"

Donnie knows I'm usually reading something, and I sympathized with his wanting to change the subject. But of all of the hundreds of books I'd read in my life, the only title I could recall at the moment was Henry Fielding's *Tom Jones.*

CHAPTER TWENTY-FIVE

"Well?" Emma demanded the instant I hung up. I glanced at the back seat to make sure Yoshi was still asleep and summarized my conversation with Donnie.

"His mother? Are you serious?"

"I don't know. It sounds terrible. But the details all fit."

"I wonder if they went to the novelty store to buy Oedipal underwear." She burst out laughing at her own joke.

"Yes, very clever, Emma. Well, what do you think?"

"Come on, Molly. Just because they're both named Sherry?"

"Sherrine. It's an unusual name. I hope I'm wrong."

"I'll ask Sherry about it when I see her tonight," Emma said.

"No! Don't do that. Sherry and Davison met in my office. If this blows up everyone will end up blaming me."

"No, they won't. It's not your fault."

"And what's worse, Sherry is my student. I do not want her to know I'm dating her ex-husband. Assuming Donnie is her ex-husband."

"Oh, right. That would make things awkward in your classroom, wouldn't it? Alright. I won't say anything to her. You know, whether she's Donnie's ex or not, she sure got herself in a situation. Did you know Glenn came back from his trip early?"

"Glenn's already back? That was quick."

"Yeah, I guess she was expecting him to be gone a lot longer. She seemed pretty stressed out about it. I hope he didn't come home and find Davison hiding under the bed. So where are you meeting Donnie?"

"Shoot. I totally forgot to ask him. He hasn't even left Mahina yet."

"Good. We have time to stop at the paddling store."

I don't remember the rest of the drive across the island. I drifted off under the spell of Emma's soothing music selection and dozed through the rest of the drive. When I woke up, we had already reached the little seaside town where we would be staying. Emma was driving around the narrow, congested streets in search of her paddling store, whose name she couldn't quite remember.

She finally located SunSport Paddling Supply in a

nondescript, sun-bleached strip mall. I followed Emma and Yoshi into SunSport and glanced around at the racks of swim shorts and rash guards and the long, impossibly narrow one-man canoes mounted along the walls. Quickly bored with that, I excused myself and went outside to look at the other shops. These were a Chinese takeout, a hot tub store, and a wine shop. I perused hot tubs and wine bottles for a while and looked into the paddling store to make sure Emma and Yoshi were still in there. They were. I stepped outside to check my messages and hurried back into SunSport.

"Emma, Donnie called again."

"Did he leave a message?"

"There's no reception here," I said, "so I can't call in for my voicemail. But I see two transcripts. I hope he's not calling to say he can't make it."

"Does that work for you?" Emma asked. "I tried one of those transcription services, but I canceled it. Most of the time it gave me garble."

"Let's see." I read the transcribed message from my phone screen. "No, it looks like he's already arrived and checked in. Here's his room number. Wow, he had time to drive all the way over and check in? We've been shopping for a while, Emma. Are you going to buy anything?"

"Not me. But Yoshi's still trying on rash guards."

"And here's the next message. It says Hi, this is Donnie. After that, it's a little harder to parse."

"What's he say?"

"According to the transcript, *I seem like I will also*

call the bathroom Birth 5. And possible when. Please, substantially. I'm gonna be a broom. Three-ten."

"He's gonna be a broom? Maybe he's getting ready to sweep you off your feet."

Emma guffawed at her own clever remark. "Oh, I am literally on fire today!"

"Emma, you are not literally on fire. Okay, I have to call Donnie back to see what the second message was about. Let's go outside. I'll try again."

We walked out to the small parking lot shared by the stores. I placed my phone at different angles but was still unable to get a signal. Out of the corner of my eye, I saw Emma do a double-take at the wine shop.

"Actually," Emma waved her hand to get my attention, "don't call back. Let him wait. You don't want to look too eager. You know he's there and you have his room number, right? I have a plan."

"A plan? Why does there have to be a plan? What are you talking about?"

"You don't want to grow old alone, do you? Here's what you do. You know what kind of wine Donnie likes?"

"I think so."

"Go in there and pick something out you know he loves. We'll get checked in, you go shower and clean up, and bring the bottle of wine to his room. Let nature take its course."

Emma took my arm and moved me toward the door of the wine shop.

"I don't know, Emma—"

"It'll be perfect. It's exactly like the story of Ruth and Boaz."

"I don't think Ruth stopped by Boaz's hotel room with a bottle of Vino Nobile di Montepulciano."

"No, but she waited until he was asleep, and climbed under the covers with him."

"What?" I protested. "No, she didn't! I mean, not the way you're making it sound."

"Oh yes she did, Molly. She let him know she was interested. She didn't leave any doubt. She got cleaned up, put on some nice perfume, and snuck into where Boaz was sleeping. And her mother-in-law was the one who put her up to it."

A woman inside the wine shop stepped out from behind the counter and beckoned us inside. We smiled at her and entered the narrow space. It was stacked floor to ceiling with bottles.

"What do you know about Ruth and Boaz?" I whispered to Emma. "You're Buddhist!"

I scanned the shelves for something reasonably priced that I could buy for myself. They didn't offer much in my preferred price range, and certainly nothing that came in a box.

"So?" she whispered back. "Aren't you the one who said an educated person should know about the world's different belief systems?"

"When did I say that?"

"At our last General Education Committee meeting."

"Oh. Maybe you're right. I guess it sounds like something I might say."

"You did say it. In fact, Molly, what do you know about Buddhism?"

"What do you mean?"

"You're an educated person. Tell me something you know about Buddhism."

"Buddhism? Uh, well, there's Nirvana, and you have a..."

I knew there was some kind of wheel. Wheel of fortune? That couldn't be right.

"Oh, this is childish, Emma. It's not a competition. Come on, help me pick out the wine."

CHAPTER TWENTY-SIX

The elevator’s close, wood-grained walls reeked of decades-old cigarette smoke and fresh suntan lotion.

“I’m not sure about this, Emma.”

“It’s only to the third floor,” Emma said.

“No, I'm not talking about the claustrophobia. Although if there were anyone else in here with us, it would be pretty tight.” Fortunately, Yoshi was down in the gift shop buying snacks.

“So what's your problem?”

“This is not my style, just barging up to Donnie’s room.”

“What is your style then?” Emma demanded. “Putting off dealing with major issues as long as you can?”

“Sounds about right. I’m an Avoider, you know.”

I drew a deep breath and wondered when the elevator's ventilation system had been checked last.

“You can’t weasel out of it now, Molly. You

already bought the wine."

"No. This is a real thing. In business communication, there's this test I have my students take, so they can find out whether they're Collaborators, Competers, Compromisers, Accommodators or Avoiders. I took the test myself. I'm a hundred percent, gold-plated, dyed-in-the-wool Avoider. I guess that's why I'm so safe and boring. That's probably what Donnie sees in me. After what happened with Sherry, I'll bet he decided to forswear all passion and excitement."

"He doesn't like you *because* you're safe and boring," Emma said. "He likes you in *spite* of you being so safe and boring."

"What if something goes wrong?"

"Pfft," Emma reassured me.

"I think you'd come out as a Competer, by the way. Those are the ones who always have to be right."

"Nothing's gonna go wrong, Molly. Listen. I don't want to hear from you until tomorrow. Unless there's some real juicy disaster. Then you have to call me right away. Anyway, here we are on two. That's my floor. Talk to you after the race tomorrow, ah?"

"Wait," I said. "What do you mean, some kind of juicy disaster?"

But the elevator doors were already closing.

I found my room and let myself in. Maybe Emma was right. I needed to take the initiative and kick things into gear with Donnie before this relationship died of boredom. Right after I finished unpacking.

I did what every sensible person does when checking into a hotel: I rolled my suitcase into the tiled bathroom to avoid picking up bedbugs from the carpet, saturated a washcloth with rubbing alcohol and wiped down the doorknobs, TV remote, and telephone. I took extra care scrubbing out the drinking glasses, thanks to a hidden-camera investigation I'd seen that caught a housekeeper washing the glasses with a toilet brush.

I pulled the bedspread off the bed and piled it in a corner, went back into the bathroom, and washed my hands for twenty seconds with plenty of soap and the hottest water I could stand. Unlike sheets, bedspreads are rarely laundered. You don't have to take my word for it; shine an ultraviolet light on any hotel bedspread, and watch it light up like a Thomas Kinkade painting.

Once the room was habitable, I pulled out a red silk blouse and black velvet slacks and hung them in the bathroom so the wrinkles would steam out. I showered, blow-dried the steam off the mirror, and set out my makeup. This was supposed to seem spontaneous, right? I had to be careful not to look too made-up. Dark brown mascara and eyeliner, not black. Pinkish-beige lipstick, the two-coat kind that doesn't come off. Foundation blended with moisturizer for lighter coverage. A touch of blush. It took me about an hour to get a nice, natural look. I spent a while debating how far up I should button my blouse, and daringly opted for two buttons undone instead of one. Finally, I unpinned my hair and ran my fingers through it to fluff it out.

I grabbed the wine, made sure I had my key card in my purse, double checked the message for the room number, and made sure my room door was locked.

I found my way to the stairs, past white stucco walls sprinkled with black mildew and orange fiberglass benches dulled with a patina of scratches. Here in the echoing stairwell, there was little chance of running into anyone. I felt vaguely embarrassed, all dolled up and walking around with a bottle of wine while it was still light out.

I was winded by the time I reached my destination, partly because of the two flights of stairs, but mostly because I was nervous. If I paused to catch my breath, I'd probably change my mind. I walked right up to the door, checked the room number, and knocked.

There was no answer. I waited. I checked the room number again. It was the right room. I undid one more button on my blouse. Might as well hang for a sheep as for a lamb. I knocked again, leaned into the peephole, held the wine bottle up next to my face, and smiled. There, I thought. Is that something a safe, boring person would do?

I felt stupid and moved away from the peephole. I didn't see any light under the door, but I thought I heard someone brushing their teeth.

It got quiet again. At last I heard, "Come in!"

The tone of his voice was encouraging. And the door was unlocked. So far so good. I slipped into the dark room and let the door click shut behind me.

The opaque hotel curtains were drawn shut and the lights were off. I stood there in the dark, feeling disoriented, gripping the neck of the wine bottle. I realized I'd forgotten to bring a corkscrew. Maybe Donnie knew that trick where you can get the cork out by banging the bottom of the bottle against your shoe.

Then again, beverage logistics didn't seem to be topmost on his mind. As my eyes adjusted I saw him lying flat on the bed, hands behind his head. I certainly hadn't expected him to cut to the chase so quickly. I was also a little put off by the fact that there seemed to be nothing between him and the bedspread.

"Hey, doll," I heard him say.

Doll? Donnie and I had never used any terms of endearment. I didn't have any pet names for him. Was I supposed to think one up now? What was wrong with simply using someone's actual name?

I took one step closer to the bed and caught a whiff of one of those heavy, cloying fragrances I don't particularly like. That was strange. Why wasn't Donnie's wearing his usual cologne, the one I liked? This whole thing was starting to feel like a mistake. As my eyes adjusted to the dim light, my brain worked in slow motion to process what I was seeing.

When did Donnie get all these tattoos? Swirls of ink wound across his shoulders and down his chest and—good heavens, was that supposed to be a scorpion?

It was like that time I'd wandered into the wrong bathroom at the airport, and my mind had time to construct the sentence, "Who put all those long sinks in here?" before I figured out my mistake.

The wine bottle dropped from my hand.

CHAPTER TWENTY-SEVEN

"Davison! What are *you* doing here?"

Davison didn't seem embarrassed at all. He grinned at me, like a kid who'd found an unexpected gift under the Christmas tree. Surprise!

He raised himself to a sitting position on the edge of the bed. I quickly looked down at my feet, but it was too late. I already had a vivid new image for my catalog of Reasons to Never Touch the Hotel Bedspread.

"No need pretend like you're surprised. I heard Dad leave you the message about him and me switching rooms."

"What message?" I shouted at the floor as I backed toward the door. "Why did you switch rooms?"

"He wanted a nonsmoking room."

"Where's your father?"

"He's all the way down in 310. Hey. Get over

here."

Donnie was down on the third floor. That information must have been in the second voice mail. The garbled one, the one Emma had talked me out of answering. I'd have a word with her about that.

"I'll get out of here and let you get dressed," I stammered, fumbling for the door handle.

"Come on, relax!" Davison's hot, minty breath was in my ear. "We don't have to tell Dad!"

I felt like I was going to pass out from the combination of embarrassment and overpowering cologne. Somehow I managed to get the door open.

"Eh, no big deal, ah?" He called after me as I fled down the hallway. "Thanks for the wine!"

Already halfway to the stairwell, I hesitated. The wine! I'd spent so much time choosing something I knew Donnie liked, good quality but not too extravagant. Should I go back and get it?

Don't be an idiot, Molly. Cut your losses and run.

I sprinted down the fire exit stairs all the way to the lobby, speed-walked to the hotel gift shop, and hastily grabbed an overpriced bottle of mediocre merlot. The stairwell entrance on the ground floor had locked behind me, so I took the elevator back up to the third floor, trying to ignore the elevator music, an instrumental version of "Afternoon Delight." I no longer cared who might see me walking around with a bottle of wine. I had mortification fatigue.

I reached my room, pulled the door shut behind

me, and deadbolted it. Davison's noxious fragrance was clinging to my skin and clothing, so I stuffed my clothes into the plastic laundry bag and took another shower. Once I had dried off and dressed again, I called room 310. The room phone rang unanswered, so I tried Donnie's cell phone next. It went right to voice mail.

Room 310 was just a few doors down. I wasn't feeling in any way amorous, but I wasn't about to let Davison ruin my plan. I buttoned up my blouse, pulled my hair back into a bun, and took the newly-purchased bottle of wine the few yards down the hall.

Donnie opened the door before I finished knocking. He was talking on his cell phone.

"Oh, here she is now," he said. "Dress nice for dinner. Don't be late. Okay, see ya."

He snapped the phone shut and pocketed it.

"Molly. You got my message. More or less. Come on in."

Donnie had the shades pulled all the way back. Hot afternoon sunlight flooded the room.

"I brought us some wine." I realized, as I handed him the bottle, that it still had the hotel's price tag on it. Great. Nothing says "I care" like a last-minute purchase from the hotel gift shop.

"Thanks, Molly. That was sweet of you." Donnie set the bottle on the dresser next to the television.

"You leave your bedspread on the bed?" I asked.

"Why wouldn't I?"

"Who was that on the phone?" I was pretty sure I

already knew the answer.

"Davison."

Did I detect an accusing note in his voice? Maybe I was imagining it.

"Hey," I ventured, "You'll never guess what just—"

"Yes, he told me what happened."

"Seriously? He told you?"

Donnie shook his head. "The poor boy is so embarrassed."

"He's embarrassed?" I repeated, incredulous. Davison was capable of remorse? This was a day full of surprises.

"Of course he is," Donnie said, "you walking in on him when he wasn't decent. Molly, I know you mainlanders can be very progressive and modern and everything, but we're a little old-fashioned here."

"What?"

"It's fine," Donnie said. "He'll be all right."

"Will he? Well. That's a relief. As long as he wasn't traumatized by the experience or anything."

"Anyway," Donnie continued, "I told him to make sure to keep his door locked from now on. You should remember that too, Molly. You never know who could be hanging around."

"Great advice."

"Well, no harm done," Donnie said, as if he were trying to convince himself. "I'm sure you didn't see anything you shouldn't have."

"I…okay, sure."

I realized it would be impossible to get my wine

back now. The good bottle, I mean, the one I left in Davison's room. If I hadn't seen anything I shouldn't have, as Donnie clearly wanted to believe, what would explain my dropping the wine bottle and leaving it there? Or worse, Donnie might think I lingered longer than necessary, and forgot about the wine. No, my Vino Nobile was a sunk cost. No point in worrying about it. Maybe Davison would surprise me and return it out of fairness and common decency. I wasn't about to bet on it, though.

"Donnie," I protested, "I thought *you* were staying in that room. I was not expecting to find Davison there. I didn't even know he was here with you."

I pulled out my phone.

"Here. Let me show you the messages I got from you."

Donnie read the transcribed messages.

"I left you this? Ah. I'm a broom, three-ten."

"Oh!" I laughed. Well, more like half-laughed, half-sobbed. "That was supposed to be I'm in room three ten! Sheesh. Next time I'll call first."

"I don't know why you didn't. You should have." Donnie wasn't laughing.

I didn't like his tone, but I let it pass. Arguing about the incident would force me to relive it. And I could tell Donnie found even Davison's sanitized version of the incident troubling.

"Well," he sighed, "you made it here, that's what matters. And it looks like we have a little time before our dinner reservation. Would you like to—"

Donnie's cell phone rang. It was the default ring tone. No frivolous song snippets or movie dialog for him. He snapped it open to check the caller ID.

"Molly, I'm so sorry. This is Travis. I really have to take this. See you at six for dinner?"

Donnie hugged me and mussed my hair a little, but he was already well into his conversation. I left him to discuss receivables with his accountant.

CHAPTER TWENTY-EIGHT

I wandered out into the humid afternoon, located the outdoor bar, and ordered the largest and most vulgar item on the cocktail menu. Equipped with an umbrella-topped, fruit-festooned goblet big enough to last me for several hours, I found a just-vacated poolside table and settled in. Tiny towheaded children, lobster-red moms and dads, and corpulent, bearded bikers all frolicked in the hotel pool. The laughter and shrieks of the children and the occasional hearty expletive from the bikers punctuated the steady rumble of motorcycles on the road past the hotel. White vog, the sulfurous, eye-stinging discharge from the island's active volcano, blurred the horizon. With all of those particulates hanging in the air, tonight's sunset would be spectacular. At least there was that to look forward to. I sipped my drink—it was tangy, sweet, and disappointingly weak—and tried to relax.

I shouldn't have been surprised that Donnie's work had followed him over here. The surprise was he was able to get away at all. This is what you sign up for when you go into business for yourself. You never truly get a day off. I'd told this to my students many times, but now I was experiencing it for myself. If Donnie and I ever did get married, I'd have to get used to it.

But right now I had more immediate concerns than the prospect of Travis the Accountant tagging along on our honeymoon.

Tonight was my much-anticipated dinner with Donnie, and instead of looking forward to it, I was dreading it. Sure, from Davison's perspective, I may have come unbidden to his hotel room all perfumed and unbuttoned and holding a bottle of wine, but why did he have to assume I was there for *that*? I mean, I wasn't, not with *him*. I was furious with myself for letting Emma trick me into this whole scheme, which now seemed desperate and sleazy. And the wine! It wasn't just the money I'd paid for it. It was the time and care I'd spent on choosing something I knew Donnie would like. *And* the money.

There was no tactful way to avoid having dinner with Donnie and Davison. Ditching them and joining Emma and her crew would be unfair to Donnie. He had arranged his weekend to come out and spend time with me, after all. Also, if I had dinner with Emma, naturally she would wonder what happened with Donnie and me, and she'd grill me about it in front of everyone. So, no. I couldn't see any way to get out of it gracefully.

I worked on my drink until it was nothing but a puddle of pale-blue slush. Then I went back up to my room to change and shower one more time. My mandarin collar cheongsam dress, black satin with red-and-gold embroidered dragons and pavilions, was hanging up in the bathroom to steam out the wrinkles.

Down by the pool, I had observed my fellow vacationers favored a more casual look. Amphibious shoes, easy-fitting cropped jeans and sherbet-colored t-shirts were the prevailing style. Something like that probably would have been more comfortable than what I'd brought. But the dragon dress, from a vintage boutique in San Francisco, was one of my favorites. And unlike some of the other clothes I'd brought over from the mainland, I could still zip it up.

Donnie had managed to secure a table out on the lanai of the hotel restaurant and was waiting with Davison by the hostess station when I arrived. The view from the outdoor tables looked like the cover of a tourist brochure. A blazing coral sun melted into the ocean, flanked by silhouetted tiki torches. The natural air pollution from the volcano rendered the sunset as brilliant and florid as the Technicolor drinks they were serving at the outdoor bar. The scalding afternoon heat gave way to pleasant warmth as the sky darkened. To the untrained eye, this might have looked like the start of a pleasant dinner.

Donnie was dressed appropriately for the occasion, in a pressed navy blue aloha shirt with a white lehua print and black trousers. Davison had thrown on a black tank top featuring an artist's rendering of a snarling pit bull. The illustration had the effect of a black velvet painting, which I'm sure in Davison's universe made it classy enough for dining out. Couldn't Donnie even make him put on a proper shirt? I suppose I should have been grateful that Davison was wearing anything at all.

The young woman at the hostess station smiled at Donnie.

"What a beautiful family!" she exclaimed. I felt a little annoyed that Donnie was somehow entitled to take credit for the three of us. Why not compliment me? Not that I'd want anyone to think I was in any way responsible for Davison. The hostess now turned her attention to him:

"You look exactly like your dad!" Donnie beamed, and Davison preened. I tried not to grimace.

I ended up sitting across from the two of them as if they were interviewing me. Donnie seemed more relaxed than he had earlier this afternoon. He was probably happy to have Davison along. Come to think of it, this was probably Donnie's unfinished business in town. Rounding up his prodigal son to come along and ruin my weekend.

Donnie suggested splitting a bottle of wine and I concurred, perhaps a little too eagerly. Davison, not yet of legal drinking age, ordered a soft drink. I fumed silently as I imagined Davison chugging my Vino Nobile straight from the bottle. Or, worse, making wine coolers out of it. The hostess left the three of us to unfurl our napkins and clank our silverware in uneasy silence. Thanks to the stiff fabric and close cut of my dress, I had no choice but to sit with my back perfectly straight and my knees together. This did not add to the comfort of the situation.

"The hotel is nice," I remarked to Donnie. "I like that they have a fridge and a coffeemaker right in the room. You don't even have to go outside if you don't want to." I hoped it didn't sound like I was planning to stock up on provisions and barricade myself in my hotel room. Which, at the moment, was a tempting idea.

"It's not bad," Donnie said. "I have a view of the pool and a little bit of the ocean."

I wondered whether he had seen me sulking out by the pool earlier this afternoon. I hoped not. I wanted Donnie to think of me as self-sufficient and unflappable.

"There was a cockroach in the bathtub when I checked in," Donnie continued when we had placed our orders, "but the rest of the room seems fine."

"I bet Aunty Molly's afraid of cockroaches." Davison was talking to his father, but staring directly at me. "I know she's scared of scorpions. Especially *big* ones."

Over Donnie's shoulder, I glimpsed Emma and her crew seating themselves around the outdoor bar.

And there was Sherry. What were they doing down here drinking when they had a race tomorrow morning? Weren't they supposed to be having bone broth and wheat grass juice for dinner and going to bed at seven? Fortunately, their backs were to us, and Donnie and Davison's backs were to them. Unfortunately, Emma had spotted me and was on her way over.

CHAPTER TWENTY-NINE

I wished I could send Emma a telepathic message: *Don't come over here. Stay right there at the bar. Better yet, leave now and take Sherry with you before anyone sees her.*

"Is that right, Molly?" Donnie asked. "Are you afraid of scorpions? You know, they're pretty rare in Hawaii."

"What?" I tried to bring myself back to the conversation. "Scorpions? They're disgusting. I hate them."

Emma was climbing down from the bar stool and heading over to our table.

No, Emma! Go back!

"Those bugs do have a nasty bite," Donnie agreed. "You have to be careful when you handle them."

Davison leaned back in his chair, tucked his fists behind his biceps, and smirked at me.

"That's right, Aunty. Careful how you handle."

"Davison," I asked pleasantly, "when do you leave?" I glanced over at Donnie and added, "I mean, when does your school term start?"

"Gotta go back pretty soon." He held eye contact with me far longer than necessary. "Better enjoy me while you can, Aunty."

I glared back, not wanting to give him the satisfaction of having stared me down.

"He's flying out Saturday night," Donnie said. "The flights were better from this side of the island. Davison, I'm glad you could get away from your girlfriend and spare a little time for your family while you're here."

"Eh, Sherry was fun," Davison declared, "but we're done."

Emma pulled up just as Davison uttered these words. She probably hadn't recognized the back of his head when she was approaching our table. Now she cast a panicked look back at the bar, where her crew members had settled in.

I had cringed when Davison mentioned Sherry's name, but Donnie didn't seem to connect the dots. Also, "Sherry was fun but we're done?" Yuck.

Sherry was still seated at the bar, her back to us. There was no mistaking her distinctive cloud of hair.

"Oh, your mystery woman has a name now?" Donnie noticed I was looking over his shoulder and turned around to see Emma standing there. "Emma, would you like to join us? We have another seat."

Davison turned an ingratiating smile on Emma. "Good evening, Professor Nakamura! Are you here for the Labor Day Race?" Emma glanced down at her outfit. She had been out on the water earlier and was still wearing her board shorts and acid yellow paddling jersey. To her credit, she refrained from sarcasm and said, simply, "Hi, Donnie. Davison, what a surprise to see you. Molly, I just wanted to come over and say hi. Well, have a nice—"

"Professor Nakamura," Davison interrupted, "You, uh, here by yourself or what? Where's your crew?" He looked past her, back toward the bar where Sherry was sitting.

"They're resting up for tomorrow." Emma deftly stepped to the side to block Davison's view. He leaned the other way, and she stepped again.

The waitress arrived with the salads, and Emma took advantage of the distraction to excuse herself. As Donnie and Davison dug in, I watched Emma speed over to the bar and urge her crew members off their bar stools. There was some initial resistance, judging from the indignant arm-waving, but Emma managed to hustle them away from the bar and shoo them offstage, to another section of the hotel. I relaxed and started to eat. I saw Davison sneak a look behind him, but by this time the bar stools were occupied by large men in leather biker vests.

Davison wiped up the last of his salad dressing with a piece of bread, popped it in his mouth, and licked his fingers. When he was finished with that, he clasped his hands behind his head, flexing his latissimi dorsi and treating me to a panoramic view of his armpits.

"Sherry was cool," he declared. "She taught me a lot." He grinned at me. "Older women, yah?"

Oh, for crying out loud. I fixed my gaze on my lap and rearranged my napkin so Donnie wouldn't see me rolling my eyes.

"So what exactly did she teach you? That you're able to discuss in mixed company?" Donnie's indulgent tone infuriated me.

"She knows a lot about computers," Davison said. "She showed me this thing online where you can search for someone by clicking on their face. You don't hafta know their name even."

Well good for Sherry, remembering what we talked about in class.

"Did you search for pictures of yourself?" I asked.

"Nah," Davison laughed. "Not me. I'm not that egotistical."

He turned to his father.

"But, ya know, Aunty Molly?"

Now what? I stared at my place setting. I wasn't feeling particularly hungry, but I was hoping the server would come by and interrupt the conversation with our entrees. What was taking so long?

"You could go to the college website and find her picture, yah?" Davison continued. "You click it to get the address, and take it to one other website with software that looks at the picture and reads her face, and it goes and looks online and it can find other pictures of her."

He paused, and I looked up, just in time for him to say:

"Even if she was using a different name."

Davison winked at me. Donnie didn't see it.

I had no appetite at all by the time the entrees arrived. I forced down a couple of bites of fibrous, overcooked ahi and pushed the remaining food around on my plate. When I thought we were finally finished with dinner, Davison prolonged my ordeal by ordering dessert, a precariously tall grotesquerie of chocolate cake and coffee ice cream, loaded with spray-on whipped cream. Donnie had a few bites. I declined, even (especially) after Davison insisted ("come on Aunty, you know you want some"). Finally, Donnie signed the tab. He invited me to join him and Davison to go and watch the manta rays. I made my excuses, muttering something about having to get up early to watch Emma's race.

CHAPTER THIRTY

I rode the elevator back up to my room, locked the door, and took my fourth or fifth shower of the day (I'd lost track). Emma's big race was Saturday morning. I wasn't actually planning to attend in person. If I wanted to catch Emma and her crew before they left, I'd have to be down at the water before dawn. The dark beach would be packed with team supporters and tourists, and, of course, plenty of little kids careening through the crowd. There would be a live Jawaiian band, or a noisy DJ setup. After their registration and last-minute checks, the paddlers would pile into their various canoes and stroke out to sea. Emma's canoe and dozens of others like it would disappear over the horizon before the sun was even up.

The women's crews would leave the bay, paddle the tough eighteen miles down the coast, and disembark. The women would get out and the men's teams would climb into the same canoes and paddle back up the coast, where they would arrive at the starting point many grueling hours later. A spectator on the beach wouldn't see anything after the canoes sped off. I'd be staring out at the empty blue water.

Emma had told me all of this on the drive over. She had assured me that my presence was not required at the start of the race, so long as I was available to help celebrate afterward. So it was well past sunrise when the hotel phone jangled me out of a deep sleep. I picked up the receiver and for a few moments, I heard big bore motorcycle engines rumbling in the background.

Then Davison's voice came over the line. Not exactly the wake-up call I would have chosen.

"Eh, Aunty. Dad wants to know if you wanna have breakfast with us."

"Oh, that's very nice of him to ask. May I speak to your father?"

"He's driving."

"What? It's only…" I squinted at the digital clock on the side table. "Ten-thirty in the morning. Where are you?"

"We're coming back to the hotel. We went fishing already."

"Breakfast with both of you sounds lovely," I said, "but I'm not quite awake yet."

The part about not being awake was true.

"Come on Aunty, we can get any kine breakfast. What you like grind?"

I heard Donnie in the background: "Speak

English!"

I didn't care whether Davison was using Standard English or Pidgin. He could have spoken Sanskrit for all I cared. I was not going to endure another meal with him.

"I don't want you to have to wait for me. You two go ahead. Tell your dad thanks anyway."

I eventually woke up for good, got dressed, and went out to wander up and down the main beachfront road. I poked around the shops, but I didn't buy anything. Crystal jewelry and floaty batik dresses weren't really my style, and I didn't need any bargain souvenir t-shirts. When I had exhausted the local shopping possibilities, I parked myself in an outdoor seat at a coffee shop. Every so often a pack of motorcycles would roar by, drowning out the already-noisy traffic.

Equipped with a tall café Americano, a view of the ocean, and a little table all to myself, I passed the time typing online faculty reviews into my phone. The one I left for Pat referred to an inside joke that would seem impossibly tasteless if I tried to explain it. My reference to Emma's Dalmatian-puppy lab coat, on the other hand, was written for a general audience. I left an absurdly fawning review for myself, and another one right after it complaining about my heavy workload and unrealistically high expectations. All of these evaluations were accompanied by the highest possible numeric scores.

The Student Retention Office uses only the numeric ratings, not the qualitative reviews. So when

Pat gives me a straight five out of five rating, and writes "Professor Barda sleeps in a coffin and awakens at blackest night to gorge on the blood of innocents," that still works in my favor.

As the sun sank to the point where it was aiming right at my eyes, Emma called. I stood and started collecting my things as I spoke to her. She refused to tell me how her crew had done in the race, insisting I come to her room to get the news in person. I assumed it must be good; she sounded excited. It only took me a few minutes to hurry back to the hotel and find her room on the second floor.

Emma was over by the window, busy on her computer. I almost tripped over her husband Yoshi, who was parked right in the middle of the floor at the foot of the bed, eyes fixed on his own laptop screen. The bedspread was piled on the floor around him and draped over his shoulders. He was eating spicy tortilla chips out of the bag, dipping each one into an open jar of mayonnaise.

"Hey, Yoshi," I greeted him, "did you paddle too?"

He slowly placed his hands over his headphones and pushed them back to expose his ears. I noticed his eyes were red. I repeated the question.

"Oh, hey Molly. No, not today. I just hung out here. I'm doing the double-hull race tomorrow, though."

"Oh, great!" I enthused, as if I knew what a double-hull race was. Yoshi plugged himself back in and resumed watching the brightly-colored cartoon ponies frolicking on his laptop screen. I watched him wipe his mayonnaise-slick fingers on the bedspread.

"Hey, Molly!" Emma called.

"Hey! How'd you do?" I stepped over Yoshi and his bedspread fortress and plumped down into the big hotel easy chair behind Emma.

"We came in eighteenth in our age group," she said.

"So do you get a prize?" I asked. "A tiara? A golden paddle?"

"We got t-shirts. We hadda buy 'em, though."

"So coming in eighteenth is good?"

"Well, it's not as good as coming in first," she admitted. "But it's an eighteen-mile race, so we decided eighteenth is good luck. It was awesome, Molly!"

"Great. I'm glad you had a fun time."

"I think even you would have liked it."

"Seriously?"

I imagined the combined effects of eighteen miles of repetitive motion, saltwater-drenched swim shorts, and the canoe's hard, impossibly narrow seat. I could almost feel the blisters.

"Right at the start," Emma said, "we saw two sea turtles swimming underneath us. And about halfway down there were dolphins, right alongside us and jumping out of the water. They were so close to us, like they—oh right, I forgot. You don't like dolphins."

"I used to like them just fine, until Betty Jackson filled me in on their, you know, behavior."

"Yeah, I know. Frat boys of the sea. Anyway, we did pretty good considering we went iron."

"What does that mean, you went iron?"

"Oh! Sorry, Molly, I thought everyone knew what it means."

"I don't know what it means."

"So in a long race like this, a lot of the crews have an escort boat, yeah? There are nine people on the crew, but only six at a time. You switch out, and everyone gets a chance to rest in the escort boat for twenty minutes out of every hour. But going iron means you only get six in your crew and everyone paddles the whole time."

"Emma, are you telling me you could have had three more paddlers in the race?"

CHAPTER THIRTY-ONE

"All of the competition over who got to paddle in this race. What did Yoshi call it, paddletics? And you could have had three more paddlers on your crew all along?"

"No need for three more paddlers," Emma insisted. "It worked out perfect. We had six seats and six crew members. And we did great."

"But why—oh, never mind." I plunked down on the foot of the bed. This was typical Emma. Kathy Banks mysteriously keels over, bringing the number of Emma's crew down to exactly six people. And Emma doesn't question it or think it seems suspicious at all. No, her response is: Great! Problem solved! Emma doesn't know how to worry a topic to death, the way Pat and I can. Pat claims it's a skill you can only get from being raised Catholic, although I have a few acquaintances of the Jewish faith who might disagree with him.

"Emma, whose decision was it to go iron? So there would only be six spots for people to race, instead of nine?"

"There wasn't any decision. We just did it."

"It was your decision, in other words."

I wondered what would have happened if Emma had gone to the trouble of hiring an escort boat. Would Kathy still be alive today, I wondered? I didn't share this thought with Emma. It would sound like I was accusing her.

"Anyhow," Emma asked, "what about you? What happened last night? I was surprised to see Davison over here."

"Yeah. You're not the only one. Good work getting Sherry out of there before Donnie or Davison could see her."

"Well, I didn't want to risk any big drama right before the race. Poor Davison, did you see when he was asking about her? He was like a sad little puppy, yah? Anyway, how'd it go with Donnie?"

I glanced at Yoshi. He was grinning at his laptop screen, headphones blocking out the world around him, fully absorbed in the antics of the candy-colored cartoon ponies.

"Let me tell you how that clever plan of yours worked out. My magical evening of romance."

"So was I right, or what? Good idea, yah? Come sit over here. I don't wanna have to twist around to see you."

I scooted the bulky armchair next to Emma, settled in, and related the events of the previous afternoon. Instead of being properly abashed, Emma burst out laughing. Yoshi glanced up briefly and went back to watching his show.

"It's not funny, Emma!" I fumed. "It's appalling!"

"Hey, opportunity knocked. Can you blame him?"

"I absolutely can blame him. And you, while I'm at it. Whose big fat idea was it not to call ahead?"

"Maybe you shoulda went for it. He's not bad looking."

"Ew, what is wrong with you?"

"What? You coulda helped him forget about Sherry. Eh, you haven't gotten anywhere with Donnie yet, right?"

"Stop it, Emma."

"I know I'll never look at scorpions the same way again."

"I'm never going to look at scorpions, period," I said.

"What does that mean?"

"I don't know! Is it time to go down to dinner? I barely got anything to eat today."

Emma peered at the clock on her computer screen.

"Oh! Yeah, it is." She stood, turned to Yoshi, and bellowed as if she were in the middle of a live fire shooting range:

"Yoshi! We're going down to dinner now!"

He glanced up, pulled off his headphones, and slowly worked his way to a standing position.

As soon as the elevator door closed behind us, I felt my phone humming in my bag. It was a missed call from Donnie. After the events of the previous day, I couldn't bear the idea of spending any more time around Davison. At the same time, I had already turned down their breakfast invitation.

"It's Donnie," I said. "He's probably calling about dinner. I don't want him to think I'm avoiding him."

"But you are avoiding him, aren't you?"

"I think it's time to take preemptive action." I called Donnie back and told him I'd be having dinner with Emma and her crew. I asked him if he and Davison would like to join us.

Emma's jaw dropped and she made wide eyes at me.

"Are you crazy?" she mouthed.

Sure, if you didn't know Donnie that well, you might think I was taking a risk. Sherry would be with us at dinner, and if Donnie showed up with Davison, it would be uncomfortable, to say the least.

But I know Donnie. He likes to have me to himself. He only attends crowded events like the Business Boosters annual installation dinner out of professional obligation. He's not a natural extrovert, and doesn't like to be put into situations where he has to socialize with people he doesn't know. At least that's something we have in common.

As I expected, Donnie politely declined my dinner invitation. Davison would be taking the red-eye in a couple of hours, he told me, and they wanted to eat near the airport so they wouldn't have to rush.

"Oh, Donnie, that's a shame." I aimed a triumphant look at Emma. "It looks like dinner's not going to work out. Tell Davison I hope he has a good flight."

"Would you like to tell him yourself?" Donnie asked. "He's right—"

"No, it's okay. I know you're on a tight schedule and I don't want to keep you. I'll see you tomorrow. I'm still catching a ride back with you, right?"

"I'm planning on it," he said.

"It worked," Emma said when I had hung up.

"See? I'm not completely inept."

"What worked?" Yoshi asked.

"Molly's cell phone," Emma said. "She wasn't getting any reception back at the paddling store. So Davison's on his way back to the mainland now?"

"Pretty soon," I said.

Two hours from now, Davison's plane would be thirty thousand feet above the Pacific Ocean. In my mind's eye I saw a jumbo jet hesitating, then spiraling down, accelerating toward the black water, billowing black smoke.

What, was I doing this again? *Stop wishing catastrophic death on people, Molly! Stop it!*

"Stop what?" Emma asked.

"What? Nothing. Just talking to myself. Out loud, apparently."

"You gonna be okay?" she asked as the elevator doors slid open.

"Yes. I'm fine. Honestly."

We walked out into the warm evening air, toward the Sunset Bar, where the rest of Emma's crew was already celebrating.

CHAPTER THIRTY-TWO

The women from Emma's crew, with their various companions and spouses, crowded around a long table at the outdoor bar. It looked like most of the party had been there for a while. Their faces shone with the effects of sun and alcohol. There weren't two empty seats together, let alone three, so Emma, Yoshi and I had to squeeze in where we could. Sherry gave Yoshi a friendly swat as he walked ahead of me. I don't think Emma saw it. Sherry motioned me toward the empty chair beside her.

It was just as well I wouldn't be seeing Donnie for dinner. I didn't like the way he seemed to blame me for the mortifying incident with Davison. And come to think of it, Donnie's following me over to this side of the island didn't seem so much like a charming romantic whim. It was more like Donnie was keeping an eye on his investment. In case—what exactly? In case some big-bellied biker threw me over his shoulder and went roaring off into the sunset? That wouldn't even make sense, because driving into the sunset from the leeward side of the island would mean going straight into the ocean.

I could puzzle this out later. Right now I had to concentrate on making innocuous small talk. Just the two of us, me and a woman who might be Donnie's ex-wife, about to have a nice drink and a chat. Nothing weird about this.

"So Sherry," I ventured, "Nice job out there today." I had no idea exactly what they did "out there" today other than paddle, but they had all made it back alive, and Emma had seemed pleased with how things had turned out. It seemed some kind of congratulations were in order.

"Thanks, Doctor B. You know, I could kinda feel Kathy's presence today. She was out there with us. I know it."

As little as I cared for Kathy, I didn't like thinking she'd been doomed to an afterlife of floating around on the ocean. Trailing after boring canoe races for all eternity sounded worse than Purgatory.

"I'm realizing I never knew Kathy well at all," I said.

"Kathy was amazing. When I first came back to school here, I was so lost, I was ready to quit. She was the one who got my financial aid straightened out, with my student loans and everything. When I got to Mahina, I couldn't even afford to buy my textbooks. I have a—a ton of student loans."

I wanted to ask Sherry whether there wasn't someone in town who could have helped her out. An ex-husband, for example? Or a grown son? But I couldn't think of any tactful way to do it.

"Back to school?" I asked. "So you'd had some college classes already?"

"Yeah. I went to college for a while back on the mainland. When I graduated high school, I didn't think about college. But I started seeing these ads on TV, and it got me thinking. They were right off the turnpike. I useta drive by and see their sign every day, and one day, I dunno why, I decided to stop in. The people at the front desk were real friendly, and they made it super easy for me to sign up."

I tried not to wince at the phrase "graduated high school."

"But you didn't finish your degree there?" I asked. "I'm sensing this story doesn't end well."

"Nah. Long story short, I ended up with seventy thousand dollars of debt. And that's right, no degree."

"That's unfortunate."

"And my classes didn't even transfer," she added.

"So which school was this?"

She told me. It took me a moment to figure out why the name sounded familiar. It was one of the group of for-profit institutions that were being sued—the case that had inspired Bob Wilson from the history department to write his indignant letter to the editor. Maybe their graduation rate was in the single digits and their classes didn't transfer, but they did one thing remarkably well: They took federal student loan money and transferred it quickly and efficiently to the pockets of their executives. Any actual education that happened to take place along the way was incidental.

"I'm sorry to hear it," I said.

"Yeah, not as sorry as me. Anyhow, Kathy didn't make me feel stupid for getting myself into this situation. She went out of her way for me, whatever she could do. She was real understanding."

"She was understanding?" I repeated. "Kathy Banks?" Was she talking about the same Kathy Banks who, the first time I turned in our departmental student satisfaction report, sent the whole thing back and made me start over because I'd turned in the canary copy instead of the goldenrod one? And then, because she had bounced it back after the deadline, wrote me up for turning it in late?

"We found out we're both type 1," Sherry was saying. "I think that's when we bonded for real."

"Type 1?"

"Yeah, cause you know how it seems like everyone around here is type two?"

I nodded as if I knew what Sherry was talking about. It probably had something to do with the way people used to get their colors analyzed, to find out whether they were a "winter" or whatever. My mother had taken me to the cosmetics counter of a local department store to get my colors done when I was a teenager. I was an autumn, the Color

Consultant informed us, and should wear warm hues like oranges and yellows.

"Oh, nonsense," my mother had rebuked the Color Consultant, whose suggestion had instantly demoted her in my mother's eyes from expert to incompetent fraud. "Molly can't wear yellow. She'd look like a corpse." Mom swept out of the department store, bristling with indignation, as I trailed sheepishly behind her.

"Type 1 diabetes," Sherry said. "Insulin-dependent. You're not diabetic, are you?"

"Type 1 diabetes. Right. What else would it mean? No. I'm not diabetic. So you can't eat sweets?" I tried to imagine not ever eating sweets. Now *that* sounded worse than Purgatory.

"Nah. You just gotta make sure to cover whatever you eat with the right amount of insulin. I mean, don't go crazy with the cheesecake or anything. It's kind of a pain, but you get used to it. You know, when Kathy—oh hey doll! You're back!"

Sherry turned her attention to Glenn, effectively ending our conversation. He was certainly dressed to attract attention. He wore a red leather bomber jacket with no shirt underneath, and formfitting, low-rise skinny jeans.

The chair I was sitting in was the one Glenn had vacated a few minutes earlier, but he apparently didn't need it back. He and Sherry seemed happy to share Sherry's single chair.

Freed from the obligation of making small talk, I sat quietly and watched the sunset. Davison was already at the airport and would be flying out in a couple of hours, so there was at least one disaster averted. Maybe I'd be able to enjoy part of this weekend after all.

CHAPTER THIRTY-THREE

Emma's husband wanted to stay downstairs and socialize after dinner, so Emma invited me back up to her room to keep her company. It was only after we reached her room and she closed the door that I realized my ears were ringing from the raucous conversation.

"So were you okay sitting next to Sherry?" she asked.

"M-hm. It was fine. And now I'm having second thoughts about her being Donnie's ex-wife. I mean, I can't picture Sherry and Donnie together at all, much less married."

"Did you ask her about him?"

"There was no way to do it tactfully. And after Glenn came back, I gave up trying to make conversation."

"So what did you do then? Sat there and didn't say anything?

"More or less."

"Really?"

"There were enough talkers around the table. If anything, I'd say there weren't enough listeners. So I was able to fill that important role."

"Yeah, sounds like our crew," Emma said. "They probably liked having an audience. But wait, about Sherry and Donnie. You were so sure on the drive over she was his ex-wife. You almost had me convinced. Like you said, how many Sherrines can there be? So what made you change your mind?"

"I don't know. I guess it's because it's so hard for me to imagine those two together. I mean, Donnie thinks it's inappropriate when people hold hands in public. Did you see what Sherry and Glenn were doing?"

"That's what I was trying to tell you. Now can you help me with this? I have to post today's results on our club website and put some kind of memorial for Kathy Banks. I shoulda done it already. My crew was bugging me about it today."

Emma went over to the desk and started up her laptop. I took my place in the chair beside her.

"What are you going to write about her?" I sure didn't have any ideas.

"I don't know. I guess I'll put, in memory of Kathy Banks. I have to put the dates. Birth and death."

"Sounds great," I said.

"But I don't know her birth year."

"Wouldn't she have put it on her club

application?"

"Yeah. Too bad I don't have the applications with me."

"Where are they?"

"Probably in a file drawer somewhere in my lab."

"Can you wait until we get back to Mahina to finish the web page?"

"No, they're all expecting me to get it done tonight."

"So then forget about the dates. Why not just In memory of Kathy Banks?"

"Shouldn't there be more than five words? Doesn't hardly seem like enough."

"How about, In Memory of Kathy Banks. She sure could tell the difference between canary and goldenrod."

"I know," Emma exclaimed. "I'll put something inspired by today's race."

"No, don't put anything corny like 'May you frolic with dolphins forever.' You'll just regret it later."

"I need a picture of her too."

"What about one of your team photos? Crop it down so you only have her in the picture."

Emma browsed the club website for a few moments, her frown becoming more pronounced.

"Something wrong?" I asked.

"Kathy's not in any of our team photos. I never noticed before."

I leaned in to look over her shoulder.

"I'm friends with Kathy," I said. "Online, I mean. Maybe she has—I mean, had something in her photo albums. You're friends with her too, right?"

"Oh, good idea." Emma pulled up the social networking website and went to Kathy's pictures.

"It feels creepy to poke around in a dead woman's photos," Emma said.

"It's just ones and zeros," I reassured her, not feeling particularly good about it myself. Emma paged through the scenic photos. We saw Kuewa's shabby, brightly painted boardwalk; a few shots of snowy mountaintops; the Bayfront on a day so clear you could see past the breakwall, clear up the coast. There were no people anywhere in the pictures.

"How about Sherry's account?" I suggested.

Emma clicked a few times.

"Jackpot!" she yelled, so loud it made me jump.

"Oh, looks nice," I said. "Kind of an action shot. What are you guys doing there?"

"We're rigging the canoe. Kathy's hair's kind of falling into her face, but you can tell it's her. I dunno. What do you think?"

Emma downloaded Sherry's photo and opened it in her editing software. She selected a square around Kathy's face and enlarged it.

"I could crop it here," she said.

"Looks fine. The resolution's kind of grainy when you enlarge it, but you can tell it's her."

"Yeah, it's not the best." Emma sighed, disappointed.

"Hey, you know what you should try? The facial recognition software. Maybe Kathy had another online photo album somewhere. You might be able to find a better picture."

"Facial recognition software? The thing your crazy student was ranting about? Is it hard to use?"

"I doubt it. Anyway, we have a picture of Kathy right here. Why don't we try it out?"

We found the site with little difficulty. Emma uploaded the photo, indicated the location of facial features with a few clicks, and chose the option to search for visual matches. It wasn't quite as easy as Davison had made it sound when he was talking about it at dinner, but it worked. A page popped up right away.

"Boo," I said. "False positive."

"No, it looks like her," Emma said.

"It's not her," I insisted. "This lady? The brunette? Click through."

Kathy Banks' dark-haired doppelganger, someone named Karolyn Beckenbauer, was the subject of a story on the website of a Midwestern news station.

Emma peered at the screen. "Why does the name of that college sound familiar?"

"That's the for-profit that's getting sued. Sherry was telling me she attended for a while. Remember Bob Wilson sent out the letter to the editor about how we're barely better than a for-profit? This is the institution he used as the example."

"Bob Wilson is the one who wrote that letter? That explains how come I just got an invitation to his going-away party."

"Sherry told me she enrolled at that for-profit after she saw their ads on TV. I'm amazed she fell for that. Who would go to a university that advertises on TV?"

"Our school has a TV ad now," Emma said.

"That's right. I forgot about that."

"Look, Molly, you were right. This isn't Kathy Banks."

"I know. This story is about someone who's brave and selfless."

"I meant because…c'mon, Molly, let it go."

"Sorry."

"Besides, Kathy was supposedly a natural blonde, remember?"

"Oh, *I'm* not letting things go? Look, you can click there to search for more matches."

We found several more photos of Karolyn Beckenbauer, including a cached portrait on the website of the embattled for-profit university. She had worked in their admissions office.

"No pictures at all of Kathy Banks," Emma exclaimed, frustrated. "What was she, some kind of spy?"

"Why would anyone put a spy in the Student Retention Office?"

"She doesn't have any online presence. How weird is that?"

"It's not that weird," I said. "The only reason you and I have any online presence is because of our jobs. If you search for me, all of my results are related to the university, or they're papers I've written, or, of course, the online ratings. If I weren't an academic, you wouldn't find anything for me either."

"How do you know? Molly, do you search for yourself?"

"Don't you?"

"Maybe. So what now? I still don't have a good picture of Kathy."

"Use the one you downloaded from Sherry's page. It's not bad."

"So you don't think that other woman is her?" Emma asked.

"No. I think it's someone who happens to have the same distance between her pupils or something."

"Yeah, I guess you're right. I mean, look at you and Sherry. You two actually do look the same. And you aren't related, right?"

"Probably not, since she's Italian and I'm Albanian."

"Hey, Molly, let's do a facial recognition search for you, and see what comes up."

"No, let's not. It's getting late, and I'm tired. Do you honestly think Sherry and I look that much alike?"

Emma shrugged. "You Italians all look alike to me."

CHAPTER THIRTY-FOUR

I came to campus early, hoping to get a head start on whatever had been piling up in my in-box over the three-day weekend. Unfortunately, many of my colleagues seemed to have had the same thought, and the close parking lot was already full. I parked at the outer edge of the far lot and had just managed to lock up my car and get my coffee cup balanced when Sherry rushed up to me. She was out of breath, as if she had been sprinting. I invited her to accompany me to my office, reluctantly putting my mental to-do list aside and shifting to small-talk mode.

"Well, that was a fun weekend," I said. "Do you think you'll do the race again next year?"

"I dunno. I don't usually plan that far ahead."

Something in Sherry's tone didn't sound right. She wasn't her usual lively self.

"Sherry, are you okay?"

"Yeah. I'll be fine. I had some kinda week."

"I can imagine. I mean, paddling for eighteen miles. And you went iron!"

"Glenn came back early from his trip."

"Yes, I saw him at dinner—"

"Oh yeah, I forgot. I wasn't planning on him coming back so quick. I thought he was gonna be gone for another couple weeks. I gotta tell you, I hadda do some quick thinking."

"It's okay, Sherry, you don't have to—"

"Dave didn't take it too well. I guess I can't really blame him."

Who was Dave now? Oh, right. Davison.

"Hey, Dave said he used to be your student. Is that true?"

"Yes, he was enrolled in one of my classes."

"And you're going out with his dad now."

I nodded. "Small world."

"I had no idea, Dr. B. Good for you!"

"Thanks." Sherry's apparent surprise at the fact that I had a personal life made me feel vaguely insulted.

"Dave told me he made a mistake on his first assignment and you let him rewrite it."

Davison's "mistake" was that he had copied his friend's paper in its entirety and turned it in as his own work. Our former dean believed that busting students for plagiarism was insufficiently "student-centered" so I had been forced to give Davison a do-over.

"I told him no way, not Barda. I mean I know you're a hard—a hard grader."

"Well, sometimes you have to give people a second chance," I said.

"Things were moving a little too fast for me anyhow. Dave wanted to bring me home to meet his father. That's not what I was looking for—hey, careful! Your coffee!"

"Oh, shoot." I tried to brush the scalding coffee from the front of my shirt. "Meet his father. My goodness, what an idea."

Fortunately, I was wearing a black blouse. Unfortunately, it was wool crepe, and was puckering where the hot liquid had splashed it.

"Yeah. I'm not looking for anything serious. And tell ya the truth, I didn't like how Dave decided I was his woman all of a sudden. He was too pushy. Kinda reminded me of my ex."

"Sherry, you don't need to—your ex? Was this the one you mentioned in class?"

"It was a lifetime ago, Dr. B. The first time I lived in Mahina, before I moved back to the mainland."

I nodded, trying my best to seem casual. I was so eager to hear more that I was sure my ears were vibrating.

"I was too young," Sherry said. "You know what I mean? Too young to get married. Too young to be a mother."

"A mother? So you have children?"

"One," she said.

"A girl? A boy?"

"Little boy. It was all too much for me. I couldn't handle it. And they were better off without me and my problems, to be honest."

I did some quick arithmetic in my head. Davison was going to be turning twenty-one. I knew that because Donnie had been talking about surprising him with a birthday trip to Las Vegas. I couldn't understand why people who lived in one of the most beautiful places on earth insisted on vacationing in one of the most aesthetically indefensible, but there it was. I had seen on the class roster that Sherry and I had the same birth year. So subtract twenty-one from my age, she would have been—

"You were so young! I mean, you must've been young. Because you're young now, is what I meant. So have you kept in touch with your son at all?"

"Nah. Honestly, Dr. B., he was kind of a little snot. Sorry, I guess I'm not very, what's the word?"

"Maternal?" I suggested.

"Yeah. What you said."

We entered the dim hallway of my building. It smelled mildewy after the long weekend with the air conditioner off.

Sherry shrugged. "I gave it all up for Mad Dog. I never looked back."

That was an interesting way to spin it. Gave it all up. As if ditching your husband and child were a selfless sacrifice for some greater good.

"Mad Dog?"

"Yeah. My second husband."

"Oh."

"Wait, no, third husband. I keep forgetting about what's his name."

We arrived at my office. "Well," I said, "here we are." I didn't particularly want to hear Sherry run down her inventory of greater and lesser ex-husbands, and if Sherry and Donnie truly had been married, maybe I didn't want to hear about that either. I fumbled for my keys before I realized my door was already ajar. Emma and Pat had made themselves comfortable in my office and were helping themselves to my coffee.

"Decision time," I announced. "You can stand around and listen to us talk about class work, or you can take your coffee and come back later."

Emma high-fived Sherry on her way out, and Sherry and I got seated.

"I wanted to meet with you about some of this stuff I've been finding, Dr. B. I kinda got distracted this weekend cause of the race and the other stuff, but now I'm back, there's some things I thought you should—"

"Women are drawn to me," came the voice of Rodge Cowper's affirmation tape through the thin wall. "I am a self-assured, confident, sexual and dominant male."

I ignored the voice, hoping Sherry would follow suit.

"What was that?" Sherry asked.

I could no longer pretend I hadn't heard anything.

"It's Dr. Rodge. He plays these—"

"Excuse me, Dr. B. This won't take long."

Sherry stood up and walked out.

"I am able to pick up and attract any women I

desire," Rodge's voice announced. I heard a brisk knock on Rodge's door.

"I read and meditate every day. I am wise and—"

All at once, the voice and the background music went silent. Sherry returned to my office a few seconds later and settled back into the visitor chair. I glanced over at the wall separating Rodge Cowper's office from mine. Still quiet.

"Thanks, Sherry. So. You were saying, about your assignment?"

"Yeah. I realized, there's so much information out there for everyone to see, if the wrong person gets ahold of it, they can do a lot of damage. The rest of my group is waiting for me to decide, and I'm feeling kind of overwhelmed, to be honest. I just wanna get through this."

"You have some ideas, though?"

"Oh, I have some ideas, all right," she said miserably.

"At this point, I'd say pick something and go with it. If you find you need to make some changes later, do that. No one expects you to get everything right on the first try."

Sherry blinked and stared, as if I had said something tremendously insightful.

"You're right. Thanks! Oh, and, uh, Dr. B?"

I looked at her expectantly.

"Never mind," she said. "It's no big deal."

CHAPTER THIRTY-FIVE

Sherry didn't come to class the next day.

I didn't give it much thought until Emma stormed into my office that afternoon, interrupting an important conversation between Pat and me.

Pat gallantly conceded the visitor chair to Emma. He refused, however, to concede my point: musicians have to work with a finite number of chord progressions, so naturally they'll end up with similar-sounding songs. You can't expect pop music to be too original, I explained, or else it's not pop music anymore. Pat seemed to believe that musicians should be able to come up with completely original compositions all the time. I asked him how many songs *he* had written, and he accused me of changing the subject.

Emma plumped down angrily in the vacated chair, and Pat perched on the edge of my desk.

"My muffler fell out this morning," Pat said when

he caught me staring in horror at the dirt crumbling from his filthy jeans onto my desk.

"And?" I demanded.

"I had to fix it in my driveway and I didn't have time to change afterward."

"Well, thanks for all the rat lungworm parasites, and the leptospirosis, and—what's that flesh-eating thing that lives in soil, Emma? Strep? Staph?"

"Staph," Emma said. "Yeah, that's kind of gross, Pat. You could have taken a shower and changed into clean clothes."

"I would've been late to class," he said.

I didn't mention the condition of Pat's car, which was the real problem. Most people don't have to duct-tape their mufflers back into place before they drive to work. Pointing out things like this to Pat tends to result in the kind of unproductive conversation where people end up making cutting remarks about other peoples' automotive choices.

"Next time you should stop by the car wash," I said. "And then get out of the car and walk through yourself."

"Hey," Emma interrupted, "are you two done bickering? I have something important to ask Molly."

"We weren't bickering," Pat said. "I was explaining to Molly that if she listened to "Holiday" and "The Shore" and "The Passenger," she'd realize they were all the same—"

"No, they are *not* all the same song. Yes, there are superficial similarities, but you can't make a chord progression off-limits simply because someone, somewhere, has used it already."

"It's not just chord progressions," Pat said. "I can't believe you, of all people, are defending plagiarism."

"That is totally unfair, Pat. I—"

"Molly," Emma interrupted, "Did Sherry come to your class today?"

"What? No, she didn't, now that you mention it," I said. "Why, what's going on?"

"She never showed for practice. We only had five paddlers today. We had someone fill in. Girl from the mainland."

"You were lucky to find someone on such short notice."

"No, Molly, we weren't. We're out on the water, halfway to the breakwall, and I see she's just holding her paddle in the air, not stroking. So I ask her what's she doing, and she says, 'I wanted to see if the boat still moved.' Like she's carrying all of us."

Pat laughed incredulously.

"She was in five," Emma continued, "right in front of me. Ooh, I wanted to crack her across her big head."

"You had your paddle," Pat pointed out.

"Yeah, my three hundred dollar Black Pearl. So we just turned the boat around and dropped her back on the shore. We went back out with five paddlers. So yeah. I was hoping you'd know where Sherry is."

"I had kind of a strange conversation with her

yesterday," I said.

"What about?" Emma asked.

"She seemed stressed out about her assignment, but she's doing well in the class. There must be something else going on. Maybe it had to do with Glenn and Davison."

"With what?" Pat asked.

"She had a thing with Davison Gonsalves while Glenn was out of town," Emma said.

"Hm. It's hard to keep up."

"Do you think she knows about you and Donnie?" Emma asked.

"I don't think so. Davison apparently told her that I'm dating his father, but fortunately Sherry doesn't know that Davison's father is Donnie."

"I still can't believe Sherry is Donnie's mysterious ex-wife," Pat said. "It's too much of a coincidence."

"I've been going back and forth on this. It's hard to imagine Sherry and Donnie as a couple, but yesterday she told me she had an ex here in town, and they had a kid. A boy, in fact. So now I'm on the Donnie was her ex-husband bandwagon again."

"I dunno," Pat said.

"You're still not convinced?"

Pat considered that for a second before he came back with,

"Six-four-one-five chord progression, and the same strumming pattern. Are *you* still not convinced?"

"Eh, you two," Emma interrupted. "Focus. What else did Sherry say?"

"I don't know. I can't think of anything else. Oh, she did go next door and tell Rodge to turn off his affirmations."

"Hooray," Emma said. "I thought it seemed less embarrassing than usual in here. Anyway, Sherry's not answering her phone. I left a bunch of messages for her and now her mailbox is full. I even called the police."

"What did they say?" I asked. "It hasn't even been twenty-four hours, has it?"

"They pretty much laughed at me. The guy wouldn't even take down the information. I'm worried. I mean, I've never even known her to be late. Have you?"

Pat and I traded a look. I knew what he was thinking: whoever did away with Kathy Banks was still out there. And now Sherry was missing.

"This is unusual for Sherry," I said. "Her attendance has been good. Except for one time when she was half an hour late to class."

"Maybe the Student Retention Office can help," Pat said.

I started to object—my reflexive reaction to anything involving the Student Retention Office—but I realized Pat was right. If anyone could find a missing student, it was the SRO. Their Customer Relationship Management system used state-of-the-art predictive analytics to flag students at risk of leaving. When one did drop out of sight, the SRO's army of Outreach Specialists would email, text, phone, and even drive out to visit the last known address. They were tireless, ceasing only when the straying student returned to the fold—or threatened to take out a restraining order.

"You're right, Pat. They're probably our best hope. For Sherry to miss both class and paddling practice is unusual. No one has class right now, right?"

"No one in this room," Pat said.

"Funny, Pat," Emma said.

"We have some time then. We can go up to the Student Retention Office right now."

"Emma and I can't go up there with you, Molly," Pat said. "You know they won't discuss your student in front of us."

"Oh, right. FERPA."

The Family Educational Rights and Privacy Act forbids revealing information about students except under very specific circumstances. Most of the time it serves as a shield, to defend against interfering parents and unstable exes.

"Last time I went up to the Student Retention Office was for that retreat," I said. "It didn't go so well."

"Sorry, Molly." Emma shrugged. "We can guard your coffee machine while you're gone."

CHAPTER THIRTY-SIX

Pat was right. Not only did the Student Retention Office hate sharing anything with faculty on general principle, but Federal law placed strict safeguards on student information. I had to do this alone.

I left Pat and Emma in charge of my coffee machine and started up the hill by myself. I wondered how Sherry's disappearance might be related to what happened to Kathy Banks. Sherry and Kathy were on the same paddling crew. Kathy's demise had guaranteed Sherry a seat in the race, but what explained Sherry's disappearance?

They both seemed to have some relationship to that for-profit education company, which had physical campuses in all fifty states and Canada. Sherry had attended one of their schools, and Kathy had a slight physical resemblance to one of their former employees.

Sherry and Kathy had something else in common:

they had both flirted with Emma's husband. I had seen Sherry give Yoshi that playful swat at dinner, and Emma had complained to me about Kathy's brazen advances. I was sure Emma was joking about cracking that woman over the head with her paddle, though. Emma would never actually do something like that. Would she?

I hadn't been paying attention to my surroundings during my trudge up the hill. One minute I was ruminating on Sherry and Kathy, and the next minute I was standing before the gleaming new entrance to the SRO's office complex. The automatic plate glass doors slid apart with a sigh, disgorging a blast of chilled air. I took a breath and strode in.

I took a quick inventory and decided I felt perfectly fine. Unlike the last time I had come up to this building, I wasn't feeling dizzy or panicky. And I knew why: I no longer felt responsible for what had happened to Kathy Banks. That was the good news. The bad news was I was sure Emma had something to do with it. I decided not to mention my suspicions to Pat. He already seemed convinced that Kathy was the victim of foul play, and I didn't want to put Emma in his crosshairs.

A Student Retention Office henchperson scurried over as I entered the lobby. She wore a ruffled red and white floor-length muumuu. Her streaked sandy hair was pinned on the right side with a crimson hibiscus.

"Molly," she said, "We're glad you're here. We've

been wanting to meet with you."

How did she know my name? I imagined a poster in the SRO's back office featuring photos of the campus's ten least cooperative department chairs.

"That works out," I said. "I had a question for you too. I have a student who's gone AWOL."

She ushered me into one of the hushed breakout rooms adjacent to the reception area. Its warm, recessed lighting was a pleasant change from the bare fluorescent tubes humming away in my office.

I stood by the wall-length saltwater aquarium and watched the fish dart around among the manicured seaweed. One fish looked exactly like a lemon. I wondered whether it was actually called a "lemon fish." As I was reaching into my bag to retrieve my phone and look up "lemon fish," I heard a noise behind me. In the aquarium glass, I saw the reflection of a woman standing in the doorway.

I knew who it was. I hadn't seen her since the day I'd shared a stage with her at the faculty development session.

"Hello, Molly." She stood in the doorway at a safe distance. "I hope you're feeling better. Um, you look like you're feeling much better."

I sighed and turned around.

"Hi, Linda. Listen, thanks for taking the time—"

"No, no, thank you for coming up to see us!"

Instead of a sari, Linda wore a simple blue "ethnic" print tunic, flowing trousers, and a chunky necklace that looked like bocce balls strung together. She invited me to sit at the polished koa table and seated herself across from me. In the chair closest to the door. Which she left open.

"We're so glad you came up to see us," she said. "We were going to contact you anyway. We wanted to touch bases about Dylan."

Why is it so hard to use the analogy properly? No one knows less about baseball than I do, and even I know you can only touch one base at a time. The term "touch bases" sounds like triangles sliding back and forth on their bases, randomly colliding like bumper cars. Which, come to think of it, may be as good a metaphor as any for the way we communicate around here.

"Dylan from Larry Schneider's class." I nodded. "Kathy Banks and I discussed his case before she passed away. Well, of course it was before, I mean it couldn't have been aft—anyway, I don't know if you have her notes or anything?"

"Yes," Linda said, "we have Kathy's records."

"So you know the class is still full, and there are several students on the waiting list. It wouldn't be fair to move him ahead of the other students waiting to get in. What I'm concerned about, though—"

"This letter is from our EEO Office." Linda slid the paper across the desk to me. "Dylan filed a complaint—"

"A complaint? About what?"

"As department chair, you are required to make sure the teachers in your department abide by the guidelines outlined in the letter in order to avoid creating a hostile learning environment for him."

I read the letter.

"This sounds like Dylan is not required to meet course deadlines. Am I reading this correctly?"

"Your teachers are expected to work with him on an individual basis to complete his work on a schedule that's mutually agreeable."

"Linda, I don't think it's going to be 'mutually agreeable' when one student gets exempted from the deadlines that apply to everyone else. How are the faculty supposed to—wait a minute, does this say he's allowed to use his phone in class?"

"His parents need to be able to contact him. Denying him the use of his phone at any time, including during class, is tantamount to discrimination."

"Isn't there any other support we can give him, other than letting him ignore the course syllabus? I mean, this poor kid was talking to me about conspiracies and lizard people. I'm worried that he might—"

"That's not your call, Molly."

"No, you're right, I'm not a psychiatrist. But don't you think the other students will think it's unfair that Dylan gets a pass when the rest of them have to follow the rules?"

"The teachers aren't permitted to disclose a student's accommodation plan to other students."

"The professors won't have to disclose anything. If Dylan's chatting on his phone with his parents in the middle of class, it's going to be pretty obvious what's going on. I'll pass this letter along to the faculty and I'll advise them of their obligation to comply. Just be ready when the other students start complaining, that's all I'm saying. Listen, there's something else I need to discuss with you. A student named Sherry DiNapoli. She's disappeared, and… I need your help."

I walked out of the Student Retention Office with mixed feelings. Things hadn't gone well for poor Dylan, I didn't think. He needed help, not a free pass to play with his phone in class. On the other hand, Linda had agreed to put Sherry on the Early Intervention list. Sherry was about to get bombarded with repeated e-mails, phone calls, texts, social media messages, and physical mail to all of her known contact numbers and addresses. Subjecting Sherry to the SRO's special brand of stalking and harassment might sound a little inhumane. But if Sherry was in trouble, it was worth it.

CHAPTER THIRTY-SEVEN

It was Pat's fault that I was late for my lunch with Donnie. I had been heading out of the campus parking lot on my way to Donnie's house, just as Pat pulled in. I saw that he was driving an aged but respectable Mercedes Diesel. Emma rode in the passenger seat. Naturally, I had to back up, re-park and go over to examine the car.

"Pat," I exclaimed, my surprise shoving aside tact, "I thought you were broke! How could you afford this?"

"The ad revenue from *Island Confidential*," he said. "It's modified to run on used cooking oil. The car, not the website."

"You get ad revenue? That's so…corporate! I don't remember ever seeing ads on the *Island Confidential* website."

But Pat did have advertisers, and apparently there were enough of them to allow Pat to buy himself a car with a decent paint job (an inoffensive tan) and a muffler that would stay put without duct tape.

"Ad revenue is what pays the bills." Pat perched comfortably on the hood. "Not even I could live on what they pay part-time instructors."

"Why do you do it then?" I asked. "I mean, not that we aren't lucky to have you."

"Library privileges. I need the databases for research and fact checking. Otherwise, you're right. It's not worth it. Anyway, you both have your ad blockers turned off for *Island Confidential*, right?"

"I don't bother with ad blockers," Emma said. "They slow down your computer."

I peered into the car's windows. The tan leather upholstery was worn to a dark gray at the edges but overall it looked like it was in good shape. This was by far the most deluxe vehicle I'd ever seen Pat driving.

"So Pat, you've been doing okay financially, yah?" Emma asked.

"Yeah, I guess I have."

"So why didn't you come to the race with me and Molly on Labor Day Weekend? Molly thought it was cause you couldn't afford to pay for a room!"

"Oh no. I could afford to go. If I wanted."

"You could?" I turned my attention from the car's interior back to Emma and Pat. "So why didn't you? It would've been fun to have you there."

"Yeah, we shoulda had someone there to keep Molly out of trouble! What's the deal?"

"It was going to be a whole weekend with you

and Yoshi, and Molly and Donnie. I wasn't up to sitting through the extended director's cut of the Patriarchal Heteronormativity Show."

"Oh, Pat," I sighed, "Heteronormativity? Is there any more ungainly, cobbled-together non-word than Heteronormativity?"

"Do you have a better one? Besides, I happen to know you used 'heteronormativity' in your dissertation."

The ensuing debate took longer than expected, and by the time I had noticed what time it was, I was already late for my lunch date with Donnie.

I had skipped eating at noon so I could enjoy my late lunch, and I had to pace myself. If Donnie hadn't been sitting right across from me, my gnocchi in gorgonzola sauce would have been a delicious memory by now. Donnie was there, however, and I was struggling to maintain the ladylike image that I had been cultivating for his benefit. Impulse control, I reminded myself (as I often find myself reminding my students) is the foundation of a functional society. The effort of restraining myself made it impossible to keep up my end of the conversation, so I dined in dainty silence.

"Heard from Davison today," Donnie said.

"So his semester is starting off well?"

"Not especially."

Having grown up among people who were frank, if not operatic, about their complaints, it's taken me a while to get used to Donnie's communication style. But I've learned. When he tells me everything's fine,

I can be sure it isn't. And if he says things aren't going especially well, that means disaster.

“Not especially?" I asked. "Is something wrong?”

“He told me he has one semester to bring his grades up. If he doesn't, he could lose his eligibility.”

“Lose his eligibility? That sounds serious.”

“Davison can’t stay on without his athletic scholarship. I couldn’t afford it.”

“So what are you going to do? You don’t want him coming back here! I mean, he’s got such a great opportunity where he is!”

“I told him to add a couple P.E. classes and drop econ. Do you think that was the right thing to tell him?”

“He should also think about retaking any classes he’s failed, if his school has a policy where the new grade overwrites the old one. That’s the quickest way to raise your GPA.”

“Good point. You should tell him the next time you talk to him. So what’s new with you?”

“Me? Well, I just—I mean, I don't know, let's see."

I searched for something to talk about, that didn’t have to do with Pat. It was a shame. Pat’s new car could run on leftover cooking oil from restaurants, and I know Donnie pays to dispose of his used oil. But I knew better than to suggest the two of them cooperate in any way. I’d found it was best to keep them apart as much as possible.

The last time Pat and Donnie had spent any time together was at the Pair-O-Dice Bar and Grill.

Donnie and I had met up with Pat and Emma for sunset happy hour. Donnie had started to tell us about his recent trip to a restaurant supply trade show in Cremona.

"I always enjoy Italy," he had declared. "The food is wonderful" —here he put his hand on mine—"the people are beautiful—"

At which point Pat had interjected,

"Hey Donnie, wouldn't it be funny if Molly actually turned out to be from some Balkan hellhole? *OW!*"

Emma and I had kicked Pat under the table at the same time. And Emma didn't hold back.

Afterward, Donnie had remarked that Pat didn't seem to approve of him. Was Pat jealous, Donnie wanted to know?

"Pat has kind of a caustic sense of humor," I had explained. "He's like that with everyone."

Which was true. Pat hadn't liked Stephen either, when I'd dated him.

In any event, I certainly wasn't about to prattle on about Pat's new car. What else was there to talk about? I couldn't say anything about Sherry. Or, worse, Sherry and Davison. And I was pretty sure Donnie wasn't interested in getting into an argument about the word *heteronormativity*.

"Wasn't this weekend lovely?" I took a piece of bread and dabbed the last of the cream sauce from my plate, hoping he wouldn't bring up that unfortunate episode with Davison.

"I'm glad you enjoyed it. It seems like I hardly saw

you except for the drive back. And you were asleep for most of it."

Donnie didn't like being left alone. I shouldn't have been surprised by that, but I was.

"Driving makes me sleepy," I explained. "And your music selection was so nice and soothing I must have drifted off. I have to listen to something upbeat if I'm going to stay awake in a moving car."

Donnie likes the same kind of music Emma does. Smooth vocal harmonies poured over a bed of languid slack-key guitar. He may as well have had sleeping gas seeping out of his car speakers.

"Anyway, you know how Emma is. She insisted on having me around for moral support. I thought our sunset dinner was, um, what a wonderful view of the sunset."

"Actually, Molly, there was something I wanted to ask you."

CHAPTER THIRTY-EIGHT

"Do you remember the computer program Davison was talking about at dinner?" Donnie asked. "The one that recognizes faces?"

"Maybe," I answered, cautiously.

"Davison showed it to me after we got back from watching the manta rays. It was quite interesting, to say the least. Technology is amazing, isn't it?"

I set my fork down. The gnocchi sat on my plate as plump and chewy as ever. But I had lost my appetite.

"I didn't think you'd brought a computer with you," I said. Donnie still uses a flip phone. He's not exactly someone who buys himself all the latest gadgets.

"Davison had his tablet with him."

"I see." I tried to appear calm. "Davison showed you the website?"

"He did," Donnie said.

"Has Davison thought of majoring in information technology? He'd probably enjoy working with computers. Maybe you should suggest it to him. It's a very practical major."

I hoped it wasn't obvious I was trying to change the subject. Or maybe I should have tried being more obvious. Either way, no success.

"Who is 'Alterity Jameson?' " Donnie asked.

"Who?" I heard myself squeak.

"Tell me about it." Donnie leaned back in his chair and waited.

"Why didn't you ask me about this on the drive back?"

At least that way we could have ended things cleanly, instead of ruining a perfectly nice lunch.

"I didn't want to wake you up," he said.

I closed my eyes and rubbed my temples. "Fine. Alright. I was in grad school. I was writing my dissertation, *Reproducing and Resisting: Hegemonic Masculinities and Transgressive*—anyway, you don't need to hear the whole title. It had to do with punk rock, basically."

"You wrote your dissertation on punk rock? I thought you said your degree was in English."

"It was in the English department. So I was immersed in the scene, doing a lot of my field work in Orange County."

"Orange County? You mean Newport Coast? Laguna Beach? Tough job, Molly."

"More like Huntington Beach. And don't laugh. Those G.G. Allin fans could be pretty scary.

Anyway, some of my grad school friends and I thought, well, that looks like fun, and how hard could it be? So we put together our own punk band."

"And now you're in charge of the management department in the College of Commerce. Quite a life change."

"I think 'in charge' might be overstating things a little. You know something? I thought it was the greatest day of my life when we got our picture in the music section of the weekly paper."

I had cause to reconsider that "greatest day of my life" thing a few years later when someone put all of the archives of the now-defunct alternative weekly online. Our photo is now On the Internet, Forever. Fortunately, our real names weren't used in the story. My embarrassing little secret was safe, or so I thought. And then this facial recognition technology came along.

"Does the name mean anything?" Donnie asked. "Alterity Jameson?"

"Alterity has to do with being 'other', the out-group, coming from a different perspective," I said. "When you're young and earnest and reading about postmodernism in grad school, it's a word you end up using a lot. It sounded much more hip and subversive ten years ago, believe me."

"And Jameson? Davison thought it had something to do with Irish whiskey."

"No. Davison is completely wrong about that. It's a nod to Fredric Jameson. You know *Cultural Logic of*

Late Capitalism?"

"Of course," Donnie said.

"Really?"

"No."

"Anyway, there it is. Now you know my embarrassing secret. I was in a no-hit-wonder postmodern punk band."

"Phallus in Wonderland. Right?"

I winced. So much for my ladylike image.

"For the record, the name was not my idea. I wanted 'Pacmanistan'. You know, sort of referring back to the Eighties. It would have been a nice reference to the fragmented recycling of trends that goes along with a civilization's transition from modernism to postmodernism."

"Sure," Donnie said.

If I didn't know better, I would swear Donnie was trying to stifle a laugh.

"Unfortunately," I continued, "the other band members were afraid the name 'Pacmanistan' could get us sued. Also, Melanie Polewski was very much into Lacan, and she lobbied hard for her idea of having an all-female band with 'phallus' in the name. Obviously, Melanie won that one. It's more, um, intellectual than it sounds."

"Were you the lead singer?" Donnie asked. "In the picture, you were front and center."

"No, I actually played bass. I think the photographer put me in front because he liked what my hair was doing. Melanie never forgave me. She thought she should've been the one—no, wait, I did sing one time. Melanie, her stage name was 'Shock Derrida', because, you know, Derrida and Lacan, right?"

"If you say so."

"She'd wrecked her voice from all the shouting. I guess there are tricks you can use to save your vocal cords, but we didn't know anything about that. So one time I did the vocals for '(Judy) Butler Did It.'"

"Could you sing it for me? Do you remember how it goes?"

Donnie was grinning now. He seemed to be taking this a lot better than I had expected.

"No. It was hard to memorize the words because they weren't intended to make any kind of linear sense. That was the whole point. It's a reference to the performative act as distinct from the content, right? Anyway, I was a disaster as a lead singer. I mean, it's punk rock, so it's not like the bar is terribly high, but I didn't even rise to loud, fast and—and awful. In my defense, I was trying to sing and play bass at the same time. Melanie didn't play an instrument, so all she ever had to do was sing."

"It sounds like you had fun. In spite of Melanie."

"You know what? We did have fun. We all thought we were being super transgressive."

"Do you still do anything musical?" Donnie asked.

"No. I lost interest when I realized how hard it is to write anything original. There are only so many chord progressions, so many bass lines, and so many melodies. It's impossible to be completely original and still be listenable."

Donnie got up. "Coffee?" he asked.

"Yes, thanks!"

Do you stay in touch with your bandmates?" he asked.

"No. I'm not even sure what they're up to anymore. The last I heard of Melanie, she was freelancing for an essay-writing company. Term-papers-for-sale-dot-com or something."

At the doorway to the kitchen, he turned back and grinned. "When does your Behind the Music episode come out?"

I let out a long, relieved breath and followed him into the kitchen.

"Donnie, I'm so glad you're not upset."

"Upset about what?"

"Well, you know, the band, the whole thing. It's undignified. I thought you'd disapprove."

The conversation paused for the whirring of the coffee grinder.

"Disapprove?" Donnie said. "I think it's kind of cute."

"Did you say cute?"

"Sure. You're usually so…you have such high expectations. For yourself, and for everyone else. I don't mean it in a bad way. You have very high standards"

"Are you calling me uptight, Donnie?"

"Not uptight. More like…persnickety."

"What?"

"I take it as a compliment. After all, you chose

me, didn't you?"

CHAPTER THIRTY-NINE

Donnie pulled me into a tight hug. I wasn't sure how to react so I left my arms limp at my sides.

"It's nice you let yourself do something silly once every decade or two," he murmured into my hair.

"Donnie, can you tell Davison that photo is not actually me? If my students ever catch wind of this I'll have to join the Federal Witness Protection Program."

Donnie released me from the hug and busied himself with the coffee.

"You want me to tell Davison that isn't you in the picture? Are you asking me to lie to my own son?"

"Fine. Tell him *I* told you it's not me. That wouldn't be a lie."

"That's a creative approach to the truth," he chuckled.

"That's exactly what Pa…"

"Exactly what?"

"Nothing. I forgot what I was going to say."

I was going to point out Pat would say the same thing to me, about being creative with the truth. At some point during Mrs. Flanagan's visit last summer, she had said about me (while I was sitting right there), "This one's kissed the Blarney Stone, so she has!" And Pat had replied, "Ma, the Blarney Stone would kiss Molly if it could!" Of course, they both thought that was hilarious. Pat doesn't realize if everyone subscribed to his literal-minded idea of total-disclosure honesty, society would collapse in a matter of minutes.

"Balkan hellhole." I wanted to kick him again, just thinking about it.

While Donnie prepared our espressos, I picked up the newspaper lying on the counter and scanned the front page. I had tried taking the local paper for a while, but the issues kept piling up unread. Taking the papers down to be recycled was an extra chore I didn't need. I never found the paper's classifieds to be of much use; the online classifieds were more up-to-date, they were searchable, and they had color photos. People like me are probably why the *County Courier* ended up having to lay off people like Pat.

"Anything interesting in the paper?" Donnie asked.

"They found a body down in Kuewa."

The headline had caught my attention because I was afraid it might be Sherry. Neither Emma nor I had heard anything from her. I was relieved to see the deceased was a man, but then I felt bad about feeling relieved about someone being dead.

"Shame," Donnie said. "Another meth lab explosion?"

"No, not this time. A hiker got disoriented in the jungle and couldn't find his way out. See, that's why I never go hiking."

"Any good news in there?" Donnie asked.

"Here's the cruise ship schedule. Want to hear the days and times you can expect crowds of hungry tourists at Donnie's Drive-Inn?"

"Visitors, Molly. Visitors. Never tourists."

"Right," I said. "Visitors." I glanced at his wall clock. It was almost time for my afternoon meeting. "Oh no, I didn't realize it was so late! Donnie, I'm sorry, I have to run."

"No worries." He transferred my espresso to a small paper cup. "Take it to go."

"Thanks. You're so thoughtful."

"Have a good meeting." Donnie sent me off with a kiss on the cheek.

I was heading down to the Bayfront. I guess you could say I was going to a "meeting," in that I was "meeting" Emma when she came in from paddling practice. Emma didn't know it yet. My real reason for being there was to avoid Cyndi from the Student Retention Office.

During one of our Student Retention Office Faculty Development Seminars (or maybe it was a Retreat or a Celebration or a Professional Development Session), the faculty were enduring the usual hectoring about being more "customer oriented," "honoring" each student's "unique way of knowing," and so forth.

If students are truly our customers, I had finally asked, and the customer is always right, why don't we let them assign their own homework and pick their own grades? That would make them happy, wouldn't it?

To my horror, my offhanded jibe had somehow metastasized into a full-blown, honest-to-goodness Student Retention Innovation. The Student Retention Office had been pestering me ever since, in hopes of coopting an actual faculty member to use as a figurehead for their latest Trophies-For-Everyone initiative.

Today I begged off once again, citing an off-campus meeting I couldn't miss. Cyndi was in a different department from Linda, and not in a position to help me find Sherry. So here I was, hiding out in the damp shade of the canoe halau, with a few minutes to kill before Emma and her crew came in. I was sure I could think of some urgent academic matter to discuss with Emma when the time came. I didn't see anywhere clean to sit down, so I stood and watched the bright blue day outside.

Something rustled behind me. I hoped it wasn't one of those huge cockroaches.

"Hey, Dr. B."

"Sherry!"

Her hand rested on the club's koa wood canoe. She gazed at it, not at me.

I had feared the worst, and now here she was, alive and unharmed, and standing in front of me. I was bursting with questions, but I didn't want to risk saying anything that might send her running off again.

"Did you ever paddle in this one?" I asked, carefully.

"Nah. Just our fiberglass one. This is for special competitions. It's traditional. They built it the exact same way they've been building them for hundreds of years."

I knew that wasn't quite right. One hundred years ago, a canoe would have been carved out of a single log. There aren't a lot of 45-foot koa logs lying around these days, and if your canoe club wants one, they have to put in a special request to the island's Department of Land and Natural Resources. If the agency approves your request, it's your responsibility to retrieve the nine-ton log from the forest. Once you've done that, it can take years to carve the canoe. This canoe, the one belonging to Emma's club, was a strip-plank canoe—easier, cheaper, and quicker to build. Still, it was beautiful. The copper and gold of the polished grain glimmered in the shade.

"Look," Sherry said, "I appreciate you getting the school to try to track me down. But you can call 'em off now. I'm okay."

"Sherry, what happened to you? We were so worried. Emma and I both were."

Finally, she turned to look at me. She had deep

shadows under her eyes as if she hadn't slept since the last time I had seen her.

"What happened to me? What happened to me is I gotta leave town."

"Why?"

"I don't want to. I have to."

Sherry stared at the sandy floor of the halau.

"Do people think Kathy Banks died of natural causes? She didn't."

CHAPTER FORTY

I probably should have been frightened. Any sensible person would have been. I should have run out into the hot sunshine, hopped into my car, and lurched away as fast as I could. But I was more curious than afraid.

I remembered what Glenn had said to Emma and me in the gym, as he was struggling to explain Sherry's extreme diet to us. It would be really bad if she took two doses of insulin by mistake.

The insulin needles and the dieters' HCG needles looked identical. Sherry knew that very well. She'd used them both. All Sherry had to do was go into Kathy's purse, or wherever Kathy kept her prefilled diet syringes, and make the switch.

"You used your insulin!" I blurted out. "That's what happened, right?"

She let out a sharp laugh. "Whoa! You're smart. Course you are, what am I saying? You're a freakin' college professor."

"I don't know anything," I hastened to assure her. "I'm only guessing."

"It wouldn't be a bad way to go, Dr. B. Insulin shock. I've been there. Your blood sugar goes way down, like when you forget to eat."

I couldn't grasp that at all. How could someone forget to eat?

"You just feel a little lightheaded," she continued. "You get confused, and then you pass out. And if you don't get medical attention right away, you're done. You don't wake up."

"I don't understand. Why? It's so irreversible!"

Had it been that important for Sherry to secure a seat in the canoe? I knew things could get competitive among the crew members, and everyone wanted to paddle in the Labor Day race. But murder?

"Look, Dr. B., I know you don't understand. You're freakin' Snow White, no disrespect. You could shoot someone in the head, and walk into the police station, and say 'Oh gosh, sorry officer, it was self-defense' and they'd sit you down and make you a nice cuppa tea and call you a cab."

I thought that was kind of uncalled for. She was making me sound like some insipid goody-two-shoes. Hey, I was an actual punk rocker once upon a time.

"Sherry, I don't understand. Things were going so well. You finally got your financial aid straightened out. Thanks to Kathy, from what you told me.

You're doing well in school. And you have the paddling."

"The paddling, yeah. I'm not happy about walking away. I think paddling's what kept me sane."

"Yes, well. So why—"

"What's done is done. I can't stay here now, can I? Look how you figured everything out. Lucky for me you're cool about it."

"Well, I wouldn't exactly—"

"Pretty soon other people are gonna start catching on," Sherry said. "I gotta look out for myself. No one else is gonna look out for me."

Her face looked hard now.

"That's how it's always been for me. I gotta watch out for myself. I can't count on things going my way. You know, me and Mad Dog could never get married officially. And we sure couldn't do it in a real church. You know why? Cause Donnie made sure to take his sweet time filling out the paperwork."

Donnie.

"Maybe he wasn't trying to mess up your life," I said. "Maybe he wanted to make sure you could stay on his health insurance. Or, you know, something like that."

That was the story Donnie had told me. When we were first starting to spend time together, and I'd found out, whoops, he was still married. He did finish filing the paperwork eventually, but by then he'd spent over a decade in marital limbo. And, of course, so had his ex-wife.

"It would've been hard for you to get medical coverage on your own, with type 1 diabetes, right?" I asked. "Pre-existing condition? Maybe he was trying to look out for you."

"Yeah, nice to think he could spare a thought for me. Makes me feel all warm and fuzzy inside. Anyway, I gotta go."

"Emma and the crew should be back in a few minutes," I said.

"I wasn't planning to see anyone. I just wanted to take one last look. I'm kinda glad I ran into you, though, Dr. B. I should thank you. Cause if it wasn't for you…anyhow, yeah, thanks."

"Sherry, wait! There's something I don't understand. Why couldn't you get an escort boat? That way three more people could have paddled in the race. And no one would have had to—"

"A what boat? Look. I found pictures of Kathy. In Glenn's stuff."

She turned her palms up. "Photographs. You need any more evidence than that?"

She paused as if she were expecting me to supply an answer to her question.

"Glenn? Had photographs of Kathy Banks?"

"I know I don't need to spell it out for you," she said. "Like I said, I did what I hadda do."

Sherry slipped out into the bright afternoon, and she was gone.

"Wait!" I called after her, uselessly. "What did you mean, if it wasn't for me?"

What just happened here? For a moment, I

wondered whether I had imagined the whole thing.

Did Sherry confess to killing Kathy Banks? Kathy, her teammate and friend? And over Glenn? If recent events were any indication, Sherry clearly wasn't that attached to him.

But she had stood there, next to the koa canoe, and said it.

Do people think Kathy Banks died of natural causes? Insulin shock. It wouldn't be a bad way to go.

And had she called her ex by name? Donnie? I had already suspected that Sherry was Donnie's ex-wife and Davison's mother. In fact, I'd defended the idea when Emma and Pat discounted it. But hearing Sherry say it was surreal.

The headache came on suddenly, with no advance warning. The inside of my head felt like a fifty-car pileup. My eyeballs throbbed with pain so intense I could barely see. I groped in my bag until my fingers closed around what I was looking for.

CHAPTER FORTY-ONE

I stared at the phone in my hand. Pat. I would call Pat.

I considered calling the police first. But what would I tell them? That an "accidental" death, one that hadn't even come to their attention, was actually a murder, and I knew this for a fact because the person who was probably the murderer sort of confessed to me? And too bad the person ran off because otherwise she could back up my story? They probably would have sat me down with a nice cup of tea, exactly as Sherry had said. And then quietly sent someone out to fetch the big butterfly net.

Unfortunately, Pat wasn't answering his phone. I left a message, put my phone back in my bag, and waited in the shade of the canoe halau.

Pat's tan Mercedes pulled up and parked just as Emma came in with what was left of her crew, now down to five paddlers. Pat waited with me as Emma and her crew hosed the canoe down and put it away in the halau, and the three of us made the short walk down the beach to Andrade's Snack Shack.

"What are you guys doing here?" Emma asked.

"Something about Sherry. Molly, your message didn't really make sense."

"Technically we're all having a meeting," I said. "That's my cover. I'm hiding out from the Student Retention Office."

"Oh, right," Pat said. "The pick-your-own-grade initiative they want you to do?"

"Exactly. Like anyone would give themselves less than an A. But now I do have something to tell you. Let me sit down first."

The Snack Shack's single picnic table happened to be empty. Over hot, salty French fries and huge cups of watery soda, I related the details of my encounter with Sherry.

"Where is she now?" Emma demanded.

"I don't know. It sounded like she was planning to go off-island."

"Why didn't you stop her?"

"Stop her how?" Pat laughed. "Was Molly supposed to run out and tackle her?"

"So listen," I said, "remember when Donnie and I first started spending time together? And I found out he was still technically married?"

"Technically married," Pat said. "Is that different from regular married?"

"You know what I mean, Pat. Sherry had left years ago, but Donnie never filed the paperwork until last year. He told me it was because he didn't want to get her kicked off his health insurance. Anyway, I had never looked at it from the perspective of the ex—"

"Right," Pat interrupted. "He was only worried about her health. Completely motivated by altruism. A modern-day Albert Schweitzer."

"What I never realized," I interrupted back, "was all those years he left the divorce unfinished, he made it impossible for Sherry to get remarried."

"Funny," Pat said, "almost like he did that on purpose—"

"Pat, let her talk!" Emma flicked her straw at him, spraying diet cola droplets everywhere. "Molly, do you think this whole time he's been hoping Sherry would come back?"

"I don't know."

"On the one hand, I would say no," Emma continued. "He's not the romantic type. I don't see him getting all gaga over someone. I mean, look at how he is with you. Sure, he likes you, but it's not like he's all head over heels or anything."

"Thanks, Emma. That's exactly the reassurance I need right now."

"But on the other hand," Emma continued, "maybe you remind him of Sherry, and he likes that about you."

"I can't imagine I would remind anyone of Sherry."

"There's a resemblance," Emma said. "You have to admit."

"Maybe physically," Pat said.

"If he was hoping for Sherry to come back, it explains how come he took so long to finalize the divorce. And when Sherry didn't come back, Donnie settled for someone who looked kind of like her, except not as skinny. No offense, Molly."

I stared out at the ocean and took a gulp from the soggy paper cup, wishing it were filled with something more comforting than diet cola.

"Do you think Donnie wants Sherry back, specifically?" Pat asked. "Maybe he likes a particular physical type, with the hair and everything, and doesn't care about any of the personality stuff."

"You guys think Donnie is actually that shallow? He just likes a certain kind of look, and the person doesn't matter?"

"Yes," Pat said.

"Come on. Who does that? I mean, I don't have a specific physical type someone has to fit before I can be interested."

"No," Pat agreed. "You're pretty indiscriminate."

"That's cause Molly looks at the inner person," Emma said. "I know it's hard for you to understand, Pat, since men are all shallow idiots."

"Men are more visual," Pat said.

"Visual. Whatta bunch of bull. Yeah, men are 'visual' when it comes to oogling the other ladies in your canoe club, but when it's time to clean anything, he's suddenly incapable of seeing dirt. It's like he's been struck blind! 'Visual' my—"

"You're still talking about men in general, right?"

Pat said. "Not anyone in particular?"

"I think it's 'ogling,' not 'oogling'," I suggested.

"Shut up. Anyway, Molly, you shouldn't feel bad."

"Oh. Don't feel bad. Okay."

"No, really. You and Donnie are a good match. Better than Donnie and Sherry woulda been. You're both professionals, you're both well-established in the community, you're both super fussy—"

"Yeah, Emma's right," Pat said. "Donnie needs someone he can bring along to a fancy dinner, without worrying about whether she's gonna put out her cigarette in the foie gras. Anyway, Donnie would never take Sherry back after she walked out on him."

"No way," Emma agreed. "Could you imagine him forgiving her? I can't."

"Uh-uh. Donnie's one of those guys that'll hold a grudge for the rest of his life."

At the other end of the sparkling blue bay, a stand-up paddleboarder was making slow, steady progress. I almost wished I could trade places with him. Why did I think talking with Emma and Pat was going to make me feel better?

CHAPTER FORTY-TWO

Emma went over to the Snack Shack to get her soda cup refilled. Pat watched her go and turned to me.

"So Molly, I realize your relationship woes are the most important thing here, but there's also the minor matter of a confessed homicidal maniac running loose. I don't think you realize what a close call you had. An enclosed canoe shed, on a deserted beach, no witnesses? We're lucky you were alive when I showed up."

"I probably would've done the same thing as Molly." Emma reseated herself at the splintery picnic table. "We know Sherry. I wouldn't have run away from her. I would have wanted to hear what she had to say"

"I was hoping what happened to Kathy was natural causes or some sort of accident," I said. "Maybe she mixed up her insulin needles with those diet drug needles. But thinking Sherry did that to her on purpose is so disturbing."

"No," Emma corrected me. "Kathy wouldn't have mixed up any needles by accident, because she didn't use insulin needles. She had a pump."

"What? I've never heard of that. Is it like a pacemaker?"

"Nah. It looks like a music player almost. You clip it on your waistband and the little tube goes right into your stomach. I remember Kathy always had to double check it before we went out. She wasn't technically supposed to go in the water with it, but she did."

"So Sherry must've taken Kathy's HCG needles and left the insulin ones in their place," Pat said. "So that Kathy would unknowingly administer a fatal dose of insulin to herself, and throw the needles away. Those prefilled needles are disposable, right?"

Emma nodded.

"That's so coldblooded. And it wasn't about who got a seat in the canoe at all. It was a plain old love triangle."

"I know," Pat sighed. "What a bore."

"Wait, what love triangle?" Emma demanded.

"Glenn got involved with Kathy," I explained, "so Sherry got rid of Kathy."

"But how did Sherry know Glenn was fooling around with Kathy?"

"Glenn had photographs of Kathy, and Sherry found them," Pat said. "Weren't you paying attention?"

"What photographs? I couldn't find any photographs of Kathy. Remember, Molly? I mean, where would Glenn—oh. Never mind. I guess we're not talking about her high school yearbook pictures."

"It is a lot to process," I said.

"But why would Sherry care so much if Glenn messed around with Kathy?" Pat asked. "She got together with Davison as soon as Glenn was out of town. If polyamory was okay for Sherry, it should've been okay for Glenn too. Fair's fair."

"Yeah, it seemed strange to me too. But I'm not Sherry. I don't know what her reasoning was. And it's not polyamory, Pat."

"Here come the word police."

"That's right, Pat. Lights flashing and sirens blaring. Polyamory is a consensual arrangement, not a synonym for cheating. What Sherry was doing was more like overlapping serial monogamy."

"You're not gonna complain about mixing Greek and Latin roots?"

"No. That etymological horse is already out of the barn. Automobile, television, and neurotransmitter are here to stay, so we can't really complain about polyamory, can we?"

Emma rattled the ice in her cup to get our attention.

"Hey word nerds, let's stay on topic. We were talking about Sherry. Here's my take. Sure, Sherry wasn't being rational. But that's normal human behavior. Who's rational all the time? Come on,

Molly, haven't you ever done anything you've regretted later? Like majoring in English?"

"Something I've regretted? Oh, let's see. You mean like walking into the wrong hotel room—"

"No, I didn't mean—"

"Imperiling my honor," I continued, "and permanently scarring my visual cortex, all because I listened to someone's lame brained—"

"We're talking about murder here, Molly," Emma interrupted. "Stay focused. You're letting yourself get distracted."

"What are you two talking about?" Pat asked.

"Nothing," we replied in unison.

"We should probably get back to campus," I said. "I think the coast is clear now."

We cleared off the table and started walking back toward the halau.

"So it wasn't about the race after all," Emma said. "Or even that other woman."

"Other woman?" Pat's voice had an urgent edge. "What other woman?"

"Remember, Molly? The look-alike? The software found her when we were looking for Kathy?"

"Who? Oh, the brown haired woman! What was her name?"

"I can't remember her first name," Emma said. "I think her last name was Galvez."

Pat stopped walking.

"What are you two talking about?"

"I completely forgot about it until now. Molly and I were trying out that facial recognition software right after I finished the race."

"We found Kathy Banks' supposed doppelganger on the mainland," I added.

"Molly means there's someone who looks like Kathy—"

"I know what a doppelganger is," Pat interrupted. "Who is she?"

"Just someone on the mainland who didn't even look like Kathy," I explained. "The software picked her up as a match."

"But it turned out to be someone else," Emma added.

"Why didn't you tell me about this before?" Pat demanded.

Emma and I looked at each other.

"Because it wasn't actually Kathy," I said. "We were looking for a picture of Kathy for her online memorial, but she wasn't in any of the team photos. The only one we could find was a candid Sherry had."

Emma and I resumed walking, and Pat quickly caught up.

"Sorry for getting all snippy," he said, "It's just that I haven't been able to find a single thing on Kathy Banks. She never got close to the other people in the Student Retention Office, so they can't tell me anything. And everyone else has been stonewalling me. I wonder if maybe this other woman is related to her. Or is her."

"No," I said, "It wasn't Kathy Banks. I did think it was kind of an odd coincidence they had the same initials, though."

"The same initials?" Pat was losing patience again. "I thought you said this other woman's last name was Galvez!"

The name hovered at the edge of my mind—something-something, four syllables—and slowly came into focus.

"Beckenbauer. Karolyn Beckenbauer! That was her name."

"What?" Pat fairly shrieked. "Emma, how do you get Galvez from Beckenbauer?"

Emma shrugged. Pat pulled his phone out of his jeans pocket and started tapping frantically on the keys.

"How do you spell Beckenbauer? Is it Karolyn with a K? Is this her? Wait a minute."

"Oh yeah," Emma said. "That's the other thing. Karolyn Beckenbauer is dead."

CHAPTER FORTY-THREE

Emma had caught a ride down to the Bayfront with one of her teammates, so she rode back with me. Pat took his new cooking-oil-fueled Mercedes. We drove behind him, marveling at the french-fry smell from his exhaust.

"You shouldn't worry about Donnie," Emma tried to reassure me. "He's still a good catch. And his feelings about you haven't changed. Aren't you having dinner with him tonight?"

"Tomorrow," I said. "I already had lunch with him today. I can't marry into that family anyway. Not after what happened at the hotel. I can't spend the next forty years enduring Davison's idiotic double entendres."

We drove past the dilapidated downtown mini-mall whose dying shops had, over time, been replaced by an array of social service agencies. This afternoon one of these was acting as a food bank.

"Oh." I felt a little sheepish now. "Listen to me with my first-world problems. Do you see that?"

A line of ordinary-looking local people (what did I expect hungry people to look like?) stretched out the door and down the block, past the mortuary, the tattoo parlor, and the internet cafe, and almost to the fire station. I tried not to look at their faces as we drove past. It must be humiliating enough to have to stand in that line, without curious drivers gawking at you.

"I shouldn't complain. My love life is a dead end, but we have jobs, and shelter, and neither of us is starving—"

"That's for sure. Yeah, I guess it's good to—hey, Molly, isn't that your student? The one who works in the library?"

I slowed down and scanned the line of glum faces.

"It's Micah!" I exclaimed.

"What's he doing standing in line at the food bank? That boy makes more than we do!"

"Micah was always such a good kid," I said. "I can't believe he's—"

"Hey! Eyes on the road!"

"Oh. Right. What is he thinking? We spent so much time in class on social responsibility and ethics. And look. There he is, standing in line to take food from people who need it! Maybe I should go talk to him."

"What, now?"

"No, not now, but I can go find him in the library later."

"Molly, you're not his mom. We teach them the best we can, but they have to make their own decisions."

"It's so disappointing. Our university went out of its way to provide a good job for him when he couldn't find anything else. And this is how he pays it forward? Ugh. I hate people."

"Yeah, speaking of hating people? Were you saying you and Donnie don't have a future together? You're sure you don't want to ever marry him?"

"I like Donnie just fine. Donnie's not the problem."

"Isn't his son doing archery?" Emma asked.

"Mm-hm. I'm not sure how Donnie managed to arrange it, but yes, Davison's attending one of the most expensive schools in the country, on an archery scholarship."

"Molly, think positive. With all those arrows flying around, you never know what might happen!"

"No, no, no. I'm not wishing catastrophe and doom on anyone. Not even Davison Gonsalves."

We pulled into the parking lot near my building.

"Do you want to stop for a cup of coffee before you go back up to your office?" I asked.

"Sure. Molly, don't write Donnie off. He's about the best thing out there. I mean what are you gonna do, get back together with Stephen?"

"Good point."

As Abigail Van Buren said, there's nothing deader than a dead romance. Every time I see Stephen at the weekly department chair meetings, I wonder afresh what I ever saw in him. He claims to dislike being chair of the theater department, but he won't give it up. Being department chair allows him to direct most of the theater's programming funds to the annual production of his original three-hour Brechtian opera, *The Drowning.* I still can't believe I ever tolerated his smoking. I don't care what he says, clove cigarettes are still cigarettes. Also, using a cigarette holder doesn't make them any less noxious, just more pretentious.

I pushed open the door to my office and went behind my desk to set up coffee while Emma got comfortable in my visitor chair. The caffeine from Donnie's espresso had worn off, and the adrenaline surge from my encounter with Sherry had left me feeling depleted. The Snack Shack does sell coffee, but it's the kind that sits out on a burner in a glass carafe for hours, to be consumed in emergencies only.

I turned on my computer and pulled up *Island Confidential.*

"You do have the ad blockers on!" Emma exclaimed, and explained to me in detail how to turn them off, as if I didn't already know. After adjusting various settings to allow ads on the site while still keeping some modicum of virus protection, I reloaded the page.

The popups and floating banners I had feared were not in evidence. The *Island Confidential* site displayed a simple column of ads along the right-hand edge of the screen. There was one for a t-shirt company, and one for an independent bookstore.

"These ads aren't so bad," I said. "Oh, wait. What are these?"

The rest of the ads touted various for-profit educational institutions. Every one of them was a member of that embattled group of universities currently defending themselves in the lawsuit.

"Emma! Look at this!" I turned my monitor so she could read it. She leaned in and read,

"Cherry Blossom Queen Controversy—"

"No, not the articles, Emma, the ads! On Pat's website!"

"Hey, that's messed up! They don't want to let this girl participate because she's 'only' half-Japanese? What's wrong with being half-Japanese? I should go up there and kick someone's—"

"Emma, the ads. Look at the ads!"

"That t-shirt's kind of tacky. What about it?"

"The other ads."

"Your future starts here…wait, isn't that our slogan?"

"No, Mahina State is Where Your Future Begins Tomorrow."

"Oh! Pat's getting advertising money from, what did Bob Wilson call them, the predatory for-profits!"

"I wonder if Pat knows," I said. "He might not."

"Should we tell him?"

"I don't know. If we did, he might feel like he has to cancel the ads, on principle. I'm glad Pat's getting some extra income out of it. Heaven knows he doesn't make anything as a lecturer."

"Isn't he supporting those idiots? By displaying their ads?"

"In a way. But the way his website is set up, it's probably pay-per-click. That means this for-profit bunch pays the ad network every time someone clicks the ad, and the ad network pays Pat."

"So every time someone clicks one of those ads, it costs those gonifs some money?" Emma asked.

"It's only a few cents, but—Gonifs?"

"It comes out sometimes."

"Because you went to Cornell."

"Can't help it. So then we should click those ads as much as possible, right?"

"Well, there's something called click fraud," I said. "I mean, you're not allowed to pay someone to click ads on your website in order to get the ad revenue, or set up some kind of automated clicking program or anything. But if a real customer clicks the ad out of genuine interest, there's no rule against it."

"Oh, well. I'm very interested in investing in my future." She reached over, grabbed my mouse, and started clicking.

Pat burst into my office, brandishing a copy of the *County Courier*. Emma quickly pulled her hand back, and I turned my monitor so only I could see it. Pat was too agitated to notice.

"Just picked up the evening edition on the way over. Your friend Sherry. She's a piece of work."

Pat tossed the *County Courier* onto my desk. The top of the fold headline screamed, KUEWA MAN IDENTIFIED. Emma and I almost banged our heads together in our rush to read the story.

The article was the follow-up to the item I'd seen at Donnie's house, about the body found in the Kuewa jungle. The unfortunate victim was now presumed to have been jogging, not hiking. The most interesting development, though, was the accompanying photo.

It was Glenn.

CHAPTER FORTY-FOUR

I stared at the photo of Glenn.

"Wow. When Sherry starts a job, she finishes it. You almost have to admire that kind of follow-through."

"Do you really think Sherry did this?"

"Come on, Emma, what do you think? Do you think she's going to let Glenn off the hook after what she did to Kathy?"

Emma shook her head. "I can't believe it," she said. "Sherry was competitive, but I never thought she was vicious."

Pat interrupted, "Am I the only one who sees a double standard here? Let Glenn off the hook? Anyone remember what Sherry was up to the minute Glenn was out of town?"

"No one's excusing her," I said.

"Kathy Banks," Pat said, "that's one. A crime of passion, maybe. But Kathy and Glenn? Now we're talking about a serial killer."

"It's a shame," I mused. "Glenn didn't deserve that."

Emma was examining the article. "Glenn Anderssen. You know, I never knew his last name. Look. It says foul play isn't suspected."

"She's clever," Pat said. "I wonder how she did it."

"I know Sherry and Glenn used to go out running together," Emma said. "Maybe he had a running accident. What if it actually was natural causes?"

She looked at Pat, and then at me.

"Or, maybe not."

"Well, class sure isn't as interesting without Sherry," I said. "Double murderer or not, it was nice to have someone contributing to the discussion. With her gone, her study group sits around the table like a bunch of stuffed animals at a five-year-old's pretend tea party."

"That's one good thing about teaching biology, ah? No one has to sit in a circle and talk about their feelings. All they have to do is shut up and learn."

"We're writing business plans," I said. "Hardly the same thing as sitting around and talking about your feelings."

"Aren't you two taking this seriously at all?" Pat said.

"Of course I'm taking it seriously," I said, "but we can't do anything about it, can we?"

"I still don't believe Sherry is guilty," Emma said.

"Well, she pretty much told me she took care of

Kathy," I said.

"Did she literally come out and say, 'I killed Kathy Banks'?"

"More or less."

"Two people have been murdered," Pat said, "and I know who killed them but I can't prove it. And as far as the police are concerned, there weren't any murders at all. Only two unrelated accidents."

"Maybe they were two unrelated accidents. Maybe Sherry was just messing with Molly when she said whatever she said. Or maybe Molly misinterpreted. You know how she overreacts to everything."

"That is not true. If anything, I'm not paranoid enough."

"Emma," Pat said, "do you think it's a coincidence that Kathy keels over, Sherry admits she killed Kathy because Kathy was messing around with Glenn, Glenn drops dead, and Sherry disappears?"

"Sure. Could be."

"The problem is, I can't go and accuse Sherry of murder in print." He brightened. "Oh, I know! Maybe I can write this up as—"

"Don't you dare write some kind of 'Cursed Paddling Club' thing, Pat. My club is already down to five. I don't want you scaring everyone else away."

"Oh. Alright. Fine."

Pat brooded for a moment. "Aah, maybe I shouldn't bother. I'm always saying I never give up on a story, but I'm about to give up on this one. It's been like banging my head against a brick wall trying to get any information at all. The people up at the hospital are still acting like they've never even heard of Kathy Banks."

"Maybe they're telling the truth," I suggested. "Is that possible? The people you've talked to were working different shifts or something?"

"No, I don't think it's possible, Molly. This is a small town with only one hospital, there's no other ER within a hundred miles, and thirty-year-old women don't drop dead in canoes every day. You'd think there would be at least one person who would be willing to talk to me."

"I think Kathy was a lot older than thirty," Emma interjected.

"They're not allowed to share any patient information with you," I said.

"I know. But any halfway-competent reporter should still be able to get the information."

"You are a good reporter, Pat. The hospital employees are simply doing their job."

"I guess there are only going to be four people in the whole wide world who know the real story. The three of us, and Sherry. Not exactly a journalist's fondest dream. Hey, Molly, what time is your class?"

"Oh, shoot, I have to go. You guys can stay here if you want."

"We will," Pat said.

"Oh, Pat, I'm going to use your idea today."

"What crazy thing is Pat making you do?" Emma asked.

"No, it's not crazy." I gathered my handouts and books. "It's a great idea. We have a chapter on persuasion and charisma, and the examples in the text aren't that helpful. I mean, most of it is about an airline most of these kids have never even heard of. So I'm going to try to bring the chapter to life by showing them this movie Pat told me about."

"It's called *The Goebbels Experiment*," Pat said. "Kenneth Branagh narrates from Joseph Goebbels' journals. In the film, you see Goebbels develop the prototype for our current political discourse."

"I think my students will love it. It shows the dark side of charisma. I think it'll be a nice corrective to all the smiley-face hero worship in the textbook."

"Do business textbooks contain anything but smiley-face hero worship?" Pat asked.

"The textbooks, yes. They actually have research and some historical perspective. They're not the same thing as those business books you see at the airport."

I checked around my office to see if I was forgetting anything, and chugged the rest of my coffee.

"Mach schnell!" Pat called after me as I rushed out the door.

I reached the classroom with two minutes to spare before the start of class. I could have set everything up and started the discussion on time, except for one thing. The whiteboard was covered with Rodge Cowper's space-hogging scrawl. In sprawling script that filled the whiteboard, Rodge had written,

"If you can't you must, and if you must you can."

And under that,

"If you do what you've always done, you'll get what you've always gotten."

And finally,

"Every problem is a gift - without problems we would not grow."

I was not in the mood to clean up Rodge's mess today. I was still reeling from my encounter with Sherry, and upset about poor Glenn. Pat had dismissed Glenn as "cute as a button, and nearly as intelligent." Glenn couldn't help it, though. Not everyone can be on the right-hand side of the distribution. Glenn's only fault was his trusting infatuation with Sherry. Why couldn't Sherry let him go and move on? Killing Kathy and then Glenn was like murdering someone and doing away with their pet guinea pig. It was gratuitous. Sherry certainly had other options in the romance department. Why couldn't she walk away?

It was time for class to start, and I was barely a third of the way through with erasing the board. This was unacceptable.

Every problem is a gift.

Well. Maybe what I needed to do was leave Rodge a nice thank-you note for his gift. I knew he had a class in here right after mine. Maybe this time *I* could "forget" to erase the whiteboard. Then Rodge would have to waste the first few minutes of his class erasing, and he'd realize what he'd been making other people put up with.

Reckless with tragedy and too much caffeine, I made a fateful decision. I would leave class today without erasing the board. See how Rodge likes it. As I scrubbed off Rodge's purple scribbles I realized I was humming Khachaturian's *Masquerade Waltz*.

CHAPTER FORTY-FIVE

Despite the misgivings I had expressed to Emma earlier, I was enjoying dinner with Donnie. A good night's sleep had helped me to put things into perspective, and the delicious cooking smells filling his house enticed me to forget my doubts about the distant future. I preferred to focus on the immediate future, which was going to include Donnie's delicious spaghetti Bolognese.

One time, it must have been about a year ago, I had fixed dinner for Donnie at my house. Since that one dinner date, for some reason, he's never been able to coordinate his schedule with mine so we could do that again, and we always end up having dinner at his place. He insists on doing all of the cooking. Tonight I'd tried to pitch in by picking up some of the groceries.

I deposited my reusable rice-bag shopping tote on his kitchen counter and started pulling things out.

"I got grass-fed beef," I said. "Beef from grass-fed cattle, I mean. That'll be nice for the sauce, won't it?"

"Perfect. It'll give the sauce a richer flavor than the grain-fed would have. Good job."

"Donnie, I'm feeling a little guilty about you doing all of the cooking. I mean, you run the restaurant all day, and when you finally get home—"

"No worries, Molly. Cooking at home isn't anything like running a restaurant. Running a restaurant is like managing a factory. Cooking is art."

"Huh. I guess that's one way to look at it."

To me, cooking is more like chemistry than art. I was never any good at chemistry.

"Creating a meal for you is very rewarding for me, Molly. I can tell you really enjoy eating."

I pulled a tub of hydroponic lettuce from the bag, popped it out of its clear plastic container, and started rinsing it in the sink. That, I can do.

"So, what's been going on since the last time I saw you?" Donnie asked.

"Oh, nothing too out of the ordinary." *Except for the part where your ex-wife murdered two people and skipped town.* "My afternoon class went well today."

"How so?"

"We're covering persuasion and charisma. So I showed them a movie about Nazi propaganda."

"That's what I like about you, Molly. Always looking on the bright side. What inspired you to show your students a film about Nazis?"

"It turned out to be interesting for the students."

I didn't feel like explaining about it being Pat's suggestion. "Goebbels pioneered the modern use of sound bites, so after we watched, I had the students try to remember some of the bits of propaganda from the movie. They were able to remember a lot of it."

"Like what?"

"For example, Goebbels got people all stirred up with the idea of endless war. *Totaler Krieg.* He got the public clamoring for it."

"For endless war?"

"I know, it doesn't appeal to me either. At all. But I guess he knew his audience. And tell me if this sounds familiar: Effective propaganda is confined to a few simple points, and these points are repeated over and over. Talking points, right? I bet we could turn on your TV right now and see Goebbels' legacy in action."

"My TV?"

"Oh right. I forgot you don't have a TV."

"There's one in Davison's room."

"Well, we don't have to go in there. Anyway, what's new with you?"

"Good news, I suppose. Do you have the onions?"

I handed him the bag of sweet Maui onions.

"Perfect, thanks. Merrie Musubis is discontinuing their Mexican food line."

"Already? That was fast."

"I understand it was popular the first week, but their sales started to decline after that." Donnie placed an onion on the cutting board and started chopping.

"I'm not surprised. Unexpected flavor combinations aren't always a good thing. Like Spam and refried beans."

I involuntarily wrinkled my nose at the pasty, flavorless memory of the Carlos Spamtana burrito.

"Speaking of unexpected combinations. Guess who's unexpectedly back in Davison's life. His mystery woman." The speed and force of Donnie's onion-chopping increased noticeably.

"What? She's in California already? I mean, she's in California now? How did that happen? How do you know?"

"I called Davison this morning. He was on his way back from the airport."

"Are you sure it's the same person? You mean the one he met here, right? Before our trip across the island?"

"He's supposed to be concentrating on his schoolwork. This is the last thing he needs right now."

"I thought she—I thought he said they were done."

"Well, it's her. No doubt about it."

"Wow."

"She dumped him. Now she snaps her fingers and he comes running back. I don't like it."

I wondered whether I should tell Donnie what I knew—or suspected—and decided I should not. If Donnie found out all about Sherry and Davison now, the Sumo Saimin would really hit the fan. Donnie would wonder why I hadn't ever said anything to him.

Why hadn't I said anything to him? Well, maybe I could have shared my suspicions with Donnie earlier, but what would I have told him? I hadn't been sure myself, not until that conversation with Sherry. So I'd kept my mouth shut, and now it was too late.

And I had something else to worry about. What if Davison got on Sherry's bad side, and ended up mysteriously dropping dead the way Glenn and Kathy had? I would have a lot of explaining to do.

"No. I don't like it either," I agreed. "Not at all."

Donnie paused his chopping and turned to smile at me.

"I like your maternal instinct, Molly. You're protective."

"Hm. Maternal instinct. There's that."

"Did Davison ever tell you anything about her? Confide in you?"

"Confide in me? No. Davison hasn't confided in me," I answered, truthfully. "I honestly couldn't tell you anything about this," I added, pushing my luck.

"Molly, maybe you should talk to him."

"What? Me? Why?"

"He won't listen to me. He thinks he can party his way through college, and everything will turn out fine. I think if he had to live my—I think he doesn't understand why his education is so important."

"Well, he is going to inherit a successful business.

If you were heir to Donnie's Drive-Inn, schoolwork might not seem so urgent. Anyway, if he doesn't listen to you I don't think there's a chance he'd listen to me."

"I think you're underestimating yourself. I know Davison thinks very highly of you. He always asks about you."

"Oh. That's very nice." I shuddered a little.

"Let me give you his contact information," Donnie said. "You should have it anyway."

I finished spinning the lettuce dry and reluctantly went to retrieve my phone.

"I appreciate it, Molly."

I opened a new contact and at Donnie's prompting typed in Davison's phone number and email address. I hoped taking Davison's information down was enough of a show of good faith. I certainly did not intend to call him.

"I think he'd enjoy hearing from you," Donnie said. "Just a quick call, tell him you're rooting for him. You're the closest thing he has to a mom right now."

I had no answer for that.

CHAPTER FORTY-SIX

I arrived at my office the next morning to find a note on my door from Dan Watanabe, our interim dean.

Please come see me ASAP. Dan

This was obviously not going to be good news. But what bad news was there that Dan hadn't already handed down? Salary cuts. Overcrowded classes. No money to replace the doors on the bathroom stalls. Last year, the administration had floated a proposal to save money by turning off the air conditioning everywhere on campus except for the administration offices. Fortunately, our librarian had pointed out it would only take a couple of weeks' exposure to the sweltering damp to reduce all of the books and computers on campus to moldy doorstops. Was the air conditioning back on the chopping block now? It had never worked that well, but still, I'd be sorry to see it go.

Dan was hunched over his desk in the dean's office, looking like he'd aged about a decade since the previous year. The furniture in the office was still fairly new, but the wood grain desktop was already separating at the seams, and the particulate filling was bulging out. Next to Dan stood a sweet-faced young man in a security officer's uniform, about seven feet tall and measuring nearly as wide across the chest.

I knocked and entered. "Hi, Dan." I peered at the security officer's little brass name tag, but I wasn't close enough to read the name.

Dan heaved a deep sigh. "Come in, Molly. Sit down."

I had encountered many different sorts of paperwork in my short time as interim department chair, but I had never seen the form Dan was holding now.

"Molly, first of all, I want to thank you for stepping up to serve as interim department chair."

"No problem," I said. "It's a delight."

"I know. You have a lot on your plate and this might not have been your first choice. But I've appreciated your efforts. You're dedicated and passionate, and you've been a tireless advocate for your faculty."

"You're speaking in the past tense. Am I being demoted?" I asked hopefully.

"No. Sorry. No such luck. But I have to ask you some questions, okay?"

I glanced over at the security officer. The young

giant quickly averted his eyes. He looked like he was about twenty. He'd probably attended high school with some of my students.

"Molly. Did you participate in a Student Retention Office faculty development session on the thirtieth of August?"

"If they had one, I must have. I don't think I've missed any sessions so far. I'm very diligent about SRO re-education camp."

Dan cleared his throat.

"Do you think your comportment or demeanor at that session could be described as unusual or alarming in any way?"

"Oh. That session." I felt a stab of pain in my right temple. "It's possible. Rumor has it I actually smiled at one of the Student Retention Officers. I guess if you knew me, you might find it unusual and alarming."

The corner of Dan's mouth briefly twitched upwards. He pulled another piece of paper from the stack in front of him and examined it.

"This week, you held classes at the scheduled times in your assigned classroom, correct?"

"Uh, yes."

"You were the one teaching. You didn't have anyone substituting for you."

"That's right."

"Did you have any guest speakers or other visitors?"

"No, why?"

"What did you do during your last class section?"

"We were discussing persuasion and charisma. I showed them excerpts from a movie called *The Goebbels Experiment.* It's all about propaganda—"

Dan nodded. "Mm-hm. I saw the movie. Very interesting."

"I'll admit, the material is kind of dark. Did one of my students complain?"

"No. And it seems like an appropriate choice, given the topic under discussion."

Dan looked up at me over his reading glasses.

"But when Rodge Cowper's class came in afterward, they saw a whiteboard covered with Nazi propaganda slogans. In your handwriting."

"Oh. I see. Well, that's, hmm."

"Social Media Monitoring has counted several instances of pictures of the whiteboard appearing in online venues."

"Social Media Monitoring? What is Social Media Monitoring?"

"It's a new department in the Student Retention Office. They just came online over the summer. Molly, you picked a heck of a day to forget to erase the board."

Of course, this was Rodge Cowper's fault. He's the one who started with not erasing the whiteboard. You couldn't blame me. Unfortunately, I couldn't explain this to Dan without coming off as a little childish.

"One thing I don't understand," Dan said. "I know 'Totaler Krieg' was Josef Goebbels' call for total war. But you, or someone, apparently wrote 'in it to win it!' right underneath. Why was that?"

"That wasn't me!" I protested. "'In it to win it!' was already on the board in permanent ink. Dan, you know me. I would never write 'in it to win it!' "

"Look, Molly. As interim department chair, you've been working hard. And doing a great job, I think, considering everything that gets thrown at you. I appreciate it, believe me. But as the interim dean of this college, I have to make defensible personnel decisions. And as a friend, I don't like seeing you burn out. I'm going to have to recommend temporary administrative leave."

"What about my classes?"

"Rodge has taught both BP and IBM in the past. I've asked him to take over for you temporarily."

"So Rodge has to teach my classes while I'm out on leave?"

"We're a small college with no resources, Molly. People have to pitch in. I'm sure my giving Rodge extra teaching probably offends your sense of justice."

"No, no. It actually sounds pretty fair to me."

"Here. I need to give you this."

It was a handout describing our Employee Assistance Program. We get those in our mailboxes at the start of every school year. I'd probably thrown mine away already. I'd always thought it looked like a great resource. For other people.

"Dan, if this is on my record, will it affect my application for tenure?"

"No. It shouldn't. In fact, if your tenure bid is

turned down, the burden is on the university to show you're not being targeted for discrimination because of this."

"Oh. Well, that's a relief. So what do I do now?"

"Go home. Read over the EAP flyer. Decide which program or programs might meet your needs at this time. Make sure you understand your options for now. Anything else you need to do, any phone calls or appointments pertaining to your obtaining the help you need, I suggest you put all of it off until tomorrow."

"So I should finish up my Student Retention Office paperwork at home?"

"You shouldn't be doing any work. Of course I'm not there to police you, so use your best judgment. Officer Medeiros here will accompany you to your car. If you need to pick anything up from your office, do it on the way down."

Dan meant right now, apparently. The young security officer stepped to my side and walked me down the hall to my office, which was now occupied by Pat and Emma and fragrant with (my) brewed coffee.

"Are you related to the other Officer Medeiros?" I asked him. "The head of security?"

"He's my cousin." Young Officer Medeiros held the door open for me as I stepped in and hastily scooped up every book and piece of paper on my desktop. Emma and Pat stared.

"Can't join you for coffee right now," I said. "Come by my house after work?"

CHAPTER FORTY-SEVEN

I woke up on the floor next to the couch. I'd been dreaming about earthquakes and collapsing buildings. The sounds of thunderous destruction quickly resolved to someone banging on the door. I was still struggling to stand up when the door clicked open, and Pat and Emma pushed their way in.

I blinked stupidly and looked at my wrist, which didn't help, as I wasn't wearing a watch. I'd fallen off the couch and barely missed cracking my head on the coffee table, upon which sat a heap of still-ungraded papers and a half-empty mug of coffee.

"It's five-thirty." Emma plumped down on my couch. "Cocktail hour. Yes, I would like a glass of wine, since you asked. Hey, I brought a video for us to watch."

"It's already five-thirty? I slept through the whole afternoon. I was hoping to get through this stack of papers."

"Why?" Pat asked. "Aren't you on administrative leave?"

"I'll have some of your Cabernet," Emma said. "The one in the purple and pink box."

"You'll drink that? Sure. Pat? Coffee?"

"No thanks. No, on second thought, yeah. I'll have coffee. Thanks."

I got our drinks and the three of us settled on the couch. Emma took a few healthy gulps and put down her nearly empty wine glass on my coffee table. I quietly lifted her glass and slid a coaster underneath.

"So Molly," Pat asked, "What happened?"

"Did they let you keep Officer Cutie Pie?" Emma chimed in. "Where is he? Is he here?"

"Emma, gross. He was like sixteen years old."

"Did you get fired?" Pat asked.

"No, I did not get fired. Thanks for assuming that, though. No, it's because, I don't know, Dan thinks I'm getting burned out. He's concerned about my well-being, I guess."

"What did you do?" Pat asked.

"Yeah," Emma echoed. "What did you do?"

"Nothing major. I forgot to erase the whiteboard after class. So Dan put me on administrative leave and arranged to have my classes covered."

"Dan's pretty efficient," Emma said. "You know he already got a replacement for you on our committee. Are you not supposed to come to committee meetings?"

"I'm supposed to stay home and rest."

"You two are on a committee together?" Pat asked.

"Committee on the Status of Women. We were supposed to have a meeting today. So who was there from College of Commerce?"

"You'll love this," Emma grimaced. "Rodge Cowper."

"Oh, that's an interesting choice," I said.

"Isn't it because of Rodge that everyone in your department has to keep your office doors open if you have a student in there?" Pat asked.

"Exactly. The Rodge Cowper Rule. So how did the meeting go?"

"Well," Emma said, "Rodge came strutting in, you know how he is."

"Covering his insecurity with a brittle shell of cartoonish machismo," Pat said. "That poor guy is a midlife crisis on wheels. Did he lick his finger and smooth his eyebrows?"

"I don't think Rodge actually does that," I said.

"Finger guns?"

"He does do the finger guns."

"So he walks into our meeting ten minutes late, right?" Emma said. "And we're having a pretty serious conversation about campus safety and putting more call boxes in, stuff like that. So Rodge busts out with, 'Hello ladies, I'm here to help you wage war on the nuclear family, the American male, and Christmas.'"

"Oh brother," said Pat.

"So Betty Jackson says, 'We love Christmas,

Rodge. You should see our version of the Nutcracker.'"

"So Dan put you on leave and took you off your committees because you forgot to erase the whiteboard one time?" Pat asked.

"It wasn't only that. The thing was, I'd left the class discussion notes up from when we went over The Goebbels Experiment."

"Paid or unpaid leave?" Emma asked.

"I think it comes out of my sick leave," I said.

"Not bad," Emma mused. "Really? All you had to do was forget to erase the board?"

"There's something else too," I said. "I guess someone reported me for displaying unusual behavior at the last SRO session."

"I don't see why anyone would complain about that," Emma said. "I thought it was the best faculty development session ever. Hey, can I move this stuff you have on the coffee table? What is this mess anyway?"

"Oh, these are the draft project proposals from the business planning class. I don't trust Rodge to do a good job giving them feedback."

"The writing, huh?" Pat asked. "Listen, I do what I can in intro comp, but I can't spin straw into gold."

"No, that's not the problem," I said. "The problem is, I'm looking at these plans, and I know some of my students are only doing this for the class credit, but there are some who are serious about trying to start these businesses. I'm seeing all of these shiny, naïve dream-bubbles that are about to get popped by the hatpin of reality."

"The hatpin of reality?" Emma rolled her eyes. "Who says stuff like that?"

I gestured at the pile of papers. "One sports bar or restaurant or shoe store after another. They do the break-even analysis, they know there's no way the business can survive, but they refuse to abandon the Dream. I don't know why we even teach this class in an undergrad program. You're not supposed to go out and start a business out of thin air. You're supposed to work in the industry for a few years first. Build up your contact list, figure out what the customers want that they don't already have. That's what Donnie did."

"Speaking of Donnie," Pat said, "does he know what happened? How are you going to explain your unexpected vacation to him?"

"Don't listen to Pat. Donnie doesn't have to know about this. You don't have to tell him anything. What's wrong with wanting to start a restaurant, though? Why is that such a bad idea?"

"We have expensive inputs and an extremely price-conscious market on this side of the island. Add plenty of competition, fickle customers, and high fixed costs—"

Pat started to make exaggerated snoring noises. I ignored him.

"If you're down near the hotels where all the tour—sorry, the visitors are, you might be able to make it on volume but otherwise, it's tough. By the way, I think you're not supposed to be looking at those. Unless you want to help me grade them?"

I got up to help myself to another glass of wine. I took Emma's now-empty glass back for a refill too.

"Hey, Molly!" Emma was holding up one of the papers. "This is Sherry's! Did you see it?"

"Emma, I don't think you're supposed to read those. I'm already in enough trouble. I don't need a FERPA violation on my record too." I returned with two brimming wine glasses and set them down on coasters.

Emma handed me Sherry's paper.

"Read this."

Sherry's proposed product was a portable device that could detect and disrupt a wireless signal.

"Well, that's a pleasant surprise. An original business idea. I'd actually buy this. Too bad it's probably illegal."

"I know! A wearable Wi-Fi jammer! I wonder if it can kill the Wi-Fi in the classroom. If it can, I want one."

"Yeah, sounds pretty useful," Pat said. "Sign me up!"

"I just busted one little princess in my class," Emma said. "She claimed she needed her laptop to take notes, so I've been letting her use it. So after class, I saw she'd been posting messages, *during* my lecture if you can believe it. So hungover LOL, BIO 101 lecture so board, spelled B-O-A-R-D, Nakamura ruined my weekend, stuff like that. If I could block Wi-Fi in my classroom, I wouldn't have to worry about any of that. Or about students who use cell phones to cheat on tests."

"How did you know what your student posted?" I asked.

"She friended me at the beginning of the semester, and I guess she forgot. So, you want us to take these papers back up to your department?"

"I want to write some feedback on them first."

"Didn't Dan tell you not to?" Emma said. "You gonna disobey your dean?"

"I'm not sure I trust Rodge to—"

"That's Dan's decision," Emma interrupted. "Not yours. Come on, let's watch a movie."

"Is it a comedy? I hope it's a comedy."

Emma's movie was not a comedy. It was a depressing drama about a doting mother making one sacrifice after another for her self-centered, ungrateful child.

"Why doesn't anyone call the daughter out on her self-destructive behavior?" I complained. "Everyone's indulging her!"

"Hit a little close to home?" Pat asked.

"Maybe. I feel sorry for the mother. I have no sympathy for the daughter. And this movie is not lifting my spirits."

"Molly, you have to watch it to the end," Emma said.

"Yeah, maybe there's a happy ending," Pat said. "Maybe the ungrateful daughter dies."

"That wouldn't be a happy ending, because it's still sad for the mother. There's no good way out of this except maybe the daughter getting a personality transplant. Come on, if Davison made a bad decision and ended up dead because of it, Donnie would be devastated."

"Well, I want to watch the movie," Pat said.

"I guess I don't understand the appeal of sad movies. Why should I pay to be depressed? I can feel depressed for free."

"Just watch the rest of it," Emma commanded. I did.

"Well, that was nice and depressing," I said when it was all over. "Thanks. Now it's too late to start grading."

"You don't have to do any grading," Pat said. "Rodge is teaching your classes, and you're not even supposed to go back onto campus."

"Yeah, Molly. Dan told you to take a break."

"You're going to have a lot of free time now," Pat added. "I know doing nothing while someone else teaches your students is probably a control freak's worst nightmare, but you'll have to get used to it."

"I think we have time for another movie," Emma said.

"Wait. Are you saying I'm a control freak? Do you both think that?"

Emma concentrated on queuing up the next movie, and Pat acted like he hadn't heard me.

CHAPTER FORTY-EIGHT

I hauled myself out of bed at sunrise to stroll down the hill and hang out at the Farmer's Market. I hadn't even been on leave for twenty-four hours, and I was already bored. The Farmer's Market is one of Mahina's few tourist attractions (or visitor attractions, if you like), and I live in convenient walking distance, but I hardly ever take advantage of it. I walked past Donnie's Drive-Inn, but it wasn't open yet.

I perused a display of papayas first. They were firm and smooth, and a day or two short of fully ripe. I had never liked papayas until I moved here and tried the Hawaiian varieties. They're smaller and sweeter than the ones you buy on the mainland, with none of the bile taste. I bought a few and moved along to a display of jewelry and hair ornaments made of plant fibers and shells. I was about to pass by, when I heard,

"Hello, Professor!"

It was Hermina, my former student. The two other women at the table with her were busy, one doing something with the cash box, the other arranging the display. None of the three women wore makeup.

It wouldn't even occur to me to leave the house without makeup, despite the many discussions I'd had back in grad school about the cosmetics industry and its perpetuation of ageist, Eurocentric beauty ideals. Pat needles me about my makeup dependence. Maybe Pat is right, and my aesthetic imagination has been colonized by unattainable patriarchally-enforced standards, causing me to buy and use cosmetics for which I have no need.

On the other hand, there was the one time I showed up to class barefaced—my car wouldn't start, and I had barely enough time to walk to campus—and I apparently looked so pale and haggard my students got together after class and wrote me a get-well card.

"Hermina!" I exclaimed. "I thought you worked up at the clinic! Did you change jobs?"

She laughed. "No, Professor, this is my family business. I still work up there."

"Oh. I might see you later then."

"Going to pick up your prescription?" The two other women were still occupied with their respective tasks, and neither acknowledged me.

"Uh, yeah. They just sent me another reminder. So what's the family business?"

Hermina explained that she and other women in her extended family made hair ornaments, earrings, and necklaces from scratch, working together for hours at a stretch. It was a time for socializing, as well as getting work done, she explained. I bought a woven ponytail holder and a necklace adorned with tiny shells. They were carefully worked, and ridiculously inexpensive. When I paid, Hermina's two relatives finally looked up and smiled at me. I felt guilty getting change back from a twenty.

I dawdled at the Farmer's Market as long as I could, and when I was done I still had the whole day in front of me. The mall didn't open for another two hours. Pat and Emma were at work, and I wouldn't be meeting Donnie for lunch until later that afternoon.

I considered violating the terms of my leave and sneaking onto campus to get the data for a paper I was working on, but I decided against it. The last thing I needed was to get into even more trouble. I could have Pat or Emma retrieve the files from my office computer. They seem to know how to get into my office when I'm not there.

I went back home, pinned back my hair with the new contraption I had just bought from Hermina, and headed back out to the clinic to pick up my prescription. It was something to do, and it got me out of the house and away from the stack of still-ungraded papers on my coffee table. The ones I wasn't supposed to be grading. Emma was right. I should pack them up, send them to my department chair, and enjoy my mandatory holiday.

As I entered the clinic I saw the pharmacy window wouldn't open for another few minutes. I heard something plop onto the carpet and looked down to see a piece of polished blonde wood, part of my new hair gizmo. I obviously hadn't put it in correctly. On an impulse, I went over to Behavioral Health, to see if Hermina was working behind the desk. She was. There was only one other person in the waiting room, a gaunt woman in a cowboy hat who sat quietly with her sinewy hands folded in her lap, staring at the floor.

Hermina flashed me her golden smile as I approached the reception desk.

"Long time no see, Professor!" she grinned.

"Hi, Hermina! I know. Look, I'm wearing the new hair device, and it's so pretty, but it keeps falling out. I was wondering if you could tell me what I'm doing wrong?" I glanced over at the lone patient, who hadn't moved. "Sorry, I don't mean to bother you at work."

"No problem. It's not busy right now. You gotta twist the hair. That makes it stay. No, do it the other way. Like this." She unwound her bun—her hair was surprisingly long—and demonstrated the correct twisting technique. With her direction, I got the thing seated securely.

"Thanks for the help. Now it feels like it'll stay put." I patted my hair to make sure.

"You have another question for me, Professor?"

"You're very observant. I do, actually. I, uh, I was

wondering. You mentioned you worked at the library for a while."

I felt a little uneasy bringing it up since I didn't know whether she had left her job there voluntarily. But she seemed to have landed on her feet, employment wise, so maybe this wasn't a huge faux pas.

"Those jobs pay quite well, from what I hear."

Her smile disappeared. "I guess so, yeah."

"Do you know, I saw the strangest thing. Down at the food bank? I thought I saw someone who works at the library, a former student, I won't say who, standing in line! Have you ever heard of anyone doing that? It seems so…"

Hermina was looking down at the desk.

"Lot of us did that thing," she said. "I couldn't apply for assistance because my paycheck says my salary too high. So I go to the food bank too."

I glanced up at the wall clock. Still a few minutes until the pharmacy window opened.

"But—"

"I'm not supposed to tell nobody. They tell me, don't tell nobody."

"You don't work for them anymore. You can tell me. I won't let anyone know I heard it from you."

"We have to donate." She looked miserable. "Almost our whole pay. More than ninety percent from the paycheck."

"Who says you have to donate? Donate to whom?"

"They tell us we have to donate to the school.

They tell us, they make it easy for us, they do an automatic deduction from our paycheck."

"Couldn't you refuse?"

"Then they fire you. Then you get nothing. I'm lucky I find a job here. I can pay for everything now, and I can help support my family. I even send money home."

"So they hire our graduates at high salaries, and they force you to turn around and donate most of it back to the university."

Hermina nodded.

"So they can say they give us good jobs, but really they don't pay us."

"It's for the rankings. They can claim our graduates' starting salaries are high and our alumni donations are increasing. Meanwhile, we're shifting our own money from payroll to the development office, and our graduates are lining up at the food bank. Well, Hermina, I'm glad you were able to get out of that situation."

"Me too. Hey, Professor, pharmacy should be open now. Hope you feel better. Your hair looks pretty now."

Peter, my former student, was the only one working at the pharmacy window. Two people were already in line. I took my place behind them and called Pat. He wasn't answering his phone, so I left a message telling him what I had just learned from Hermina. As I hung up, I noticed the large sign posted on the wall: Please No Cell Phones.

I dropped my phone back into my purse. I'd done

enough rule-breaking for now.

CHAPTER FORTY-NINE

"Hey, Professor!"

Peter was inches away from me, on the opposite side of the pharmacy window, but he spoke with the same clear, ringing tone that used to carry his off-topic observations to the far corners of my classroom. Certainly the people waiting in line behind me could hear every word.

"It'll be just a minute. You're here to pick up the contraceptive ring, right, Professor? Do you need instructions on how to insert it?"

"No, that's not mine."

"What? Sorry, I can't hear you through the glass."

"That's funny, I can hear you loud and clear. My prescription is for—could you check my record again, please?"

I didn't want to say it out loud: anxiety medication. For that matter, I couldn't imagine any prescription I would want announced to the entire clinic. We have patient privacy laws for a reason.

Peter leaned over and peered at his computer screen. "Oh, sorry. The contraceptive ring was for Professor Jackson. You know her, yeah?"

I nodded. Poor Betty.

Peter stood and grinned. "She told me factory's closed. She said she told Niall if he wants any more kids they'll have to outsource to China. You seen her kids? Wow, they're getting bigger!"

"They are." I wondered why Peter seemed to find it remarkable that small children would grow larger. That's what children do. Even I know that.

"You ever notice how they're the same color from head to toe?" Peter persisted. Their hair and skin and eyes, everything? All golden brown. Like they're made out of caramel. Professor, you don't have any kids, do you?"

Peter hadn't changed at all. I wondered whether there might not be more fitting career choices for an extroverted blabbermouth than small-town pharmacist.

"Do you need my patient number?" I asked.

"Nah, thanks. I have it right here."

Donnie and I had never talked about whether we wanted children (additional children, that is; Davison isn't negotiable). We don't have those Where Are We Going with This Relationship kinds of conversations. I'm in favor of children in a general sense, being necessary for the stability of our various social and economic systems, but I could never picture myself as a mother. I couldn't begin to imagine having four, like Betty Jackson and her cheerful husband Niall.

Peter disappeared behind the tall shelves and returned with a small brown bottle and several different forms for me to sign.

"I have to see your driver's license, Professor, sorry."

I pulled it out and showed it to him, and out of habit kept my thumb over the weight. Which was silly, since Peter had my entire medical record right there in the computer.

"So you got me mixed up with Betty Jackson?" I asked.

He laughed. "I guess it's cause you were both my teachers. And you're both young and pretty, for professors."

"Oh, Peter," I said. "So close."

"May I advise you about your prescription?" he read from the screen.

"Please," I said. I wasn't planning to take it again, but who knows? I might need it in an emergency. And Doctor Spinner hadn't told me anything. All I knew was what I had found online.

"Doctor says start with a half tablet at first, and if you feel okay with that dose after one week you can work up to a full tablet."

"Start with a half tablet," I repeated.

"Don't take it with alcohol."

"No alcohol. Got it."

"Don't drive or operate heavy machinery until you know how you react to it. It might make you drowsy. Sometimes people get something like the manic phase of bipolar disorder. That's the most dangerous because you don't recognize the danger yourself. You lose your sense of fear. That's rare, though, and it happens mostly with people who already suffer from depression. If it happens, discontinue the medication and seek medical attention immediately."

"Thanks. It's helpful to be informed in advance. So do I pay at this window, or—"

"You know, my buddy's girlfriend takes this," Peter said. "She has a stressful job, and it totally helps her deal."

"I'm glad to hear it." I glanced back at the growing line of customers behind me.

"She's a dispatcher for the county," Peter continued. "She's the one who picks up the phone when you call 911. She gets a lot of those goofballs who think it's funny to call when there's no emergency."

"That's terrible, Peter. Well, I don't want to hold up the—"

"She was telling us, this one time, not that long ago, she got a call from the bay front, so she sent a vehicle down, and when they got there, there was no emergency. Hardly anyone there, too. And guess what happened next! When the responders got there, this scary-looking skinhead comes running up and starts cussing them out. They hadda get out of there quick!"

"This was at the Bayfront?"

"Yeah! Was after dark, too. Scary!"

The story had clearly mutated in the repeated telling, but I had no trouble recognizing Pat from Peter's description. Paying someone else to cut his hair is too bourgeois for Pat, so he shaves his head instead. It does make him look kind of scary, especially if you don't know him.

"Maybe they dispatched two vehicles by mistake," I suggested, "and the other one got there first?"

"Yeah! She said that's exactly what she thought at first, but she checked and all the vehicles were accounted for. There wasn't even an ambulance available. She had to send a fire truck instead. But firefighters can do first aid too. Did you know that? You know, sometimes I think my job is stressful, cause I have to work quick and be super-efficient all the time, but it could be a lot worse, huh?"

Peter glanced over my shoulder at the long line behind me.

"Uh-oh. Hey, Professor, it's great to catch up, but I have to get to my other customers."

I stopped by the grocery store, the post office, and the dry cleaner, finishing my errands and arriving back home by mid-morning. I wondered about the strangely disorganized state of our county emergency services. I knew Peter's story about the fire truck and the supposedly nonexistent ambulance could make a good business communication case, if only I could figure out exactly what kind of miscommunication had caused the mix-up. I had heard Pat arguing with the dispatcher over the phone. What had been going on at the other end? Stress and human error, or something else?

I put the last of my dirty clothes in the washing machine, started it, and looked around my house for things to do. Everything was already clean and well organized. Maybe I'd have another look at those student papers. Mark them up with a little bit of useful feedback, and then have Pat or Emma take them back to my department. I was supposed to be avoiding stress, but I decided it would be more stressful for me not to look at my students' papers. Rodge would probably give them all A's without reading anything. He'd get rave reviews from the class, no one would complain to the dean, and my students would learn nothing.

I brewed myself a cup of coffee and settled onto my couch. I was glad I'd chosen leather; it felt cool in the midday heat. Sherry's paper was at the top of the stack, where Emma had left it. Stapled to the back of her proposal was an article from one of the tech blogs, something about wireless security. I read through the attachment twice and sat staring for a long time at the last paragraph of the article. I set it aside, and got through the rest of the class papers, making at least one helpful comment on each.

I went back to Sherry's article and read it all again. I wished I could talk to her. But she was probably thousands of miles away by now.

CHAPTER FIFTY

Donnie still didn't know about my being out on administrative leave. I was considering telling him about it at lunch, but as soon as he opened the door, I decided it could wait. It was easy to see something was bothering him. He may as well have had a miniature cartoon storm cloud hovering over his head. Either I had become good at reading him, or this was exceptionally bad.

I followed him back to the kitchen. Either there was some problem with the restaurant, or something was up with Davison. If anything had happened at Donnie's Drive-Inn, I would have already heard about it through the usual gossip channels.

"So, what's the news about Davison?" I asked as Donnie busied himself at the stove. "Everything okay with his school?"

I watched him chop and stir and deglaze, admiring his cooking skills as I might admire a trapeze artist or a glassblower.

"I'm glad you asked, Molly. I'm worried about him. I only know what he tells me, and his story keeps changing, but I think he's going to lose his scholarship. He might even end up getting kicked out of school."

"What happened? What did he do?"

"That's the problem. It doesn't sound like he's doing much of anything, especially his homework. This is such a good opportunity for him, and he's squandering it. I don't know how to fix this."

"Sometimes," I ventured, "when people have to endure the consequences of their actions, it can good for them. A learning experience."

I knew I had to tread carefully here. As far as I knew, nothing good had ever come from telling a father that his beloved son is a spoiled jerk.

Donnie shook his head. "I see what you're saying, Molly. About consequences. But this doesn't only affect Davison. You have no idea what kinds of favors I had to call in to get him set up over there. If he gets kicked out now, it'll be worse for me than for him. It seems like he's happy to goof off all day with his girlfriend. I don't know. He might be feeling like he's in over his head. Maybe I should try to do something to build his confidence."

"I don't think that's what you want to do," I said. "Build his confidence, I mean."

Donnie poured something into a pan and began stirring.

"Why not?" he shouted over the sizzling.

"Marginal students have poor metacognition, and they tend to be hugely overoptimistic about how much they're learning and understanding."

I hoped Donnie hadn't noticed I'd just implied his son was a marginal student with poor metacognition. "Betty Jackson, from psychology, was telling me about some research that shows if you take struggling students and try to bolster their self-esteem, it can backfire. There's one study, I think the title is actually something like *An Intervention That Backfired*."

"Are you going to tell me something that doesn't work? Because I'd like to hear about something that *does* work."

Donnie was facing the stove, stirring energetically, so I couldn't see his expression. I could guess it wasn't happy.

"Yes. Just listen, please. I'm trying to tell you, encouragement is fine, as long as you don't overdo it and give him a false sense of security."

Donnie turned around to face me.

"So you're telling me he doesn't need someone to build his confidence. What he needs a kick in the `okole."

"That's not exactly what I was trying to—"

"No, I think you're right. If I could get away from the restaurant, I'd go out there myself and do it. But I can't. I wish…"

Donnie twiddled some dials on the stove, placed lids on pots, and came over to where I was sitting at the counter. He sat down next to me, placed his hand on my shoulder, and looked into my eyes.

"Molly, you know it's hard for a kid who doesn't have a mom."

I nodded.

"I'm glad I met you, and there are a lot of reasons for that. Not all of those reasons have to do with me."

This wasn't the first time Donnie had said something like this to me. I wasn't expecting a Browning sonnet or anything, but it might have been nice to hear some declaration of frank affection. Instead of variations on, "I need help wrangling my hooligan son, and I think you're up to the job."

"I know," I sighed. "You want to do what's best for Davison."

"I hope this doesn't frighten you, Molly, but spending time with you, it's started to feel like we're a family. Even though Davison's not here all the time, I think having you in our lives is good for him. And I know it's good for me."

"That's very nice, Donnie. Of *course* you're not frightening me."

I wondered whether he could tell I was lying.

Donnie let his hand trail from my shoulder down to my hand. "Molly, I normally wouldn't ask you for a favor like this, but what's your schedule like this week?"

"My schedule?" I stammered. "You're asking me what my schedule is?"

Donnie gave my hand a squeeze.

"When are your classes?" he persisted. "This

week? What times do you have to be on campus this week?"

Not only did I not have to be on campus, I wasn't even allowed to come within five hundred feet of it. Donnie's eyes gleamed. Those weren't…tears? I sighed.

"I don't have any teaching obligations this week. I'm actually on kind of a mini-sabbatical right now."

Donnie pulled me close and whispered into my ear.

"I love you so much, Molly."

CHAPTER FIFTY-ONE

"Maybe Davison won't want to meet me," I protested. "We can't force him, right?"

Donnie handed me his phone. "Tell him you'll buy him dinner wherever he wants. He'll show up. I guarantee it. I'll give you a credit card. You can put all the expenses on it."

With Donnie sitting beside me at his kitchen counter, I grudgingly called Davison and explained his father's plan for me to come out for a quick visit. I described Donnie's plan in terms chosen to make it sound as dull and inconvenient as possible, and I gave Davison several opportunities to decline.

"I understand if you're too busy," I told him, followed by "I know this is very short notice and you probably have other plans" and finally "really, feel free to say no."

Unfortunately, the prospect of dinner on Dad's dime was apparently too good to turn down.

Once it was clear Davison was bent on accepting my invitation, I suggested some agreeable dining establishments that had been among my favorites during my time in graduate school. Donnie nodded encouragingly as I laid out various options. A pleasant and reasonable Afghan restaurant lay within an easy walk of Davison's school. The retro red-banquette restaurant on Route 66 was a landmark, having been in operation since 1955. Within a short drive lay dim sum, pho, the Mexican cuisine I missed so dearly—

But Davison had his heart set on a faux-Italian chain restaurant adjacent to the shopping mall.

Twenty-four hours later, that's where I found myself eating dinner.

My minestrone soup had been thickened to the point of being mucousy and tasted of stale dried oregano and not much else. Swollen, overcooked rigatoni floated glumly among the tomato shreds and oregano flecks. A Sumo Saimin Bowl from Donnie's Drive-Inn would have been preferable, by several orders of magnitude. The highlight of the meal was the bottle of Chianti Classico I was sharing with Sherry.

I had insisted Davison invite Sherry to join us. It did feel a little strange, sitting right next to her after everything that had happened with Kathy and Glenn. On the other hand, the arrangement was preferable to the prospect of dinner à deux with Davison. To get through that I would have needed that bottle of Chianti Classico all to myself, wineglass optional. Also, I did want to talk to Sherry.

While I picked at my soup, Sherry tucked into her gluey fettuccine Alfredo. She had apparently abandoned her austere paddler's diet, although to me she looked as skinny as ever. Davison powered through one course after another, noisily relishing every morsel of his fried lasagna appetizer, glazed apricot chicken breast, and super-sized tiramisu.

At least we were spared any awkward silences. Davison rambled on about the misadventures of his archery teammates, the beer-soaked hijinks of his frat brothers, and the perfidy of his teachers. (At one point he declared that his English professor was a Nazi, which made me wonder what my students were saying about me during my enforced absence). He also threw in some incomprehensible (to me) commentary on football, which was apparently going on at the moment.

I tried to hold up my end of the discussion with an occasional remark about the value of the experience Davison was getting in college, and the importance of taking advantage of his once-in-a-lifetime opportunity. Sherry was surprisingly quiet, probably regretting her candor during our last meeting in the canoe halau.

Davison polished off his block of tiramisu and licked his fingers.

"Hey, you girls wanna walk over to the mall? There's some shoes I need to get."

"Do you mind if we stay here?" I asked. "I think we 'girls' would like to catch up. We can meet you back here whenever you're done." This plan seemed to be agreeable to everyone. Davison left for the adjacent shopping mall and Sherry signaled for our waiter. We ordered a Seven and Seven (Sherry) and a bourbon straight (me).

"So Sherry. I'm glad we can catch up."

She half smiled. "You coulda called."

"I didn't have your number."

"Dave woulda gave it to you. You two must be pretty close. He talks about you a lot. You're almost like his mom, huh?"

"I suppose that's one way to look at it. Anyway, it's better to reconnect in person, don't you think?"

"Sure!" Sherry agreed. She was starting to let her guard down. "Especially with an open tab."

Except for the part about having to spend time with Davison, this wasn't a bad deal for me. Donnie had arranged a first class flight to a small regional airport (LAX gives me panic attacks), along with a decent rental car and a comfortable room at a local hotel. It was no worse than going to a conference. Thanks to my temporary exile from campus, it wasn't like I had a lot to do back home in Mahina.

"You liked your fettuccine?" I asked.

You didn't need to be an elitist hipster snob (as Pat claims I am) to be put off by the menu offerings. If Dante Alighieri could see this, I thought, he'd write an extra circle of Hell into the Inferno especially for whoever thought up these culinary slanders against his countrymen. I wondered what punishment would suit putting glazed apricot chicken breast on an Italian menu. Probably an eternity of having to eat glazed apricot chicken breast.

"You know, Dave likes this place," Sherry said. "I think it's cause they give you a lotta food. Me, I dunno. For me, the secret is, don't think of it as Italian food, and make sure to get a good bottle of wine to wash it down. I mean, I grew up with real Italian food. Any resemblance is purely coincidental, like they say in the movies."

"This wouldn't have been my first choice," I admitted.

"The restaurant's pretty to look at, though," Sherry said. "One day I'd like to do my house like this."

I glanced around the dining room. The "hand painted" faux-Tuscan furniture looked dated and cheap, as if it were bought on clearance from one of those mall furniture stores sometime in the mid-nineties. The sponged walls, in golden and olive hues, had probably looked elegant twenty years ago. Well, each to her own. Sherry probably wouldn't like my Frida Kahlo fridge magnets.

"So you took time off just to come visit Dave?" she asked.

I'm visiting someone named Dave? Oh, right. Davison.

"That's right," I said. "Davi-, uh, Dave's father is concerned about how he's doing in school, but he couldn't get away from his work. So I'm here to check up on him, give him a little pep talk, say hello.

And I was hoping to talk to you too."

I wasn't about to administer the "kick in the `okole" that Donnie had pinned his hopes on. But I did have a plan.

"We're fine. Dave's roommate's cool with me staying in their dorm. It's just for a while."

"Sherry, I need to ask you something. About what happened with Glenn and Kathy."

She stared down at the tablecloth.

"I don't like to bring it up, but it's been—it makes no sense to me. I mean, I never thought Glenn had you so under his spell that you would—well, you know."

"His spell?" Sherry scoffed. "What are you talking about?"

"Okay. You found out that Glenn and Kathy were having an affair. But what I can't figure out is, why didn't you just walk away? What am I missing here?"

Sherry stared at me. Her lips trembled for a second, and then she lost it.

"What are you missing?" She was laughing so hard that people were starting to stare.

"What's so funny?"

"Dr. B.," she gasped. "I thought you had it all figured out. You're not even close!"

CHAPTER FIFTY-TWO

"So I didn't get all the details right. Maybe you can explain it to me?"

I was a little stung by Sherry's slur on my powers of induction.

"Sure." She took a gulp of her Seven and Seven. "I'll tell you how I figured it out. So Glenn hadda leave for a business trip. Remember, before the race? I came to see you in your office? You know it's all cause of you that me and Dave met to begin with. Remember?"

"I can't take the credit for that. Anyway, Glenn?"

"Yeah. So his business trip was him going to collect payment for a job. But he came back early. And he was pretty pi—he wasn't too happy. Cause he went all the way out there, he wouldn't tell me exactly where, though. Somewhere on the mainland. Glenn told me he did the job and was supposed to get paid, but the guy didn't wanna pay him. That's all he would say. It put him in a real bad mood, though." Sherry leaned in and lowered her voice. "So the day he came back, he was rushing around and didn't unpack right away. He left his bag in his workroom and went right back out again. So I'd just took a shower, and I'd ran outta deodorant. I thought no big deal, I'll borrow some of his. I went and looked in his travel bag. I saw a file folder there, and maybe I shouldn't of, but I looked inside."

"And that's when you found the photos of Kathy?"

"Yeah. Two of them. One of them looked like one I'd posted online. Where our crew is rigging the canoe. So I'm the one who took the picture and posted it, and now he has a copy of it. How weird is that, huh? He had another picture of her too, a headshot. It looked like it was from a driver's license or something like that. Kathy had dark hair in that one. And not only that. I found a printout of one of my emails. It was the announcement from when Kathy died. Now if youda been me, what would you do?"

"I would have been frightened," I said. "I'm not sure what I would have done."

"Well, I was mad at first. Like, who does he think he is, going through my stuff?"

"The nerve," I agreed.

"But then it hit me. I'd just read that article, the one I turned in with my paper. Did you read it?"

"Yes, I did. The one about how you can use a wireless device to hack someone's pacemaker remotely. Or their insulin pump."

"Exactly. Well, Kathy had an insulin pump. And you know Glenn, he was always playing around with his electronics. You know, I didn't really think about how he was always screwing around with that stuff. I was like, yeah, boys and their toys, whatever. But after reading the article, and finding Kathy's pictures and death announcement in his bag—he wasn't playing around. Kathy was dead, and he's the one who did it. He figured out a way to get the job done without getting his hands dirty."

"Glenn?" I exclaimed. "Your Glenn? I mean—"

"Yeah. I told you he was into electronics, didn't I?"

"You did," I admitted.

"He was helping me write up my business idea. Remember?"

"I do remember." Sherry had told me Glenn was good with electronics. And, having met Glenn in person, I had dismissed it.

"I've been thinking about this a lot," she said. "I haven't talked to anyone about it, though. Don't tell Dave. Poor kid, he's such an innocent."

"Don't worry, I won't. So now *you* didn't kill Kathy. You're saying *Glenn* killed Kathy, by hacking her insulin pump."

"You thought *I* killed Kathy?" Sherry stared at me.

"No, I didn't think you killed anyone. I never thought you did." That wasn't quite true, but it was all I could think of to say. "So you figured it out when you read the article about hacking the insulin pump, and saw the photos of Kathy in Glenn's suitcase, and the email."

"Uh-huh. And I figured his 'job' had to do with that. Someone hired him to get rid of Kathy Banks. Made me wonder what she did. Mess around with the wrong woman's husband, probably."

"So the last time I talked to you, back in Mahina, why did you tell me you'd killed Kathy?"

"I didn't tell you I killed Kathy. Why would I tell you that?"

"Well, you told me I'd figured out how you did it. I asked you if you'd used your insulin—"

"Oh yeah, that's right. And I did."

I shook my head. "I'm still confused."

"I didn't use the insulin on Kathy," Sherry said. "I used it on Glenn."

CHAPTER FIFTY-THREE

"Glenn knew." Sherry sipped her Seven and Seven. "I don't know how he knew, but that night when we came home from the race? I could tell something was different. You know that diet us paddlers were doing? He'd never been real supportive of it, but that night he said to me, hey, baby, don't forget your injection. You don't wanna let yourself get fat just cause the race is over."

"He said that?" Grounds for justifiable homicide right there, as far as I was concerned.

"And when I opened the medicine cabinet, I saw my things weren't exactly how I left them. He'd done something to the needles. I could tell."

"So what did you do?"

"I made up some story about how I wasn't gonna do my injection right then, cause I'd switched to doing them in the morning. That bought me twelve hours. I was so nervous I didn't sleep that night. I watched Glenn till it started to get light out. Then I got up and grabbed five of my insulin pens. I use the 31 gauge, they're real fine. They slip in nice and smooth. I gave him all five, one after the other. I shook him awake, and we went out for our morning run like always."

"You were smart. You made sure not to have a body in the house. He'd probably be hard to move."

"Look, sorry Dr. B, but it was him or me, you know? It was self-defense."

"No, I understand. You didn't think you could go to the police?"

"I thought about it," she said. "I did. But they wouldn't of done anything. What could they do? It was safer to take care of it myself. I mean, Glenn didn't think twice about blowing up Kathy's insulin pump. I knew I was next, and I didn't have a lot of time. He's a professional, Dr. B. I didn't know him at all. His whole pretty-boy act, that was for this job. And now I think about it, I'm pretty sure Glenn Anderssen wasn't even his real name."

"You can call me Molly. You're not my student anymore."

"Dave calls you Aunty Molly." Sherry grinned. "Can I call you that?"

"Please don't."

"So anyway, Glenn? We were out on the trail about two miles from home when he passed out. And I'll be honest, I felt bad for a second. But I remembered what he did to Kathy, and how he used me. I was disposable to him. I was just there to help him finish the job."

"It must have been more than that. He didn't have to start a relationship with you. If he'd wanted to, he could have just befriended Kathy directly. She wasn't averse to male attention, from what I could tell."

"No. No, I was thinking about this. No, he couldn't. Cause the boyfriend is always suspect numero uno when something bad happens. Right? No one ever suspects the *friend's* boyfriend. He hadda get close to someone who wasn't his mark."

"Oh. I see your point."

"Same reason I hadda leave town. They find Glenn, if anyone gets suspicious, who are they gonna look for first? The girlfriend."

"Did you hear they found him?"

Sherry went a little pale. "They ID'd him?"

"Yes. It was in the *County Courier*. It said they didn't suspect foul play."

Sherry drained her glass.

"I didn't mean anything to him." She looked around for someone who could bring us more drinks. "You know what? If he'd of gotten paid when he was supposed to, he probably wouldn't of come back at all."

She was probably right.

A waitress came over.

"Evening, ladies. Sisters' night out?"

"She's visiting from Hawaii. Can we get another round?"

"Aloha and welcome to California!" the waitress

smiled and left to get our drinks.

"So anyway, when Glenn went down, I said, you know, kinda loud, 'Hang on, baby, I'll go get help.' In case anyone could hear. I turned around and ran back home, got dressed, and went up to school. That's when I saw you in the parking lot."

"So when I talked to you that morning, you'd already…"

"I was on autopilot. It didn't hit me till later, everything that happened. You know, I thought I had it all set up. I was gonna finish up my college degree, finally. I was back on my beautiful island. I had a great guy, or that's what I thought. And I had the paddling. When all this happened, it made me feel like the elevator doors opened and I'd stepped in, but the elevator wasn't there. Know what I mean?"

"Sherry, why did you say, if it weren't for me? When I saw you in the halau. What did you mean?"

"If it wasn't for you? Oh, yeah, right. If it wasn't for you, I wouldn't have been reading those blogs and stuff, that's for sure. The thing about the wireless insulin pump hacking thing was still in my mind when I found the photo of Kathy. Kinda rang warning bells for me. Otherwise, I probably would've said something right to Glenn's face, like, hey, what's Kathy's picture doing in your suitcase? Who knows what he would've done then? But thanks to you I knew enough to keep my mouth shut."

"That was smart."

"You know, Glenn was always telling me about how wireless stuff wasn't secure. He said I shouldn't use the Wi-Fi at the coffee shop unless I wanted everyone seeing all my private email and stuff. That's why he liked keeping things on paper. I guess he'd know, huh? Hey, Dr. B., can I ask you something? I mean, Molly?"

"Sure."

"Do you know who hired Glenn to kill Kathy? Who wanted her dead?"

"There was no such person as Kathy Banks. Her name was Karolyn Beckenbauer."

CHAPTER FIFTY-FOUR

I glanced back at the restaurant entrance, hoping Davison would take his time shoe-shopping.

"Karolyn Beckenbauer worked in the admissions office of one of the branches of your former college. She started to notice they were doing things like steering students to take out loans from their affiliates, misrepresenting the terms of the loans, paying recruiters by headcount, all kinds of things they weren't supposed to be doing. You know, what they did to you, they did the same thing to all of their students. Their whole enterprise runs on collecting student loan money, and whether or not you get an education out of it isn't a concern for them. They pocket the money, and you're on the hook to pay it back. So Karolyn made copies of the training materials, the employee manuals, internal emails, everything. Then she went to the Feds. That's when she first appeared in the news, as a whistleblower."

"Whoa." Sherry's eyes widened.

"Now, right as the trial was getting underway, Karolyn Beckenbauer died in a traffic accident. That's what the news reports say. Pat thinks she was actually put into witness protection. That company, the holding company for all those for-profits, stood to lose billions in federal aid they'd collected over the years. Of course they'd want to keep her quiet."

"So ya think she had a bunch of plastic surgery like the mob guys do?"

"I don't know. There is something different about her. I didn't even believe it was the same person at first. What do you think?"

I pulled out my phone and brought up the photo of Karolyn Beckenbauer from the news article announcing her death. Sherry took the phone from me and held it at arm's length.

"Oh yeah. This is different from the picture I saw in Glenn's folder, but yeah. There she is with the dark hair." She squinted at the tiny picture. "No, no plastic surgery. Her face is the same. She's not wearing any makeup here, and her hair is kinda blah. She got some kinda major makeover, huh, with the frosted hair and everything?"

Sherry handed my phone back to me.

"Looks like she made the most of her new life," Sherry said. "I bet Karolyn Beckenbauer never had a chance to do the things Kathy Banks did."

I hoped if ever I were given a chance at a fresh start, I would use it for something more worthy than making people redo their paperwork and flirting with their husbands.

"So anyway," I continued, "one month after Karolyn Beckenbauer supposedly passed away, Kathy Banks started working in our Student Retention Office. It would have been a perfect assignment for Karolyn. She already knew how to do that kind of administrative work, and our university is about as remote and off the beaten path as you can get."

"So how did Pat figure it out?"

"That facial recognition website. Emma and I started with your picture of Kathy Banks, and that's how we found Karolyn Beckenbauer. You know, without that picture you posted, we could never have discovered Kathy's real identity."

"So Kathy was in witness protection. That explains how come she never let us take her picture."

"That must be why Emma couldn't find any team photos with Kathy in them. It must be one of the rules. You don't want the bad guys to track you down just because—"

Because someone carelessly posted your photo online, I stopped myself from saying.

"They musta really wanted to get rid of Kathy," Sherry said. "Setting Glenn, or whatever his name was, up here with a house and spending money, musta cost them a lot."

"I'm sure paying Glenn's expenses was a lot cheaper than having to give back billions of dollars in financial aid."

Sherry fumbled in her purse—auburn suede with long, swinging fringes—and pulled out a box of tiny mints.

"Man, I'm dying for a smoke. Remember when you could smoke in a restaurant?"

She offered me a mint, and I took it. Who knows, that minestrone may have had some hidden garlic in it, although I had detected no flavor.

"Now it makes sense. Here I'd thought how strange it was she was such an important witness in this major trial, but she ended up falling victim to this quotidian love triangle. I knew there was more to the story."

"I wonder if Glenn found her picture online," Sherry said. "On my page. Cause I didn't know how to work the privacy settings. Otherwise, how would they of tracked her all the way to Mahina?"

Sherry rested her forehead in her hand.

"He probably used that software to find her. You and Emma started with Kathy and found Karolyn, Glenn coulda started with Karolyn and found Kathy. It was me. I was the one who gave her away."

I shrugged, not sure what to say.

"That's how he did it." Sherry seemed near tears now. "Glenn saw from my pictures that me and Kathy were paddlers, and he probably started hanging out down on the Bayfront on purpose. The Bayfront is where I met him."

I felt a shadow fall across our table. It was Davison, back from his shopping trip.

Sherry sat up quickly and dabbed her eyes with the cloth napkin.

"Hey doll," Sherry said. "You did good, huh?"

Davison was carrying plastic bags from a sporting goods store and a video game shop, as well as a large white paper bag printed with a black and white photo of what looked like half-naked Hitler youth.

"The brave hunter has returned." He leaned over and kissed Sherry on the mouth.

I still had one more thing to do. This was going to be a little tricky. I waited for Davison to come up for air.

"So Dave," I said, "sorry you couldn't join us for a drink. You're turning twenty-one this year, though, right? When's your birthday?"

He wiped his mouth with the back of his hand. "It's November thirteen." He moved closer, rested his hand on the back of my chair, and grinned down at me. "I'm a Scorpio. You shoulda figured *that* out, Aunty."

I scooted forward in my chair to break contact between his hand and my back.

"November? Are you sure? I thought it was December. December thirteenth, right?"

"No, Aunty, it's November."

"I'm sure you said December," I insisted.

"I'll prove it. Look, here's my driver's license."

He set his bags down on the floor, pulled out his wallet and handed me the rainbow driver's license.

"Oh, you still have your Hawaii ID. You should get your California one if you're going to live here.

But that's such a nice photo of you. Sherry, have you seen this?"

Davison had been too cool to smile when they took his picture. It looked like a mug shot. I handed the license to Sherry.

"Cute, huh?" I managed to say. Davison seemed pleased rather than inconvenienced. Of course he did. First, he had been proven right about his birthdate, and now here I was gushing over his photo.

Sherry glanced at the driver's license, smiled, and started to hand it back to me. Then she grabbed it back.

I held my breath.

"Hang on," she said. "Your name is Davison Gonsalves? You're *Davison Gonsalves*?"

"Yeah?" He seemed confused. "But I like to be called Dave."

She sat still for a long moment, gazing at the drivers' license in her hands. She uttered a remarkably apropos expletive and handed Davison's license back to him. She wasn't looking at him. She was glaring at me.

"So, you and Donnie, huh? You're together?"

I tried to think quickly. Now Sherry knows. But does Sherry know that I know? Not necessarily, but it's possible. I shouldn't overdo the fake surprise, in any case.

"Uh, yes. We are."

She pressed her lips together and nodded.

"You and Donnie. Yeah. Figures."

That didn't sound like a compliment.

"Well." Sherry stood up, brisk and sober. "I think it's time for us to get going. Thanks for dinner, Molly. Dave—*Davison*—has to get back and finish his homework. Come on, buddy. What's in the bag? Let me see. Oh, no. No, you do not need any more games. You're already wasting way too much time on those. We're gonna go back and return these right now."

Sherry didn't actually drag Davison back to the video game store by his ear, but for some reason, that's how I remember the moment.

CHAPTER FIFTY-FIVE

I wish I could wrap up this story by revealing I saved Kathy Banks' life. But I have to give credit where it's due.

The marshals were fast. They were able to whisk Kathy away in an ambulance before the real emergency responders showed up in their fire truck. When Pat went up to the hospital to ask about her, no one could tell him anything, because Kathy was never there. If she had been taken to the hospital, she would have been an easy target. Glenn could have finished the job as she lay in her hospital bed.

Then there was Sherry.

She was the one who had unwittingly put Kathy in danger to begin with when she posted Kathy's photo online. That was how Glenn found Karolyn/Kathy's new whereabouts and identity in the first place.

On the other hand, Sherry found the article

describing how someone could control an insulin pump from up to half a mile away, releasing an overdose of insulin and sending the victim's blood sugar plunging to a fatally low level. Sherry knew Kathy wore an insulin pump. And when she discovered Kathy's photo and death announcement in Glenn's suitcase, she put two and two together. She stopped Glenn before he could make a second attempt on Kathy's life.

Kathy Banks, aka Karolyn Beckenbauer, survived. Pat tells me we can infer this from the news stories about a surprise "key witness" testifying in closed court.

The case will drag on for years. And Karolyn Beckenbauer (or whatever her current alias is) will have to stay underground for the rest of her life. She's probably hiding out in Amish Country or something by now, trying to convince some woman's husband she's a natural redhead.

Over dinner the other night, Donnie relayed some good news. Davison's grades had improved tremendously, and he was set to get off academic probation by the end of the semester.

"I'm so glad you went out to see him, Molly. He completely turned around after your visit. Something's definitely changed for him."

"All he needed was a little maternal encouragement," I said.

Donnie beamed at me.

"Speaking of that. I never told you this before. Davison is hanai. That means he was adopted."

I know what hanai means. Sometimes Donnie over-explains things to me like I'm some kind of clueless tourist. Sorry, I mean clueless *visitor*.

"Davison's adopted? But everyone says how much he looks like you."

"He was my sister's baby."

"Oh. Well, that's good."

"Why is it good?" Donnie asked.

"Um." I stared down at the golden-crusted veal Milanese on my plate. "What's good is you, you're comfortable sharing things with me. Because sharing and honesty are important. That's what I meant. Anyway. None of this changes how I feel about Davison."

"I'm glad to hear you say that, Molly."

"So your ex, Sherrine? She wasn't Davison's biological mother?"

"No. She wasn't. We wanted to have children, but she had some health problems that would have made it dangerous—"

"Oh right. Type 1 diabetes."

Donnie put down his fork and stared at me.

"Yes, Sherry did have diabetes. How did you know?"

"Ah! How did I know?"

And, more to the point, why did I say that? Why couldn't I keep my mouth shut and listen? See, this is what happens when I say things out loud. I have to stop doing that. I stared at my plate and concentrated on sawing off a piece of veal with the side of my fork.

"I knew because…I just watched *Steel Magnolias* with Emma and—with Emma. Did you ever see it?"

"I don't remember. The title sounds familiar, but no. I don't think so."

"In the movie, there's a mother and a daughter, and the daughter, well, the whole plot hinged on how dangerous it is to get pregnant if you have diabetes. That was the first thing I thought of when you mentioned the high-risk pregnancy."

Donnie nodded, apparently satisfied with my explanation. I fairly collapsed with relief. I'd have to thank Emma and Pat for making me sit through that depressing movie.

"I'm impressed you put that together. You're a very intelligent woman, Molly."

"Yeah, you'd think."

"I'm glad we talked about this." Donnie smiled. "There shouldn't be any secrets between us."

"Oh, I agree. Absolutely. No secrets. Ow. My head! Donnie, I'm just going to go get some ice from your freezer, if you don't mind."

ABOUT THE AUTHOR

Like Professor Molly, Frankie Bow teaches at a public university. Unlike her protagonist, she is blessed with delightful students, sane colleagues, and a perfectly nice office chair. She believes if life isn't fair, at least it can be entertaining. In addition to writing murder mysteries, she publishes in scholarly journals under her real name. Her experience with academic publishing has taught her to take nothing personally.

Thank you for taking the time to read The Cursed Canoe. If you enjoyed it, please consider telling your friends or posting a short review. Word of mouth is an author's best friend and much appreciated.

Mahalo, Frankie

Want to be the first to learn about events, promotions, giveaways, and new releases? Click here to sign up for my newsletter.

www.ingramcontent.com/pod-product-compliance
Lightning Source LLC
Chambersburg PA
CBHW032100180726
48284CB00002B/376

* 9 7 8 1 9 4 3 4 7 6 1 5 2 *